ZOË APOSTOLIDES

THE HOMECOMING

S
SALT

CROMER

PUBLISHED BY SALT PUBLISHING 2025

2 4 6 8 10 9 7 5 3 1

First published in Great Britain in 2025 by
Salt Publishing Ltd
12 Norwich Road, Cromer, Norfolk N R27 0A X

www.saltpublishing.com

Salt Publishing Limited Reg. No. 5293401

A CIP catalogue record for this book is available from the British Library

I S B N 978 1 78463 339 4 (Paperback edition)
I S B N 978 1 78463 340 0 (Electronic edition)

Typeset in Neacademia by Salt Publishing

Printed and bound in Great Britain by Clays Ltd, Elcograf S.p.A

ZOË APOSTOLIDES was born in south London in 1990. She began her career in magazine and newspaper journalism after graduating from the University of Oxford, and has written for a variety of print and online media. She is the author of several works of non-fiction and this is her first novel.

To Debbie and Chris, for the best of homes, and
to Marco, for the one we're building

"Life is a dodgy and uncertain business, and a monster with a smiling face may live or work right next door to you. Dislocation is central, and so is loss. Loss befalls us all; loss is half the human story. Mostly, we experience moments of joy and transcendence a couple of seconds after they have already begun to fade, and our knowledge of such exalted states consists largely of their existence being held in memory. Adult human beings live with the certainty of grief, which deepens us and opens us to other people, who have been there too." —PETER STRAUB

Elver Estate

ELVER HOUSE

Conger Brook

1762

Remains of chapel

Fountain

Summer house

Main entrance

Side entrance

N
E
W
S

THE HOMECOMING

CHAPTER ONE

E LVER HOUSE HAD seemed funny on Saturday night when we sat over dinner. A mystical, strange sort of name nestled deep in a county neither of us had been to. The map showed few roads and large swathes of avocado green; a place where net curtains twitched and eyes watched every sign of movement from the post office to the pub. A place I'd tell you about next month when we met again, painting the picture of myself as a city interloper confused by the lack of tubes and buses, thick sandwiches and smoke. We'd laugh about the village in the way Londoners, even adoptive ones, do.

It was less amusing now I was here. The rain gathered itself as though for a tantrum, hurling great splashes on the windowpane. Everything had been so familiar between Kings Cross and York, a journey I'd made back and forth a hundred times. It was the change that threw me: crossing the platform to board the connection and settling down in the cold as the engine chugged and spluttered and we snaked our way north-east. The light was fading as we approached Newcastle and I craned my neck to spot the steel skeleton, wings flung out wide, a patinated anchor funnelling the wind to its foundations. We paused, the doors opened and people disembarked in a whoosh of cold air. And then we were off again, proceeding along the coast. An hour passed. I closed my eyes and pulled my hood over my head.

When the train shuddered to a stop in the station I was the only passenger along the platform, hauling my suitcase along as a fine mist spread out, hovering a few centimetres above the ground.

The car park was empty, the sun just setting over the horizon, the trees great towering sentries across the single-lane road. You remember how I packed my waterproof inside the suitcase, and how you'd said better to pop it in the rucksack? Well, you were right.

Water ran down the neck of my shirt. It was the last week of October. Just a month ago we were on the pebbly beach, eating melting lollies and slapping on Factor 50. I looked around, past the tiny café – closed, of course – and the deserted bus stop. Laura had booked a cab, but there was no sign of anyone either side of the concourse and I strained my ears for the sound of a rumbling engine. Nothing.

This, I suppose, was how it began. Not on the train and not back in London, when I was asked to come, but here, in the gathering dark of an autumn evening.

The agency had given me the address, but it wasn't much use as walking was out of the question. That much I knew – the drive alone would take half an hour. I left the station and spoke to the guard. He stood against the railings, looking out into the night, smoking contentedly. He frowned slightly when I mentioned the name of Miss Carey's house; my heart sank. To come all this way, separated from everyone, hours from home, was one thing if it was going to be comfortable, pleasant. The way he grimaced suggested that it wasn't.

I hadn't met Miss Carey, nor even spoken to her on the phone. Not so unusual, especially for a woman her age. The fact she hadn't hassled me was reassuring: she had my number, after all. The agency agreed the time and place, the hours.

She said she'd feel more comfortable if you'd agree to stay in the house, my editor said, apologetically. *I can find you a hotel if you prefer. I suspect she's just lonely. It's five days – what do you think?*

Would you do it, Laura? I asked.

I wish, she said. Laura had three children under four – two had chicken pox. *Let me know anyway. We agreed the start date a month ago and Richard was meant to do it, but he's pulled out. I don't want to let her down, she sounds sweet.*

Tell her yes, I said. *It'll be good to get out of the city for a few days.*

That's my girl, said Laura, and hung up.

⌘

The project details were brief: autobiography, start to finish, 20 hours of interviews. I'd get all the information I needed and then, back in the city and over the course of the next few months, I'd write her memoirs.

No word on Miss Carey herself – what she wanted to discuss, if and when she'd worked, whether she was still married or single or widowed, had children or did not. Unusual, yes, but not unheard of. I'd travelled to meet clients in all sorts of places.

It's important to note early on that I was looking forward to the assignment. I remembered every client I'd ever worked for: not the detailed specifics of their stories, but the way they spoke, the hesitancy or brashness of their voices, the way they glossed over life-defining events or cried as they recounted them. It's no easy thing having a stranger rock up one day, asking questions and writing it all down. I tried, always, to keep that firmly in mind.

Whether I liked them personally or not was immaterial, though the majority were friendly enough, interesting and interested. Often their children had commissioned the book, keen for a memento, a legacy, something to look back on. Those were the toughest nuts to crack: the ones who hadn't sought out our services themselves. Usually, though, we got there in the end.

I checked the time. No wonder the taxi wasn't here; I saw with some surprise that the train had been early. Glancing behind me I saw it now, quietly waiting on the platform, as empty as it had been for an hour before we'd arrived. Passengers had disembarked steadily at every stop beforehand until I was the only one left. The lights were still on, and I wondered who might soon be arriving to catch the service on to its next destination. I'd never heard of any of these places – small villages with names so quintessentially British they seemed plucked straight from a Miss Marple novel. *Fisherman's Deep. Idlecombe. Kings Lock. Hollydale. Harts Close.*

Outside the train concourse the road was silent now: no glare of headlights or screech of tyres, no sirens, no buses exhaling as they paused briefly to let commuters off or pick them up. It was close to six and the dark was settling, bedding in. Perhaps the place would be livelier in the glow of morning, when the weather was better. Then I remembered Laura's email, arriving just as I left, and sighed. *Heavy rain forecast tomorrow and Sat. Hopefully it'll clear by Sunday. Don't imagine she'll want to be out in such bad weather . . . Shall I send wellies?* And then a laughing-face emoji.

Ducking into the station waiting room, the noise from outside dropped quite suddenly as the door swung shut, a thick silence engulfing the small space. It was immaculately clean, the plastic benches attached to the wall the only splash of colour.

There in the corner, beside the exit, was a noticeboard behind clear Perspex. Leaflets and posters were arranged neatly, tacked up so as not to obscure one other. There was an advertisement for a village fete, some six weeks ago now, a garden sale of household furniture, and the number of three local handymen. Prominent among them was a notice about bird-watching tours led by someone called Amanda, and another asking members of the Conger Brook Historical Society to contact Jim about the winter timetable.

I smiled, feeling my shoulders relax as I scanned these portraits of village life, snapshots of comings and goings, events, ways to make weekends and evenings brighter. Atop several notices an identical crest hovered, which I took to be the town's emblem – a logo of sorts. Inside an elongated circle ran a stretch of water through which tiny waves were drawn in thin pencil, the water writhing within its own current. I peered closer, frowning. Perhaps not waves after all – the illustrated lines were thicker than that. They were swimming in a school. Swordfish maybe, or snakes.

I shivered, feeling the damp of my sleeves and my arms goose-bumping. I turned away from the board just as a pair of headlamps lit up the road from afar, like the eyes of an animal in the gloom.

CHAPTER TWO

T HE CAR SEEMED to round various bends of a long road, but eventually it turned into the station car park. I waved at the driver, sticking my head out of the door as he wound down the window.

"You Ellen?" he called. I nodded. "Lady who made the booking said you looked like Wednesday Addams."

I laughed. Thanks, Laura. I'd tried to throw a bit of colour onto my cheeks that morning, but she was right. There was a marked contrast between my hair, black as compost, and the skin beneath it that made me look almost bloodless.

"I'd have said more Snow White," he said kindly through the window, as he pulled the handbrake up with a jerk, jumped out and slammed the car door shut before coming over to meet me. "I'm Steve," he said. "What a bloody night." He was smiling. "Lemme take that, pet."

He lifted the case over a large puddle and clicked a button on his key. The boot sprang open. He beckoned at me to climb in and I pulled open the back passenger door. Now there was someone else here, I realised how loud the wind was. We were mostly communicating through signals, but he was saying something.

"What?" I cupped a hand over my ear as he ran back round to the driver's side.

"Jump in the front."

I did as he'd asked, placing my soaked rucksack down between my feet. The car was warm, throwing out great waves of heat from the dashboard vents. I sighed as it washed over me.

"Sorry," said the driver, closing his own door. "You sit where you like. I only ask because most people get sick in the back. All these twisty roads. I didn't want you feeling ill the whole way there, too polite to say owt."

Steve tapped something on his phone and the screen sprang to life. I could see the thin black line indicating the route, and all around us large swathes of green, a straggling course of blue, a single cross over a lone building indicating a pharmacy. "When you say, 'the whole way there'," I began, and Steve laughed again.

"Yep. It's not exactly far as the crow flies, nothing is round here." He turned the key in the ignition and the engine rumbled beneath us. "Just takes a while through the lanes, you know?" I nodded, knowing. "And some of the roads aren't really, like, roads at all. Just rocks and gravel. Gotta go slow. I got stuck in the mud last year – had to ask a farmer to pull me out with his tractor. Reet faff."

My phone buzzed, finally. Some signal, at last. Not a lot, but it would do.

All ok?

Good thanks. Am in the taxi, thanks for booking. Should be there soon.

She was decent like that, Laura – always had been. We weren't a big team of freelancers but she'd hired us individually, after three separate interviews: she took care to make sure we were alright, especially when the assignment was a little more involved.

You're with Steve, right? The cabbie. I spoke to him earlier today.

Yep, I tapped back. *On our way. Will message once I'm there.*

Steve hummed a little as he rounded the bends. I could see nothing from the windows now – barely a distinction between tarmac and hedgerow. We were still on the main road.

"First time in Conger?" he asked, popping a Polo into his mouth and offering me the packet.

"Yes, that's right." I said. "I'm here for work."

Over the years I'd found it was good to keep things vague. The idea of a ghost-writer arriving to compose a person's memoirs usually aroused all sorts of curiosity, and anyway most clients preferred not to broadcast the fact they'd not written it themselves. Fair enough.

Steve nodded. "And you?" I asked. "Do you live here in the village?"

"Always have done," he said. "There's not much work round here anymore, but we do alright. It's a nice little place." He fiddled with the radio and tuned to a station playing soft jazz. "Will you get to explore much?"

"I doubt it, to be honest. I'm only here a few days."

"I suppose you'll be busy. But if you do get the chance, a bit of downtime might not be a bad idea. We're in the pub most evenings, you should come and say hello. We're normal, I promise." He chuckled. "None of your May Day dances or Rose Queens or whatever. We won't be propping up the bar in deer masks or burning you in a wicker man or whatever."

"That'd be nice," I said, laughing. After the silence of the train station and the creeping fog I was glad of this, the amiable chitchat. "I'll see what I can do. But yeah – I'll probably be quite busy."

Steve nodded. "I bet. You're a solicitor, I take it?"

I turned to look at his face, happily nodding in profile to the music. The radio had started stuttering as we took a left off the main road, but he didn't appear to mind. "No, actually," I said. "What makes you ask?"

"Just Miss Carey, is all," said Steve. "It was always way too much for her, the estate." He twiddled the dial on the dashboard and the jazz came through a little more clearly. "She was going to hire someone, last I heard, go through some paperwork. Tie up loose ends. I imagined you were here to help with all that."

I thought about this for a moment. From what Laura had said, I was aware my new client was retired, but she could have been a sprightly 70-year-old for all I knew. Perhaps she was in the process of selling up. But Steve seemed to be suggesting something else – a vulnerability.

"You said it was too much for her . . ." I began, as we turned off yet again. Now I could see what he meant about the roads. The suspension protested as we bumped over a raised hillock. Ahead of us, the car's beams provided a spotlight for the driving rain. "I didn't get the impression it was that big."

"What, Elver House?"

"Yeah. I thought it was . . . I'm not sure. A cottage."

Steve laughed, though there wasn't much mirth in his voice now. "They just called it that to make it sound quaint, like, way back when. Nar, Elver's no cottage." he said.

And he left it at that.

CHAPTER THREE

WHEN WE WERE children and we were apart, I missed you with a kind of physicality I'd never known before and haven't known since. At home, perched on the edge of the sofa watching the same films we always watched; I saw Bill Murray dashing through the Natural History Museum, Chief Brody staring through his binoculars for any sign of a shadow under the surface. I looked, constantly, out of the window, expecting to see you coming up the path, bursting through the front door like Marilyn Monroe from a birthday cake. We'd grown up surrounded by each other as cubs did; I knew every like and dislike, every swing and roundabout of your personality. You were a key hidden under a plant pot and only I knew it was there.

You were a member of the swimming squad and the second netball team. You were an average Wing Attack. You were hopeless at English which many thought odd, because you read a lot. It was your maths that won you the place at our school. You pressed flowers from your parents' overgrown garden and drank orange juice from its glass bottle in the fridge, which infuriated your mother. You spent stolen pound coins on hair grips that were quickly then lost, and had an irritating habit of crunching cans of Coke between your hands when you were finished.

In the summer, you'd drag an inflatable beach toy from the shed onto the slate slabs under your window. It took you an hour to puff enough oxygen into the bulbous grey shark, its dorsal fin rising and fall with each exhalation, your dad calling out to you to knock it off before you gave yourself an aneurysm.

You ate cereal for breakfast and slurped the milk from the bottom of the bowl, white slops of muesli laced with sugar. You licked the whisks, covered in icing, which your brothers left in the sink after baking. You loved baths filled with soft white bubbles. You slept with a retainer, and could not turn off the light without at least half a glass of water beside your bed. You were frightened of small dogs but loved animals. By the time your 10th birthday came, you had learnt how to raise your right eyebrow, and were enjoying the new, particular facial expressions that could be conjured up using this trick.

I awoke with a start, my forehead damp with condensation from the window. We'd stopped. Turning bleary-eyed to look around, I saw Steve switching off the sat-nav and opening the glove compartment.

He turned and smiled bashfully. "Haven't been down here in a long while," he said. "Signal cut out. Just give me a mo."

I nodded sleepily and pulled out my phone. Nothing. It was almost seven now. I stared uneasily at the absent bars on the screen, the total lack of connection. Steve traced a finger over a line in the map, nodding, and glancing to his left – though what he was looking for was beyond me. Though I squinted, I could see nothing through the sheets of water.

After a couple of minutes he put the car into reverse, backed up the lane to a crossroads and swung the car round to the right.

"This should do it," he said. The radio was nothing but white static now, and he snapped it off. His hands drummed on the steering wheel as he peered ahead. "The next one," he muttered, almost to himself. We crept slowly along, dipping into potholes which splashed up around us. "Should be any minute now."

A larger car would not have fitted, I realised, let alone a truck or lorry. The lane was just big enough to let us pass, and even then Steve wound down his window and tucked the wing mirror in. I took a sip of water from my bottle and wrapped my scarf a little tighter round my neck. Steve's affable conversation had all but vanished now. I thought about you, at home, the candles arranged haphazardly around the fireplace, a chaos of clothes and books, small bowls and plates on the table. You'd have the radio on and in the background the washing machine would hum its soothing spin. I wished you were here, wished you wanted to be.

I knew it must be difficult, driving in this weather, especially along lanes that looked as though they saw little if any traffic. But as the minutes ticked on I noticed Steve's hands, the way they gripped the wheel, and the set of his shoulders as he hunched before it. Several minutes passed as we edged along the track. There was no sense of jollity in his tone as he stopped, finally, looked over my shoulder and said flatly, "Righto. Here we are."

I looked out onto the side of the road, where a thin wooden board stood at an angle, hammered into the earth. A single word was hand-painted onto the white background. *Elver.* There was nothing beyond it but a dark, narrow path set between thickets of gorse and nettles.

"Can't get the car up there, pet," said Steve, not meeting my eye. "Sorry. I'll help you with the case. It's just a tad further up though, you can't miss it."

"No problem," I said, and paid him, watching as he scribbled a receipt. "I'll manage. Thanks so much."

He hopped out of the car and retrieved my case from the boot. "Straight up," he said, pointing. "Can't miss it, as I said. It's a muckle of a thing." He paused. "Hope the work goes alright."

I pulled my hood up and thanked him again. He stopped as he prepared to climb back into the car, then reached down into the recess of the door and pulled out a card. "My number," he said, gruffly. "In case you need a lift back to the station, once you're finished. Or just, you know, for anything."

I wondered briefly if he was asking me out – in a strange, awkward sort of way. And then I met his eyes and I knew that wasn't it.

CHAPTER FOUR

M Y CASE WASN'T big but it took some navigating over the bumps and dips in the path. I'd taken just a few steps when I heard the gentle rumble of the car engine; Steve was reversing again, heading back up to the crossroads to turn around. The beams of light flicked twice as he waved from the window – a pale hand just illuminated by the amber glow of the dashboard. I waved back, trying to appear cheerful, and extracted my phone, flicking on the torch and straining my eyes up ahead to gauge the distance.

I began to walk, eventually picking up the suitcase by its handle and carrying it, my shoes squelching through the mud, leaving deep prints in their wake. The torch beam swung in time to my steps. It couldn't be too much further.

Five minutes passed before I saw the trees up ahead, great pines reaching towards the sky. The path led directly through them, and I sighed, checking the signal bars on my phone. As expected, we were back to zero.

Not only was this much more remote than I'd been expecting, but the struggle wouldn't end here, and I knew it. Many of our clients feel unsure about the process, at least to begin with. They reveal little about their motivations, still less so about themselves. I'd encountered people with such a deep-seated suspicion of strangers that it seemed incredible they'd contacted one of their own free will. And it wasn't as if I was there to value their property, fix the boiler or tend to the garden. Memoir-writing, by necessity, requires a deep dive – a lengthy process of revelation. There's no use being coy about it.

I'd been feeling tired, hungry, a little daunted by the prospect of settling into Miss Carey's home. Now, for the first time since arriving in Conger Book, unease replaced it all, and I felt my scalp prickle at the sight of the narrow, dark path. I turned left and right, hoping to see an alternative – a turning, perhaps, another signpost directing visitors any way but through what appeared to be not just a copse or a brief line of trees, but a forest.

It is also, I think, important to note here that I wasn't a frightened sort of person – not then. If anything, I went into most situations feet-first, fearless to the point of stupidity, at times. I took risks and, usually, no harm came of them. I'd learnt to trust my gut, to know when to stop. It hadn't always been like this, but I enjoyed the feeling of solidity that being in my mid-thirties provided: a sense that the ground would keep shifting, but that the major quakes might, at last, be behind me. And I loved the variety of my job, the fact I never knew from one week to the next what I might be doing or where I might be going. The idea of booking tickets to a train station I'd never heard of, packing a small bag for the days I'd spend here and leaving my flat behind – I liked it. I had nothing to tether me there, no anchor weighing me down. I liked the free-floating nature of my days, the ability to go and do as I pleased. It felt self-sufficient, rudderless, lacking in any kind of restriction.

I wished, not for the first time, that I'd asked Laura for more information. The years spent doing this job, moving from client to client and confidently navigating my way round towns and cities had all but removed any sense of caution, any need for clarification. That confidence had always stood me in good stead, and now I cursed myself for being so gung-ho. There was nothing but hedgerows ahead, and it seemed beyond foolish to walk through here, at night and on my own, without any real knowledge of what was waiting on the other side.

The path was a little smoother here, at least, covered over by thin pine needles, and the case rolled easily enough as I placed it down and set off. Holding the torch straight in front of me, I counted my steps as a distraction, reminding myself that this wasn't an urban alleyway but the middle of nowhere. Any company I had here was limited to owls, mice, badgers: nothing else.

A hundred steps became two hundred. I avoided looking to either side of the path, worried that if I did so I might panic. Instead I kept my eyes firmly ahead, willing the house to appear, praying for a glimmer of light. My ears strained for the sounds of a snapping twig, a rustle of leaves.

I forced myself to think of something else, to notice the beauty of the place. Here, just a few hours' by train from London, was an area of land unspoiled by machines, by tall buildings or redevelopments. Nature had been allowed to do its thing, to run riot. The shrubbery was waist-high in places bordering the path before the forest. Here there were fallen trunks at either side of me, toppled by age or lightening or bent double by the wind. Instead of being cleared quickly away, tidied up, they lay where they'd lie for weeks, months or years more, a home for insects I'd never heard of, a playground for snaffling mammals. And above it all, the deep blue of the night sky was speckled with stars, spread in joyful abandon like food on a picnic rug.

The trees started to thin, and as they did the torch reflected off something to my right. I peered closer and saw a square tin on a stick, the sort of post box found on driveways in America, with *Carey* written in curling script on the side.

It was half-open, the edges of a package sodden from exposure to the elements; inside, I could see a bundle of letters and postcards. I shone the torch ahead and my hand stilled as it scanned the horizon.

There, up ahead at last, was Elver House.

I had expected a squat little thing, perhaps covered with ivy. Original windows, a garden brimming with dahlias, nasturtium, a farmhouse-style door. This couldn't have been further from such cosy images, and I stared for a full minute at the black mass before me, too preoccupied with its incongruity here, in the middle of the woods, to notice for a moment that none of the lights were on.

Elver was taller than it was wide; it had at least three floors, perhaps four. Creeping vines curled up its face, almost obscuring the brickwork on the right-hand side. Circular, porthole windows like those on a submarine pitted the uppermost level and above them, the domed roof rose with peaks like little church spires, jagged and turreted.

Steve had been right. If Elver was a cottage, Balmoral was a camper van.

Fumbling for my case I pressed ahead, pushing the wrought-iron gate, which squealed in protest, and walked slowly through the choked weeds of the forecourt. A ruined fountain, its curled lip long since run dry, forced me to swing round to the edge of the gravelled path, holding my torch high, waiting for any sign of movement behind the dark windows up ahead. If she'd been waiting up, half-asleep, perhaps she'd heard the sound of the gate.

The ground was uneven, rough, and trenched through with puddles. As I came closer to the house I paused a moment, alert and watchful, every sense on high alert. There was water some-where, over to my left. Its cascade was continuous, its path, I could hear, broken by rocks. Although I couldn't see them, I knew these rocks would be sprinkled with moss, springy and clumped like mats across the stones. We'd spent our childhood, you and I, crossing the stream at the end of your garden, picking off the drenched tufts and throwing them at one another. As the wind cut across the forecourt the smell of mulch, decaying plants and fallen leaves combined with the mineral, earthy scent of the water.

The grass soaked through my trouser legs. I ran the torch up from the uneven facade along the front of the building to the roof, where I could see several cracked, broken tiles lying precariously in some strange balancing act between waiting to fall and staying put. In some places the coverings had been blown off completely, exposing the dark beams of thick trunks, the house's skeleton laid bare.

Everything about the situation, I realised, felt wrong. I was a practical sort of person – organised, adaptable, able to blend when

I needed to. I could barely remember a time where a job had troubled me, or when my gut had so viciously kicked in to warn me off. I thought back to the bus journey, the one we'd taken through Morocco in the dead of night, and the sick knowledge we'd felt when it terminated far from where we'd expected, a quiet road, dimly lit. I'd known then and I knew now that some deep, primitive part of myself, the reptile brain, was broadcasting red flags, stop signs.

But then, I realised as I walked slowly forward and peered through the first set of ground-floor windows, it was natural to be afraid. There appeared to be no one here. It was late, and my usual channels of communication were cut. It would be stranger not to panic, to feel relaxed in such unusual circumstances. Through the glass of a pair of small doors, the light revealed a series of bookcases and an old wooden ladder for reaching the uppermost volumes. I steadied myself against the handle, hovering my torch over the beige stone. It too was old, cracked, at odd angles. Heavy and impenetrable, but nature seemed determined to find a way inside.

I wrenched my foot from the mud and pressed on, pausing before the front door, steeling myself, and knocking.

No one answered. I rapped my knuckles again, moving to the side to peer through the next set of windows. These were streaked with dust and muck, and I wondered – briefly – how an old woman could live out here in this crumbling wreck of a house.

After the third knock I tried the handle and found, to my surprise, that the door swung inwards.

By this stage, and looking back on it, I was too wired, too tired, too scared to fully appreciate how truly bizarre it all was; so high on adrenaline after the quiet of the woods, and the shock of the house itself, nothing felt surprising. It felt like a video game, where all I had to do was reach the next level. First the country lanes, then the path, the rain, the stuffed post box, the ruined exterior of Elver House.

I don't think, if I'm honest, that anything more would have shocked me at this point. It had all been so bewildering, so other to the way I normally worked, and this reception – if you could call it that – so in keeping, really, with everything else that I almost laughed as the heavy oak of the door knocked against the back wall and I found myself on the threshold of Miss Carey's home.

CHAPTER FIVE

"Hello?" I called out. "Miss Carey?"

Nothing happened, and I flicked the torch off for a moment to let my eyes adjust. With a thrill, I realised the signal had crept to a bar, just one, and I dropped my case and rucksack to the ground, pressed a key on the home screen, scrolled down. There was Wi-Fi, too, accessible without a password: relief. I called Laura.

"Ellen? You there?" Laura's voice crackled down the line. In the background, I could hear the faint sound of music fading to the low voice of a newsreader.

"I've just arrived," I said. My relief at hearing a familiar voice lasted seconds. "Laura, there's no one here."

"What?"

"There's no one here. I knocked but nobody answered. And now I'm standing in the hallway. It's pitch dark and I had to walk through an actual forest to get here and –"

"Ellen, you're cutting in and out, but did you say you went inside?"

"Yes. The lights were all off. I knocked and I've called out to her but no one's here. The door was open."

"Right." I could hear the cogs turning as she took this in. "Err. Look, Ellen, d'you think you could try the bell again?"

"There isn't a bell."

"Wait outside until she comes down? I'm not sure how great it'll look if you've just let yourself in."

"Laura, it's chucking it down, I'm soaked through and covered in mud. There's no bell. I did knock. The wind's pretty strong, though. She might not have heard."

"Alright. I get it. You're knackered. Look, at least you're there now." Laura sounded mildly concerned but I could hear her bemusement. "She might be asleep. No one locks their doors round there I bet. And she might have gone to bed."

"Why would she go to bed? It's barely eight. And she was expecting me."

I cast my eyes once more around the hallway. Two doors led off one side and another opposite; all of them closed. Their brass knobs looked dull, polished by the hundreds of hands that had passed over them.

"We definitely said today," Laura agreed. "Ok. Better idea. You wait there, where you are. I'll ring the house phone. If she's asleep and hasn't heard you, I'll explain what's happened. That way you don't need to go creeping around in the dark, and we won't risk frightening an old woman half to death."

I nodded.

"Ellen?"

"Sorry, yes," I whispered, suddenly aware this was, as Laura said, the most likely scenario. Miss Carey was asleep. "Yes, do that."

"I'll speak to you in a minute. Keep your phone with you."

Like there was any chance I wouldn't. I ended the call, flicked the torch back on and decided, on an impulse, to close the door. Whatever happened, I wasn't going back outside to wait. If Miss Carey wasn't here – if we'd somehow got the dates wrong or she was ill, gone to stay with a friend, or anything else – we'd deal with that. I'd just have to change my clothes, find somewhere halfway warm and call Steve for a lift back to the station.

The shrill of a telephone sounded from a small table along the hallway. I could hear it from above, too, up the stairs and along the hallway somewhere in the distance. It rang once, twice, five times, and then cut out. My own home screen lit up as Laura phoned back.

"Ellen?" Bemusement had vanished now. "You're still there?"

"Yes," I said. "No one answered?" My teeth began to chatter.

"No," said Laura slowly. "No answering machine either. Look, I'm so, so sorry about this. Are you ok?"

"I'm fine," I said, and I realised as I said it that it was true. Somehow, the confirmation that no one was home was a relief. Whatever had led to this misunderstanding was immaterial: Miss Carey wasn't here. The idea of climbing that steep flight of stairs to find her, possibly waking her to the sight of a stranger, was almost worse than the walk through the woods. Knowing I was unlikely to have to do that was curiously calming.

"There must have been a mistake, I guess," I said. "But look, Laura, I'm here now . . . I'll stay put for a bit in case she's popped out." I couldn't imagine a less likely scenario. The house looked, at least from the outside, totally unoccupied. "I'm hardly breaking and entering, she invited me after all."

"I'd much sooner get you a cab back," said Laura. "Give me a sec . . ." I heard tapping sounds and then a sigh. More tapping. Seconds turned into minutes. "Yeah. I thought as much. There's a couple of later trains tonight but you'd be waiting for a connection til 6am anyway. I could send a car and get them to take you to a hotel. Let me see . . ."

"No," I said suddenly. "No, Laura. Cars can't get up the driveway here." I'd have to walk back through the woods again, and now I'd done it once, I wasn't about to do it again - not tonight. "Let's wait until tomorrow."

"What?"

"Let's wait. She's not here, but she might come back. And you wouldn't believe the weather, seriously."

"So, what, you just stay there? In the house?"

"I guess so. It's very tucked away. No neighbours, no one close by. I can't really emphasise how remote this place is . . . And look, I'm cold, my feet hurt and I need to eat something." I didn't want to tell her about the woods again, worried how my voice might sound.

"You cut out for a moment there."

"I'll stay put and head back tomorrow. Don't worry about booking a car, I got the number of the guy you sent before. Steve. I'll text him, ask him to come and get me first thing. That way I can warm up a bit, get some sleep and head back to the city tomorrow."

Laura sounded dubious, despite the crackling of the line. "I don't know, Ellen," she paused and sighed, clearly thinking it through. "Ok, look. Keep your phone nearby. Write a note and pop it on the front door explaining that you're inside, will you? Just in case she does come back. I'll try Miss Carey again on the landline in an hour . . . Maybe she *is* upstairs."

As she spoke, my eyes travelled up the carpet runner to the first floor and I swallowed. I hoped she wasn't. Through the banister I could see the sweep of a handrail turning in on itself, rising higher. There must be at least ten rooms up there, in the dark.

"I'll explain the situation when I get hold of her," Laura continued. "But if she doesn't arrive, you head back to town and we'll sort another way of doing this..."

There was more tapping, the sound of mouse-clicks. "I've no email for her either. Don't suppose she has one. Just the house-phone number: I can see the notes confirming the dates and times we spoke . . . For heaven's sake, El. I'm sorry. It's bloody strange. This has literally never happened before."

I closed my eyes, nodding again, though of course Laura couldn't see that. "I'll speak to you tomorrow, then." I said.

"Absolutely, first thing. Charge your phone, warm up a bit, and have a rest. Text Steve and you'll be out of there nice and early. And any problems give me a call immediately, my phone's under my pillow. Share your location with me, too."

"Will do," I said weakly. We hung up.

I'd never felt more alone – and that was saying something.

CHAPTER SIX

I BEGAN TO move along the wall, finding a light switch. In the milliseconds before the hallway was illuminated I tensed wildly, my eyes caught on the thick-set hulk of a silhouette on the right side of the corridor. Three pendant lamps sprang into a warm glow and I felt myself exhale. A grandfather clock, ticking patiently.

The wind was barely audible now through the thick wood of the door, and though I could hear the rain lashing the glass to my right and left, it sounded altogether cosier now that I was out of it: it sounded, almost, like home. Downpours on weekend days in a house about a fortieth of the size of Elver; anoraks and wellies for treks up Scafell Pike, trudging against the flow of traffic on the way back from shivering swims in Windermere. Outdoors, soaking, covered in muck and slime and huddling together like penguins on the back seat of an old Ford Mondeo. The scrape of butter across a crumpet when we got back, the four of us ravenous, no prisoners taken. Shared bathwater and fires and an adult – a parent, an aunt, a granddad, a second cousin, they were interchangeable – reading aloud from a book, any book, until the two sets of bunk beds fell silent.

If something had come up, and Miss Carey was no longer available for our interviews, so be it. I'd hole up here tonight. Laura would deal with the fallout and we could sort something else. By this point I was so tired I barely cared. The adrenaline began to leech out of me, and in its place remained only a longing for tea, a shower and bed. It felt so wrong walking through someone's house when they weren't here, but there wasn't much I could do about it.

Turning the knob of the door immediately to my right, I paused on the threshold before stepping inside. The room was large, its high ceilings a soft buttery yellow. The hallway light spilled inside to reveal an ornate fireplace, the sort of old-fashioned kind three people could lie down inside. The walls bore tasteful, impersonal paintings of country scenes: a harvest, a hunt, a pair of fishermen on a boat. Others had hung there once, judging by the faint silhouettes that remained. On first glance it would have seemed as clean and comfortable as any hotel, though the overall effect told me little about Miss Carey.

And yet as I stepped into the room my foot crunched over something and I jumped back, startled. A scattering of trinkets and china figurines lay sprawled across the carpet, some already shattered, one newly decapitated by my foot. I stared at them, frowning, then looked to the window. Had the wind forced its way inside and toppled them? I bent down and collected as many of the fragments as I could, cupping them in both hands and placing them on the mahogany coffee table.

The thick, plush pile of the carpet bounced slightly under my feet. Two deep L-shaped sofas were turned to create a square around the fireplace. I peered closer, noticing a boot-print on the upholstery. It was large and muddy, and had clearly been there some time. I passed a finger over the print and a dusting of dirt flaked off.

Despite these anomalies the room was in good order – I was reassured by the plumpness of the cushions, the well-stocked coal scuttle, the pile of neatly stacked firewood. In a way, it was almost better that Miss Carey wasn't here, that I didn't need to make small talk, that I'd done my best to accommodate her project but the mistake, once this had all been cleared up, was entirely hers.

I felt stupid now for my panic at the forest, the silent path, the terrible weather. What had happened was unexpected, inasmuch as I'd anticipated that my client would be here, of course. But now that I was out of the rain, out of the dark, the house was fairly clean and comfortable, I felt myself relax. Yes, it was odd to be spending the night here, but Laura was aware. I had Steve's number and whatever had happened, I'd be out of Conger Brook by the morning.

Closing the door behind me, I crossed to the other side of the entrance hall to find a library: the embossed spines winking at me in the soft glow of the light. A ladder rested against the far corner. My entrance caused a cloud of dust to leap into the air, tumbling and spinning to rest on the ground once more. There was another low coffee table placed in the centre of the room, and a thick-set wooden desk by the windows which doubled as a set of doors leading out into the grounds. It must be beautiful in the summer. On the coffee table sat a pile of newspapers, magazines, a set of coasters – all neatly arranged, their circular discs positioned on top of one another with precision.

The final door, towards the rear of the hallway, revealed a kitchen, large and clean, with multiple worktops and pans of varying sizes hanging from small hooks on the walls. A polished oak table took up much of the space, eight chairs tucked beneath it. There was no sign of life, no teaspoon in the sink, bowl of fruit, no dishcloth slung over the handle of the cooker. It was well-equipped but empty. Beside the fridge, a calendar hung lifelessly from a small hook. It was open to the correct month, though, and peppered with handwriting, notes, reminders. October was illustrated with a picture of a squirrel, almost camouflaged, hopping among auburn leaves.

I backed out and realised the time had come. If I was to stay here, really, actually sleep in this woman's house, I needed to buckle up and find a room to do it in. I couldn't put it off much longer. The boards, with their smart runner on the staircase were thick, well-trodden in the middle. I'd no desire to go poking around and wanted only to find a guest room, but placing one foot in front of the other seemed to take a long time.

Upstairs the layout was much the same as below. The hallway gave off onto three rooms either side of the corridor, with a bath-room – I could see the enormous tub from where I stood, since the door was open – at the end. A stopped clock on the wall opposite showed a time of half past one.

I knocked at the first door on the right and turned the knob slowly. Despite everything that had happened there was still, evidently, the chance that Miss Carey might have slept through my arrival, through the phone ringing, through the muted banging and crashing of my ascent.

"Hello?" I called, as I pushed open the door, "Excuse me . . . Miss Carey?"

Whatever I'd been expecting, it wasn't this.

The room was ransacked – there was no other word for it. It was clearly a study, or had been: a high-backed chair had been tipped over and one of its legs broken off; an Anglepoise lamp lay shattered on the wooden boards, and the drawers of the desk had been pulled out completely and left on the floor. Only the books on their shelves remained untouched.

I stared for a moment and then, on autopilot, I pulled out my phone. My hands were freezing, and they shook as I dialled Laura again. I spun around quickly, checking behind the door as the call connected. I backed slowly from the room, every sense on high alert as I scanned the dark corridor.

"Alright, Ellen?" Her voice was reassuringly calm. "How're you doing?"

"Something's happened here."

"Go on," she said. I could hear her exhaling. I imagined her happily ensconced on the porch, kids safely in bed and vape in hand.

"I'm upstairs and there's stuff everywhere. It looks like a break-in." I described it to her and paced outside, back to the hallway. "Furniture broken, glass on the floor. It's a mess. But she's not here."

"Shit," she muttered. "*Shit*. Could this get any weirder . . . I'm sorry, Ellen, really I am . . . You must be completely freaked out."

"A little," I lied. I was seconds from losing it completely. "I just want to get out, to be honest."

I turned back to the trashed study and paused, staring. The

footprints silhouetted against the threadbare carpet were my own; fresh imprints in the thick dust. As I stared ahead, I saw too that the upended chair was covered in dust, the shards of lamp thickly coated.

"It's weird," I said, "but I don't think it happened recently."

Laura said something and the line began to break up.

"Sorry, love," she came back on. "What did you say?"

"Whatever happened in here didn't happen tonight, I don't think."

"Did you hear anything when you came in?" Laura asked.

"No, nothing."

"Ok. Can you go into another room for me?"

I went to the bathroom across the hallway, treading carefully. Towels were hung neatly over a rail. A mug on the basin contained a tube of Colgate and a single toothbrush.

"It looks fine," I told Laura.

"That's good. And another?"

I turned again, making my way along the corridor, my ears straining to catch a sound, the creak of a board or rustle of clothing. The next door opened into a bedroom, a thick eiderdown covered over with a mantle and two plump cushions. A dresser stood against the back wall. An empty vase, its glass dirty and smudged, was positioned on the mantelpiece above the fireplace. Dirty water clouded its bottom. It was clearly a spare bedroom; there were no personal items anywhere.

"It's fine," I said into the phone, whispering again though I'd no idea why. "Nothing broken. It's fine."

Relief was making me giddy. Laura exhaled.

"Right, here's what we're going to do. From what you've said, there's no immediate danger, right? No one's in there with you."

"No," I said slowly. "I don't think so."

"So what I'll do now is ring around and see if there's a taxi company who can come and collect you tonight. Bugger the connecting train and the waiting around – better than being there, at this point. I'll get someone to take you all the way home, alright?"

Laura sounded more in control now, less bewildered. "It might take me a little while to get hold of someone and persuade a driver out there, but I'll make sure they come to the door, whatever it takes, and I'll have them call me when they're outside too. How does that sound?" I heard the sound of her laptop booting up.

"Perfect," I said. "Thanks. I'll wait to hear back."

We hung up quickly after that. I stood in the doorway of the bedroom, looked back down at the hallway and, making up my mind, returned to fetch the case and bag.

Once back inside the spare room I shut the door, firmly, and placed the heavy case before it. Hopefully it wouldn't be too long and I'd be out within the hour. But however long it did take, there was no part of me that wanted to wait downstairs, with its long, ancient-looking windows and the summer doors leading onto the lawn. Had I even checked them, when I'd been inside? Why would I have? The main, outer front door had been open, so why not those too?

Pushing the thought aside I turned on the bedside lamp, shrugged off my drenched jumper and trousers and began to change. At least there was only one entrance and exit here, and the room was sufficiently far along the corridor that I'd hear anyone approaching. I tried to reason with myself, to find another explanation for the wreck of the study. Perhaps Miss Carey was redecorating - in the process of clearing the room out. Maybe it had always been like that and I just wasn't to know.

Whatever had happened, it was concentrated within that one room, and the rest of the house - mostly - seemed fine. I had no idea who this woman was or how she lived, and Elver gave little away. In any case, it was no longer my business. In an hour or two, I'd be out of here and speeding back to London.

Sitting down on the bed I was struck by its softness, by the thick swathes of the duvet underneath the dust cover. I lay back and reached for my phone again. My alarm that morning had gone off at four; I was exhausted. And still the rain showed no signs of stopping.

The window looked out onto the eastern side of the grounds, and though I couldn't see it I could hear the far-off babble of a stream, water coursing over rocks and pebbles. It was soothing, a repetitive, calming, incessant beat as the swell passed over smaller stones and sent them scattering with the sound of a clock's ticking.

I wondered how much Laura would have to beg, borrow or steal to get any driver up to the front of the house – it was, I knew, pretty much impossible and unless they were aware of another route here I'd be walking back through the forest again. But at least, this time, I wouldn't be on my own. Laura would insist that whoever arrived would meet me at the house, and I was sure – once she explained the situation, perhaps greased the wheels a little with a generous tip – that they would do so.

I closed my eyes, allowing the day to melt away, just for a moment. My hands were folded across my chest, my phone tucked neatly between them like a medieval queen buried with her crown. I'd rest until it rang.

CHAPTER SEVEN

A SHUFFLING AND then a pause. A sound like something being dragged along the wooden boards. In the halfway house between sleep and waking I heard it, and my mind – already alert to threat – scanned the possibilities. It was too regular, too rhythmic to be an animal. Too big. But it was patient, almost. Feet, moving slowly. Not in shoes, though, or barefoot; slippers? I felt myself charged, like a cat scanning for danger on a busy road, my ears ready and waiting.

Eyes snapping open and breath coming quickly, I was fully conscious once again in a matter of seconds, a pulse beating maniacally through the tense muscles of my neck. The shuffling paused, stopped, started again. It crept closer until I heard it reach the bedroom door. I clenched my fists, felt my chest tightening. The knob turned with aching slowness and, although the suitcase protested, it began to scrape its own way across the floor. The door knocked against the back wall as it opened fully, and I stared at the figure, lit from behind by hallway lamps which were blazing out.

"I warn you," said the figure, "that whatever you want, you won't find it here. I have a panic button. The police have already been called. Now you'd better tell me, and quickly, exactly what you're doing in my house."

I sat up, staring at the woman advancing on me. She was petite, slightly hunched. She paused, looking straight at me. I could make out very little of her face in the glare cast from the hallway.

"Miss Carey?" I said, swinging my legs off the bed.

She took a step backwards.

"My name's Ellen. I'm from the ghost-writing agency." I switched the bedside lamp on again.

The woman peered at me disbelievingly and then, like clouds parting, her face cleared. "The ghost-writer."

"I'm so sorry. I was planning on leaving, but the storm . . . I thought you'd have been here. The plan was to wait until I could catch the next train back to London . . ."

"I spoke to another woman – Lauren, Liz, something like that," she said faintly.

"Laura, my editor. She told me you were expecting me."

Miss Carey ran her hands across her eyes and reached out a hand to steady herself on the end of the iron bedstead. She looked to the floor, then back at me, taking me in properly now we weren't in the shadows, just as I stared back. Her hair was cut into a smart, thick bob, a brief cascade of short shining grey; her skirt was almost professional, uncreased, chosen carefully. On her feet she wore a pair of green slippers.

"Yes," she said, "I was expecting you." I was already dialling Laura as she spoke, trying to nod reassuringly. She looked almost ill, pale in the harsh hallway light. I noticed her eyes, the heavy lashes, the deep blue irises like the ocean's midnight zone. She must once have been very beautiful.

"Hello?" Laura's voice was crisp and tight, clearly stressed. I imagined she was having trouble finding someone willing to drive from Elver to London at – what time even was it? I glanced down as I put the phone on speaker and saw it was close to one in the morning.

"Laura, you're on speaker-phone. Miss Carey's here."

Laura's manner changed abruptly. "Miss Carey?"

"Yes," I said.

There was a brief silence. "Hello?" Laura said uncertainly.

Miss Carey sighed. Turning to me she spoke clearly, less frightened now. "My dear, I am so, so sorry. It's my fault entirely."

"Miss Carey, it's Laura, Ellen's editor at the agency. I'm sorry if we've startled you. I've been trying to reach you on the landline."

"I've been out," she said softly. "I just returned."

"Ellen," said Laura, sounding more than a little concerned now. "Is everything ok?"

"It's fine," I said. How many times this evening was I going to say that? I looked back towards the older woman, who'd moved to sit in the wicker chair by the window. "Miss Carey?" I asked clearly, so Laura could hear me. "I really am sorry for coming in like this. The car dropped me off some time ago and the door was open. I didn't want to startle you, but I came inside. The weather was awful . . ."

"Terrible," she agreed softly. Her pale face seemed to hang above the rest of her body: there was a look of such vulnerability about her now, such guilt, that I forgot momentarily about the fear of just a few hours before, the dark forest and the empty, freezing house.

"And so I came in to wait. Laura was looking for a car to take me back to the city tonight. I was waiting to hear from her and must have dozed off." I managed a shaky laugh. "This isn't normally how I meet new clients, by the way."

Laura, sensing the mood shift, laughed too. "There's no harm done, Miss Carey. I'm just glad you're there and everything's all right. Would you like me to have someone collect Ellen, and we can reschedule the interviews?"

I almost laughed at the idea I might return here, if Miss Carey decided to pick a different week, if she wanted to get back to us in a few months, if there'd been a change of plan. There was no way I'd be doing this again. Perhaps sensing this, the woman shook her head vehemently; the wicker chair creaked with the force of it. When she didn't say anything, however, I turned the phone off speaker mode and lifted it to my ear.

"Hi, it's just me. I think Miss Carey would prefer to continue, if that's alright with you." I looked to her for confirmation, and she smiled weakly. "She doesn't want to reschedule."

"Jesus Christ," said Laura quietly. "And she seems . . . ok? Did she mention where the hell she's been?"

"Not yet," I said carefully. "I called you straight away. I'm sure we'll come to that."

"And you're happy to stay? I've tried every blood taxi service from here to Scotland and no surprises, we didn't have any takers. But Ellen, if you'd prefer, we can still arrange it for tomorrow morning, ok?"

"Thanks," I said, "but honestly, I'm happy to stay."

"Did she mention the burglars?"

I'd almost forgotten that. "No. As I said, we've literally just met. There'll be an explanation though."

There was something in the set of Miss Carey's shoulders, the blades thin as a bird's, and the way she sat, arms folded, looking out of the window. Her face was angular, agreeable, innocent somehow. Her skin, like mine, looked as though it had never been exposed to proper, strong sunlight, like she had been cocooned, sheltered from the elements. And yet her voice, when she'd found me here in bed, had demonstrated a strength that contrasted with the fragile frame, a power.

I didn't want to leave her, didn't want to have come all this way for nothing. She and Laura had agreed the date weeks ago and, although the welcome was bizarre, she was here now. We'd get it done. I thought about how I'd explain all this to you, tomorrow perhaps, once the light had risen over the forest and everything seemed calmer. Perhaps you'd answer, perhaps I'd leave a message. Maybe you'd ring back. It felt unlikely. I had to leave it, to forget.

When I ended the call, we both stood up. "Well," Miss Carey said shakily. "I know it's late, but . . . a cup of tea?"

"Should we call the police back? Just to save them coming all the way—"

"That won't be necessary," she said. For the first time, I saw the hint of a smile playing on her lips. "I was bluffing."

CHAPTER EIGHT

T HE HOUSE FELT utterly different now we were here together. Miss Carey looked up at the severe overheads in the hallway. She pressed a smaller, hidden switch that illuminated several table lamps at once. Now the place looked warm, relaxed, cosy even. I walked behind her as we descended the stairs: she moved slowly, cautiously and, I noticed in the downstairs hallway, with a slight limp.

"What must you think of me," she kept saying. "Turning up and no one home."

We entered the kitchen and she set to filling the kettle, placing it on the Aga and clattering about with crockery, with tiny, ornate silver spoons retrieved from a hidden drawer in the tall oak dresser. "My mother's," she explained, smiling weakly. "And only to be used by very special guests."

There were no windows here save for the back door and no way for the light, were there any, to enter. I saw my own reflection in its narrow panes of glass - pale, eyes bright with anxiety. My hair, never very neat anyway, stuck up at odd angles and I could feel the imprint of the bedspread on my cheek.

My nap, however short, had re-focused me, and I found myself fascinated by her as she moved from cooker to fridge, depositing things on the table and placing coasters neatly before us both. There was a certain balletic quality to the way she held herself: rigid, almost - quite upright. I saw her wince as she placed her weight on her ankle, but otherwise she seemed well.

It was clear she'd had a shock, though. The china cups clattered slightly as she set them down. But when she smiled she did so with her whole face, and her eyes were kindly and shining in the semi-darkness. Each of her fingernails was painted a deep, luxuriant red.

"There you are, dear," she said, pushing a plate of biscuits towards me. Several were broken, and they looked a little faded but I plucked one up, realising how hungry I was, while she poured the tea. I knew exactly how I must look opposite her: the dark bottoms of my jeans splashed with mud, my skin and eyes puffy from sleep. You used to say, not unkindly, that I looked like a sort of mad professor. It was true I wasn't the tidiest of people, but this was far below the usual image of vaguely presentable I'd have chosen for a first meeting with a new client.

"So," she said now, settling herself, "let's start again, shall we?" She held out a hand theatrically and I grasped it, grinning back.

"Catherine Carey," she said. She gestured around her. "My home, Elver House. My marbles . . ." and here she indicated her head, "totally lost."

Playing along, I held out my own hand. "Ellen," I said. "Marbles also totally lost. I've never been discovered asleep in bed by a client before. Like the Goldilocks of ghost-writing."

She chuckled. "So you're who they've sent. To record my memoirs."

I nodded. "Exactly. Did Laura explain to you how it all works?"

"Oh, bits and bobs," she said. "Though I expect I've forgotten most of it. I must have spoken to her, and to another of your colleagues a good month ago, maybe more. Please," she indicated the plate of biscuits again and poured me more tea. "Tell me first about you. And tell me where you've come from. Did you have a good journey?"

"It was easy enough," I said, through a mouthful of Hobnob. "About four hours to the Junction from London, then the second train. It was good to get out of the city, actually. And I love long train trips."

"I do, too," she said softly. She smiled. I continued. "And then Laura had a taxi pick me up from Conger Brook."

"It's quite a schlep," she said. "You must be tired."

"Well, I had a nap . . ."

"Indeed," she said, and grinned at me shyly. "You live in London, but I'm guessing you're not from the city."

"Did the accent give it away? I moved about a decade ago. I grew up just outside Kendal."

"I've never been," she said. I was momentarily surprised by this, and then checked myself. She'd not visited Cumbria, but I'd not been to Northumberland. Both of us the same, despite growing up so close, at either end of the country's waist, its slimmest part.

"My memories of it are pretty distant now. I left for university and then went straight to the capital. Like everyone else."

She nodded, sipping her tea. "Not quite like everyone else," she said softly.

"Have you lived here long, then?"

"Oh yes. I was born here. In fact, the story of my life is as much a story about this house. My great-great-great, and probably some more greats, grandfather built it in the mid-18th century."

"It's beautiful," I said. "Perhaps tomorrow you could give me a tour."

"I'm sure we can arrange that." She tucked her hair nervously behind her ears and leant her elbows on the table. She had the air of someone, despite her age, who had never been ill in her life: there was a frailty to her, but underlying it a deeper sense of robustness too, of good health and cheer.

I spoke before considering whether it was wise or not. Curiosity – or fear, more likely – got the better of me. "Miss Carey . . . when I was looking around earlier, I noticed . . . Well, the study upstairs."

She looked blankly at me.

"It seemed as though something had happened there."

"How do you mean?" she said evenly.

I wondered whether to drop it, brush it off. But it had been so chaotic, so at odds with the rest of Elver. The chair on its side, one leg broken off and the splinters sticking up like switchblades.

I'd only just met her, and yet I knew Miss Carey had not been responsible for that.

"It was in a bit of a state," I said. I avoided looking directly at her, unsure how she'd react. There was a pause, then—

"I don't go in there much," she said. I glanced up and her; the expressionless face gave nothing away. "I wouldn't be surprised if it's a mess. We can work downstairs, if that suits you. In the library, or the drawing room."

The broken china figurines came to mind, the boot-print on the sofa. "The library sounds good," I said. I'd no desire to press the subject, and it was clear she didn't want to talk about it.

"Now, as I say, I've forgotten most of what your young man told me over the phone." I supposed she meant a member of the sales team at the agency. "Blame my age," she said. "But I'm keen to hear how it'll all work. We discussed the ins and outs of it so long ago now . . . I should have taken notes." She pushed the plate towards me again. "Give me the spiel."

I took her in: the neatly combed hair, the startling dusky blue of her eyes set against the pallid, tired-looking face. She could have been mocking, but I detected no unkindness in her comment.

"Right." I said, "Yes. So, the intention is to spend a few days with you here at the house. Discuss your life, your upbringing, childhood, family, and anything else you'd like recorded." I paused, chewing the Hobnob. "Try not to see them as interviews. I imagine you'll soon forget about the recorder anyway. Look at it as one long conversation. A sort of extended coffee with a friend."

She gave me an appraising look and nodded. "And then?"

"Well, at the end of the week, I'll return to London. Once I'm there, I'll transcribe what we've discussed and begin to shape a sample for you. A structure with chapters outlined, that sort of thing. And a few short pages for you to read through."

She considered this a moment and then nodded again. "Very well. And if I don't like it?"

I was prepared for this. They always asked. "Chances are, at first, you won't like it. We'll work on it. You can tell me some names of authors you like, and other autobiographies you enjoyed, and I can try and emulate those. Before I get going on the rest of the book, you need to be happy with the samples. Saves us both a lot of trouble later." I smiled at her. Sweetly, I hoped.

"I must say, I was most surprised when I heard about the company. One never really imagines anyone besides a celebrity or public figure having their memoirs recorded."

"That's true," I said, feeling on more comfortable ground now. "And yet for most of us it's really important to get our experiences down. It can bring back all sorts of memories. Sometimes it's even quite cathartic."

She nodded slowly. "All those diaries people keep for years, sometimes with the most mundane entries . . . but sometimes not. They're snapshots of a time and place, aren't they?"

"Exactly," I said. "You're the only one who's lived your life, whatever twists and turns it might have taken."

"Indeed," she said gravely. "You're absolutely right, Ellen."

I paused, and the silence elongated. She seemed so contrite, so totally different to the woman I'd first encountered upstairs.

"Miss Carey," I said, "It *was* today, wasn't it? Our meeting. Did we get it wrong? I only ask because if so, I need to apologise – and also let my editor know, too. We want to make sure this sort of thing doesn't happen again. It can't have been very fun for you, finding me upstairs like that. I'm sorry."

She gave a bark of laughter and stood, moving slowly to the calendar beside the fridge. She lifted it off its hook, jabbing her finger at the squirrel among the leaves, the page opened at October. She pointed to the week commencing the 26th. Today's date was circled, with the name of the agency printed inside the ring. "To Elver" it read. "Writer arriving today." The word "today" was underlined three times.

"It was absolutely my fault, Ellen," she said. "I do write things down, but sometimes . . . Well, I forget. In any case, I should be apologising to you." She glanced out of the kitchen doors at the rain driving against the panes. "What a frightful night to be caught inside an old woman's house, and no one here to greet you. That'd be a good way to start the book, in fact. An empty house and a lunatic creeping up on you while you sleep."

"Were you . . . visiting friends?" I was tentative asking the question, and saw immediately I'd good reason to be. Miss Carey's face fell and her lips became pursed.

"I was out walking," she said shortly. She placed the calendar back on its hook and stood by the fridge, hands clasped.

Trying to lighten the mood, I nodded enthusiastically. "You're a braver woman than me," I said. "I was drenched after 10 minutes tramping through the forest."

Miss Carey said nothing, simply stared ahead.

For reasons I didn't understand even as I spoke, I tried again. "It was very late – to be out walking, I mean."

"I don't sleep much," she said. "People don't, at my age. I'm 87, you know. I can never drift off without a long walk in the evening." I thought back to her shuffling steps, to the slow pace with which she'd come down the stairs. The way she'd clutched onto the banister. She moved more briskly, this time, to the sink.

"You'll be tired, I expect," she said. "Do take the guest room upstairs, the one we met in." She laughed shakily. "I saw your case up there. Do you have everything you need, my dear?"

I nodded, smiling back at her, and understood myself dismissed. "I'll head up now," I said. "Thank you for the tea. Goodnight, Miss Carey."

"Call me Catherine," she called after my retreating back.

As I climbed the steps, in the early hours of that Friday morning, I thought of my regular weekends: walking from south-east London up all the way to Tufnell Park, through the townhouses of Camden and on past the lock. I was never alone there; in every corner, every alleyway Londoners smoked, chatted, sat, read, ate or nodded as I passed. Last week I'd sat and watched a dog chasing a ball, unable to stop himself in time and lurching into me, his collar a thick red leather. He wagged and dove into the water, chasing scattering ducks that had been floating neatly around a tinfoil food container.

On Mondays the tube platforms thronged. People formed orderly queues at Canada Water and loudspeakers announced there was another train right behind this one so please don't shove. Some commuters took out their headphones to listen, others read newspapers, books. Some kissed. There was so much direction, so much purpose, it felt like everything unfolded exactly as it should there.

In the bathroom, the small cabinet under the basin revealed toiletries wrapped in torn, dusty paper. *Wright's Old Tar, Imperial Leather, Lifebuoy toilet soap.* The glass bottles were time capsules with peeling stickers describing what had once been Vaseline hair tonic, Yardley's hand lotion, thick set as concrete, Pond's cold cream. There was no shower, just a creaky standalone bath: underneath the taps, its pale cast-iron was streaked with water stains. Even now, as I watched, small droplets leaked down relentlessly, pooling around the drain.

Like the rest of the house, the guest bedroom had a completely different air to it now. The water running down the glass felt homely, reassuring. The lamp gave out a halo of orange, a circle of softness. I pulled my pyjamas and a paperback I'd brought from the suitcase and went about preparing to sleep.

The day, at last, was about to end.

CHAPTER NINE

I'D FORGOTTEN TO set an alarm or draw the curtains. The light woke me, changing with remarkable speed from deep indigo to periwinkle to the pale grey dawn of late October. How piercing it was, as it gathered force for the new day. As I lay in bed and watched it, almost-bare branches tapped the glass of the window lightly at the top. The lower portions, near the sash, revealed the gently undulating lawn and the edge of the ruined fountain, all the way down to the stream, which I saw now for the first time as a ribbon of silver in the distance.

The duvet, though thick and comforting, had an earthy, musty sort of smell. I pinched its corners and felt the hard edges of feathers like twigs. I'd fallen into it last night and passed the small hours without waking once, a deep and dreamless sleep.

I checked my phone; the clocks had gone back an hour during the night, creating the present from the past; I'd forgotten it was happening. Laura, of course, had been in touch. *Hope you slept well. Text when you're up and about. Hope it goes well with CC.*

Beneath it I saw a message from you, tapped out hurriedly, I could tell, from the spaces between words and the odd spelling mistake. You hoped the first day went alright. You asked how the journey was. The message had come through at 3.30am, and I could imagine you there, in the one-time spare room we'd slept in so many times. You'd be rocking in your chair and typing with one hand. I typed back about the train and the rain and the big, old house – Georgian, I said, knowing you'd want a picture.

I shouldn't have responded, really: it was so strange to omit things from you, to give a part of the story but not the whole. It felt dishonest somehow. But you had taken the time to remember where I was going, and you knew I'd see the message when I woke.

The first thing I noticed, swinging my legs from the theatrically high bed, was the cold. It was freezing, and I didn't chill easily. The air seemed charged with it almost – thick, like it had hung around in this same room without moving for weeks. I made a mental note to ask Miss Carey to switch the central heating on, and glanced around for the radiator. How had I not noticed this last night, when my clothes were all but drenched? There was no heater to be seen. Sighing, I turned to the fireplace and stopped.

The large, deep-set hole in the wall was clean, its grate pulled to one side; I could see the brush marks where the ash had been removed. Beside it stood a large basket filled with roughly chopped logs, scraps of bark and newspapers twisted into long tubes for kindling. And yet there, among the half-burnt scraps of old coal that remained in its centre, there was something else, something that doused me with a cold quite unlike whatever the room itself could inflict. It looked, for one sickening second, like *hands*. Folded over one another.

Perhaps I'd just stood up too quickly. I turned around for a moment, barely noticing what I was doing, and began to make the bed. I piled the cushions one on top of the other, took a sip of water from the bottle on the beside table, smoothed the duvet and pulled the cover on top.

And then, turning sharply again I moved forward, reaching into the hearth, and brushed the coal from a pair of latex gloves. They were clammy and cool to the touch, and I recoiled as soon as my fingers made contact with them. Just an ordinary pair of gloves – intact, without holes or rips. There was nothing about them that ought to have repelled me and yet I'd reacted like they'd burned. I pinched them out, pulling them from the grate before tossing them into the waste-paper bin. Then I washed my hands and sat down before the fireplace again, determined to bring a bit of warmth to the room.

I remembered the last time I'd done this – building a fire from scratch. We were 27, camping in a field in Spain. I'd reassured you I knew how to do it before Googling it when you went to find somewhere to pee. It was early evening and we'd been walking all day; our boots and jackets covered in dust and mud, and in our backpacks we'd nothing more than spare tops, a mini camping stove, a toothbrush, chocolate and a bottle of unknown but high-percentage spirits. I got it going in the end, the fire, while you pitched the tent and poured bottled water into a pan for pasta. How did I do it? I pushed the field, the golden dusk from my mind and focused. A tepee-like structure. Small, dry bits of bark, perhaps. A splash of the vodka, maybe. We were idiots then, but it worked. I shook my head, trying to clear it.

I built the cone-like structure in the grate. There was a box of matches beside the basket and I lit one, propping it up inside the tented scraps and blowing softly through the gaps. It took quickly and crackled. I fed the long blue flame a small piece of the rolled-up newspaper and watched as it snaked along the edges, blackening the print like a glass of water just spilled and spreading. After ensuring the bottom of the grate was open, its little hatch providing plenty of air, I placed a small log on top and watched, satisfied, as it hissed like an exhalation.

I turned and faced the door; immediately took a step back.

Miss Carey stood framed in the doorway, wearing the exact same clothes as she had last night. Her eyes were glassy but her mouth was pulled down into a scowl.

Had she opened the door while I was busy with the fire? Why hadn't she knocked? I immediately crossed my arms, defensively it must have seemed. I was in pyjamas, and was more than a little unnerved at the idea she could have been standing there for minutes, watching as I blew on the flames and muttered to myself.

"I was just . . ." I pointed at the fire. "It was chilly in here." She said nothing, so I tried to smile. "Did you sleep well?"

Her eyes moved from my face to gaze out of the window. The

light was stronger now; it was almost eight. She stared blankly out at the lawn or the trees or the brook in the distance.

"Miss Carey?" I remembered her parting words the night before. "Catherine?"

With an obvious effort she shifted her gaze back to me. "Good morning," she said eventually. She looked exhausted. "Not terribly well I'm afraid. You don't, at my age." Her eyes caught the fire and she frowned. "I'm sorry. The heating here is abysmal. We have central downstairs but it's always been impossible getting these rooms to a decent temperature. I suppose I've rather gotten used to it."

"It's no trouble," I said, bending down to toss another log onto the grate. I stood for a moment and then, deciding, picked up my wash-bag and made as if to leave the room. "I'll just get myself dressed and ready, and then perhaps we could begin in half an hour or so?"

"Begin?" She looked from me to the fireplace and back again.

"The interviews," I said, carefully. "Or we could wait a little, if you'd prefer. Did you want to have a rest, perhaps? If you didn't sleep well. I could go for a walk and come back a little later."

I hoped she wouldn't agree to this, but her face relaxed. "Oh," she said, "Yes. That might be better, if you don't mind. I rather feel I ought to lie down for a while. Perhaps we could begin after lunch? Would that suit you, Helen?"

I nodded, mentally calculating how long that gave me. "It's no trouble."

If we started at half past 12, I reasoned, I could explore the house, walk into the village even, and be back in time for an afternoon's work. There was no use starting now, when Miss Carey was clearly tired.

"How long will we need, do you think? This afternoon, I mean."

"A good couple of hours," I said, trying to sound casual. The truth was, at this stage, I had no idea. Until Catherine Carey told me what, exactly, she wanted from this memoir I was in the dark. Better to err on the side of caution, though. "Oh, and it's Ellen. Sorry." I tried to sound light-hearted. She simply nodded and turned.

I was just leaving the room when something occurred to me. "Catherine," I said to her retreating back. "I just wanted to check . . ."

She turned around on the landing, her eyes still holding that strange, vacant look.

"When I was about to light the fire, I noticed there was something in the grate. Just some old gloves, but I popped them in the bin. Was that alright? Sorry, I ought to have checked with you first."

I didn't expect her to mind, of course. They were thin plastic gloves, hardly something she could be fussed about keeping. I'm not even sure, now, what made me ask. Simple curiosity. Nosiness, probably.

Catherine frowned again. "Gloves?"

"Yes, just old plastic ones. I can show you if you like."

She took a step back, and then another. Her hand flew, suddenly and with a speed I'd not expected, to her throat. She made a strange, gasping sound.

Alarmed, I moved forwards, but her eyes – placid and distant just moments before – had transformed. She stared at me with a kind of wild, furious intensity and once again, for the second time that morning, I moved away.

"I'm sorry," I said, bewildered. "I can get them out of the bin, I didn't mean—"

"Leave them," she said abruptly. And with that, she turned around, holding onto the banister, and began to descend the stairs. I watched her, embarrassed and clutching the wash-bag, until I heard the strange, shuffling noise of her slippers on the flagstones below.

It was going to be a long week.

CHAPTER TEN

E LVER HOUSE APPEARED smaller in the daytime, and smaller than it looked from outside. In the dark, it appeared out of nowhere like a large black boulder, a blot on the horizon – tall, imposing, unwelcoming. Now, as I stepped out onto the drive once more and looked up, I supposed it must have six or seven bedrooms, judging from the windows ranged along the second and third floors. I could make out the drawn curtains of my own bedroom on the second floor, the contact-lens solution perched on the sill along with the wash-bag.

Above my room, I could see a row of four nondescript identical windows. Their panes were dark and dirty, like they'd not been washed in months, covered in a moss-like green grime off which the weak sunshine seemed to reflect. No wonder, when the rain appeared such a feature here. It wasn't falling heavily now, but in a thin mizzling mist that snuck up across the lawn and seemed to curl itself around the trunks of trees, buffeted by the wind. The turrets of the roof were little spires, running along what must be an attic across the entire width of the house. There were birds' nests sticking through the thin arched crevices of the eaves.

The deep pool of the fountain in the centre of the forecourt was entirely dried up, deep and scattered with dead leaves, but there was a faint glimmer of once-tossed copper coins. I peered down, leaning over the side and extricated a few of them, turning them over in gloved hands. Nestled among the modern silvers and golds was an older coin. I freed my hand and traced a finger over its braille-like script: a shilling. Behind me the windows were pearly in the midday light, their glass catching the intermittent rays and winking down.

It was, in its own sad, decrepit way, quite beautiful. I could well imagine the long line of families, complete with housekeepers, maids and butlers, gardeners, governesses and drivers, who had probably once lived here. And I was right, I made a mental note to tell you: it was Georgian. Above the heavy oak front door, the one so inexplicably open the night before, was a keystone engraved with the year 1762.

Since our encounter on the landing, I'd not seen Catherine again. I'd poked my head into the kitchen on my way outside: the teacups from last night were stacked neatly on the draining board, though, and there was a jug of coffee – warm to the touch – on the Aga. In the light of day, I noticed another stopped clock, this one paused at twenty to seven, beside a small door. This led into a pantry where I found, to my surprise, a well-stocked larder filled with oats, various types of pasta, tins of tomatoes and beans, glass jars crowded with pickled cucumbers, carrots, beetroot. The packaging on the tins looked at least 20 years old, if not more, though the oats looked fresh enough. There was a whole shelf dedicated entirely, it seemed, to what looked like rollmops: limp, semi-translucent slithers hung suspended in brine, as in a museum.

It was the most comfortable part of the whole house, I realised with a jolt: the first area I'd seen that had an air of lived-in personality. I liked it. A pair of old muddy boots sat on the threshold to the back door, their laces patterned with cobwebs. I tried the handle and was relieved to find it locked. At least not every door here seemed open to whoever trudged off the lane and poked their head in. I'd turned, coffee in hand, and pulled on my rain jacket, wellies and gloves.

It felt good to be outdoors, despite the rain. Straight ahead I saw the dense jungle I'd walked through yesterday and noted with a sense of pride that the trees were indeed very thick either side of the path. While the house looked utterly different in daylight, that stretch of woodland was undeniably lonely and unsettling, day or night. I turned left and set off through the long grass, passing the dry fountain. Soon the grass grew higher still and I was grateful for the waterproof trousers I'd grabbed at the last moment. Every few steps my foot would sink down into a patiently waiting puddle, a dip in the earth covered over by foliage and dead leaves.

I'd never been anywhere so noisy. Or, I should say, so naturally noisy. The wind made triumphant, whooping sounds as it skirted the corners and rounded domes of the roof, demanding entry at the doors. In the trees the magpies chattered at one another like maracas. The thin whine of mosquitos pervaded the air in certain patches, gathering in almost-beautiful swarms over the small pools and stagnant lagoons that punctuated the estate, and indeed the land that stretched for miles around it. Water boatmen skated across the blackness, leaving barely a ripple in their wake.

Over to my right, some four hundred metres away or more, a flash of pink: hydrangeas, tall and majestic, swaying in the gusts of wind that whipped across the ground. Their splayed petals were upward-facing cups, ready to collect water and drink it down. The autumn might have bedded itself in, but the first frost of the season hadn't yet arrived, and they looked bright and healthy even from a distance.

I kept walking until the house became distant through the rain, kept walking until, with a start, I realised I'd been following the sound of the stream.

If I hadn't been watching my steps so carefully I'd have walked straight into it. The lush green gave way quite suddenly to a drop of about three feet. I looked down at it, realising that the noise of it – a churning, droning sort of sound that would have made conversation difficult unless you were shouting – had drawn me in but that I'd not sensed how close it was.

The trees either side, their trunks thick and gnarled and roots spreading right down to the bank, seemed to bounce the sound off themselves. The echoes had ricocheted back as I trudged unknowingly forward, following the noise without realising it. The stream wasn't especially wide, around two metres or so, but it was swollen and rapid, its endless waves leaping and shimmying over large rocks. It coursed along its journey away from the house, heading out towards a river, presumably, somewhere far away outside the estate.

The rain began a steady beat now, throwing itself with drama onto the already disturbed surface of the water. I ducked under the nearest tree and sat down, pulling out my phone and dialling Laura's number. As expected, she picked up on the first ring.

"Well?"

"Where to begin," I laughed.

"Oh God." She sighed theatrically but I could hear the edge in her voice. "Tell me."

"Not much to tell yet. We've not started."

"It's gone nine – is she not up yet? And what's that noise?"

"It's the rain, Laura. And the stream. This is the wettest place I've ever been."

"Where's Miss Carey?"

"Back at the house, I assume. Laura, she's . . . weird. All that stuff last night . . . And then, this morning, I caught her just standing in the doorway staring at me."

Laura's laugh was full, throaty, and descended quickly into a violent round of coughing. "I mean . . . so many of them are barmy but this does take the biscuit, doesn't it."

"She was much nicer last night, oddly," I said. "Maybe she's not a morning person. I'm having a walk now. With any luck we'll get cracking this afternoon."

Something broke the surface of the water, ducking down as quickly as it appeared. I spun round. A flash of grey bobbed up a few feet downstream, then another. As soon as I spotted one, another emerged. I stared as Laura chattered on.

"You still there?"

"Yeah, sorry. Saw something in the stream . . ."

"A fish?"

"I've never seen one like that."

She laughed. "The city girl speaks."

"I'm not a city girl."

"You are now."

There was silence as I stood up and moved closer. The rain seemed to be abating somewhat. As the water dipped and turned I saw, with a wild glance to my right, the top of a long tail curling out, round and back into the stream with a light splash.

"It's a snake. There are snakes in here." I stepped backward instinctively. "I literally just saw one."

"I don't know if snakes swim, Ellen."

"Of course they bloody do."

"It must be something else. Listen, I've got to head off in a second – there's a team call with that Scottish woman, you know the one—"

The speed of these things was remarkable. They weren't big, exactly, but now I stood at the stream's edge I could see them, hundreds of them, thin worms as fine and mobile as strands of wet clay. They slithered over one another, boneless and agile, wrapping themselves round rocks, moving haphazardly through the currents of the brook.

"They're eels," I whispered, though I wasn't sure why my voice dropped.

"Oh, stupid," I heard Laura tapping away on her laptop. "Of course. Sorry, of course they are. Not eels though - elvers. Baby eels."

"Elver House," I said quietly.

"Yep. That explains it. I thought it was a funny name. That'll be the Conger Brook."

"I've never even heard of a conger. Or an elver," I said.

Such strange creatures, their bodies shot through with long black lines so that they looked like plastic biros. I continued to stare.

"Well, now you have, love. Don't they have all kinds of things in those lakes of yours?"

"Mostly carp and pike. I've seen bloody *eels* before Laura. Just not like this."

I heard the whine of a coffee machine. "Listen, I'm heading off. Text me later, let me know how it goes. Hope she's chattier this afternoon."

I hung up and squatted down next to the brook. The rain started again and, with a collective swish of what seemed a thousand long tails the elvers, clear as tape, darted back into the depths of the water as the first heavy drops crashed down.

CHAPTER ELEVEN

HALF AN HOUR later I was back in my room, peeling off the layers and draping them across a chair close to the still-glowing fire. I placed another log onto the hearth and rubbed my palms together, checking the time. The house was utterly silent, save for the moans of the wind through the missing roof tiles. I decided to take my laptop downstairs, where Catherine had said there was central heating, and see to some work before we got started.

The corridor was deserted. I walked past the ransacked study, its door now closed, and stood for a moment at the top of the stairs, trying to work out which of the remaining rooms was Miss Carey's. Perhaps it was upstairs: I glanced through the banister and saw another floor twisting up ahead. If our welcome had been more natural, our introduction beginning when I'd knocked on the door and she'd opened it, I might well have taken a look around. As it was, the last thing I wanted was for her to find me somewhere she'd rather I didn't go. Perhaps this floor – the one where I slept – was more of a guest area. Upstairs, I imagined, was out of bounds to me.

I wished I'd looked around for longer last night. There was the guest bedroom – where I slept – and beside it the bathroom, at the end of the corridor. The study was to my right. The idea of Miss Carey, whose walk was slow and whose stick was well-used, deliberately making life more difficult for herself struck me as unlikely given her age. Then again, in these grand old houses it was probably uncommon for the guest room to be so close to the master bedroom. She *must* be upstairs.

The library was warm and welcoming, the carpet so soft and luxurious it seemed designed as a direct contrast to the soaked, uneven ground outside. The broad desk held nothing but a paper-weight and a great bankers lamp; a thick Chesterfield chair was tucked neatly underneath. Across the desk was a day sofa with a blanket draped invitingly on one arm. The magazines and news-papers fanning out had been removed. It was the perfect reading room. I closed the door behind me, made me way to the desk and sat down.

The view from the window revealed, in the distance, the crooked outline of the old iron gates. Now, in daylight, I could see that these, rickety as they were, were the strongest part of what passed for the estate's enclosure. A totter-down brick wall, no more than four feet tall, stretched in either direction along the edge of the perimeter, some two hundred metres away. I realised that having walked to the brook this morning I'd not yet reached the eastern-most border. Another question for Catherine Carey. I'd never been anywhere so vast, a place one might conceivably get lost in the grounds.

I opened the laptop and was reassured, once again, that the Wi-Fi had no password. I connected and five strong bars appeared, incredibly, in the right-hand corner of the screen. I could have wept. I opened my in-box and started work.

For the first time since I'd arrived, the sound of the rain was pleasant on the windows, a steady beat which, coupled with the heat thrown out from the radiator, made for a surprisingly tranquil environment.

I dealt with the simplest things first. There were four messages from different clients, each asking for small changes, clarifications, and brief edits to phrasing or dialogue. These were easy fixes, and I moved through them quickly, pinging the revised documents back and copying Laura in too. I responded to another, newer customer, and advised him I'd be back in town next week. Generally people preferred to meet in person, but I added a postscript. If Catherine and I were to spend the afternoons talking, as today, we could always do a video call instead in the morning. I'd let him know.

It was dull, easy work: admin, but the normality of it felt good. I sat back, stretched, and opened another folder on my desktop.

This was Mr Phillips' book, three quarters finished. Not his real name, of course. A retired Tory MP who'd taken great delight in explaining why the miners' strike had failed during the first minutes of our first interview, and wanted to use this as a slightly cack-handed metaphor for his own misspent youth. Laura had told him she felt the two of us would get on, but half an hour with Mr Phillips had revealed the opposite. I could have been a robot, a faceless Dictaphone and he wouldn't have cared, I don't think.

Despite this, it had been a fun project. One of the best parts of the job, really – that silent bearing witness to someone else's musings, the stories they tell themselves, the narrative they've constructed of their own life and what happened in it.

I liked Mr Phillips, perhaps more as a specimen than a person. He was so essentially a product of his time, his age, his gender. He spent the first hour of our time together asking me to repeat myself ("I didn't catch that, my dear – nothing personal, just the accent") and regaled me with stories of his time at Durham University in the 1950s. Initially confused, I soon realised he believed I'd grown up there: I told him I'd been to the town just twice in my childhood, as it was 80 miles away and on the other side of the Pennines. He grunted, frowning as I explained that my parents had thought the place bad luck when the Mondeo packed in on the A688, and we'd had to roll it along to the hard shoulder.

Mr Phillips barely seemed to notice me at all, unless I asked him something he didn't want to answer, in which case he'd wave his hand as at a fly. Otherwise he responded to me with the sort of rehearsed, oft-repeated tales I'd heard so many clients trot out. Not everyone wants a warts and all memoir, after all.

I pulled on my headphones and clicked play on our seventh interview, the penultimate one, where Mr Phillips had described a storm. I was in the middle of a chapter where his personal life had imploded, and had asked him what else he remembered of the time. I watched droplets scurry down the windowpane as I heard my own voice, disembodied, on the recorder.

So she had left, by this point?
    Yes. I suppose I deserved it, really.
    It must have been incredibly painful.
    My dear – he'd always called me that – *you have no idea. I barely got out of bed for a week. Told the boss I had the 'flu.*
    And did you know she wouldn't be coming back?
    Oh yes. I'd told her not to.

There was a pause on the tape. Pauses are incredibly useful. I used to cringe when clients stopped talking, and now I almost relished it. So often we feel the need to fill a silence, but I'd learned over the years to leave them, to smile through them, or pretend to take a note. More often than not, the truth came tumbling out into the void.

I couldn't trust myself not to do it again. She deserved better.
    Deserved better?
    Yes. She would only worry – every time I went away. Fret about me doing it again. And I probably would have, to be honest.
    When you say you'd do it again, do you mean that you'd be unfaithful to her?

A leap of faith there, Ellen. I flinched as I continued typing, even though I remembered how he'd reacted to the question. It was risky though. He hadn't used the word himself and hearing it spoken so bluntly could have thrown him entirely, clammed him up. I might have had to spend hours bringing him back round after that. But no: he'd seemed almost relieved.

Yes. I would likely have been unfaithful to her again.

And so you decided that it was better not to try and mend the relationship?

There wasn't much to mend, by that point. We were in our sixties. I barely noticed her around the house, if I'm honest.

I scrolled down to the section about his wife, who we were calling Camilla. Pausing the tape, I jotted down a few notes to myself before amending a paragraph about the divorce. Just as I'd known it would, Mr Phillips' voice boomed out when I hit play.

But you'll have to find a way of rephrasing all that, my dear. I don't want to hurt her. Better just to say we separated and have done with it.

And this was in – I heard the rustle of paper on the tape *– 1987?*

That's right. The year of the storm. He laughed. Fitting really.

Tell me about the storm.

Oh, it was ghastly. Awful. We'd never seen anything like it. I thought the roof would blow clean off. Winds of 100 miles an hour, cars thrown upside down, windows shattered.

I remember reading about it. People died, didn't they?

Several. I can't remember how many. Certainly more than 20. It was the worst storm the country had seen in 300 years.

What did you do?

The only thing we could. Push the sofa against the front door. Hunker down. Avoid the top floor. I remember running out to the off-licence for candles and toilet paper.

When did it hit?

Mid-October, sometime. I can't remember the date. We knew it was on the way, but most people missed the worst of it because they were asleep. Of course the most terrible, violent part of it came around three in the morning.

Why do you say "of course"?

There was a pause on the tape.

Well, the worst things often come then, don't they.

It wasn't a question.

CHAPTER TWELVE

I LEANED BACK and rubbed my eyes. It was close to midday: I'd been here, transcribing and editing, for the best part of two hours. Time for a break. Time, in fact, to go and find Catherine and persuade her to sit down with me. I grimaced as I stood up and crossed into the hallway. Mackintoshes, scarves and hats hung limply from pegs beside the door; wax coats seemed almost to stand on their own, their green coverings taught as skin.

My phone buzzed in my back pocket. I checked it briefly, saw it wasn't from you. Sighing, I pulled my wellies on where I'd left them, by the front door, and turned the handle.

The door didn't move.

I stared at the brass knob, as polished by previous hands as the others, and turned it the other way. Still, nothing. Crouching down, I peered at the gap between the door itself and the lock, and saw a thick rectangular piece of metal drawn across.

I stood up, forced myself to slow my breathing. I turned the handle of the knob once more, in vain, rattling it in case there was some mechanism I'd missed.

There had to be an explanation. Maybe she'd gone out and assumed I was still on the grounds. Why leave the door locked, though, in that case? The weather was awful. If Catherine Carey had gone out, where to and why, at 87, in this pouring rain?

I glanced to the left and right, hoping to see a hook, a row of keys hanging neatly by the door. There was nothing. I swore under my breath and tried, though by now I'd no idea why, to turn the doorknob again, heaving my weight against the oak and pushing inwards as I turned. I'd seen the deadbolt, though.

And then, for the second time that morning, I turned around and there she was. Catherine stood not five feet behind me, and this time I didn't have time to pretend. I shrieked, my hands flying to my mouth, and tripped backwards against the door.

"I'm sorry," she cried, moving forwards as fast as her age would allow her. "I didn't mean to startle you."

I stared at her.

"I didn't hear you," I said. "I was just . . ." I gestured at the door. "It's locked."

"Yes," she said, placing one hand against it. "I've had some trouble recently." She pulled a set of keys from the pocket of her cardigan. "Strange people coming by . . . I wouldn't say 'prowlers', probably just bored teenagers but . . . well, you can't be too careful."

I wondered which teenagers would be bored enough to come this far out just to play a game of knock-down-ginger on an old woman. But then I remembered the shoe-print on the sofa last night, and the disarray of the study upstairs. So why had the door been unlocked when I'd arrived?

"Did you want to go outside, Ellen?" she asked now. She put the key in the lock and the bolt scraped back. I smiled and held out my hand, stalling her.

"It's fine," I said. "In fact, I'd just finished some work, and wondered if you'd like to begin now, if now's a good time?"

"Begin . . . the interviews?" she said, her smile fading somewhat.

"Yes," I said carefully. "If that's alright?"

She nodded, just once, and turned toward the library. "It's what you're here for, after all. Let's make a start."

And she passed through the door, into the book-lined room, and settled herself on the sofa. I followed, slowly so as not to rush her, and sat as before at the old desk. At last, we were about to begin.

"I've never done anything like this," she said, and frowned. "It feels ridiculous somehow."

I opened the recording app and hit the red button. "It often does," I said. "It can be strange talking about yourself. I suppose in some ways we do it all the time – chitchat about our lives with friends, or at the hairdresser's. This is slightly different."

"Yes, I suppose it will be," said Miss Carey. She placed her hands on her lap and I noticed again the shape and colour of her nails – the luxuriant red nestled inside clean cuticles. Her small frame seemed to sink into the thick pile of the sofa. I smiled and gestured to the bookcases.

"It's a beautiful room," I said. "You're very lucky. A beautiful house, in fact."

"It is, isn't it," she said. "Easy to get lost. Good for a game of hide and seek." She flashed a smile. "It'd take months to find whoever you were looking for."

"I imagine you've read every novel in here," I gestured to the shelves.

She followed my hand and seemed to take in the spines for the first time. "My father's, mostly."

"Tell me about him."

"His name was Alfred. He spent a lot of time in here. He liked reading."

"How old would he be now?"

"Let me see . . . He was just a baby in the First War. His father was killed at the Somme, so he never knew him. He had siblings, though, and they remembered their dad. Naturally, my father was the last of his parents' children. He'd be over 100 now."

"It's fascinating, isn't it. The loss of life, the scale of it."

"That war . . ." Miss Carey said, and trailed off. "It was meant to finish everything, but it was just the start. So many young men, gone in seconds. So many vanished and often in totally run-of-the-mill, unheroic moments. Not the sort of letter mothers and fathers ever wanted to receive, but for some, the pain was worsened by learning how their sons had died. The sheer waste."

"Did your grandmother ever learn how her husband died?"

"Well, yes, and that's what was so upsetting. He contracted pneumonia. Imagine nowadays – you'd be right as rain within a week or two. It was different then. No antibiotics and nowhere to recuperate even if you had them. He burned up in the trenches, my mother was told, and the fever was so high he was hallucinating. It appears to have been quite common but . . . yes, as I say, a waste."

Outside the rain was blown with a gust against the windowpanes. It was impossible to see much beyond the glass – the swaying shapes of the trees were walls of green, punctuated by the brownish gravel of the driveway. The window was slightly ajar and the deep, mulchy scent of wet earth drifted into the room.

"And meanwhile, miles away, the Careys were living out the war here?"

"The Careys?" She frowned. "My father's family, you mean?"

"Yes, sorry. I just want to try and get a parallel view of life for the family here. For your father, I suppose, after the war."

"Oh, no. I wasn't clear. My father didn't live here. No, Elver came from my mother's side of the family."

I nodded, chastising myself. Never assume: first rule. She smiled at me shyly. "My father's name was Carey: I never married. The house and the land was the property of my mother until her death. And then it passed to me."

"And how long had your mother's family lived in the area?"

"Oh, years. Centuries, Ellen. Elver was built in the mid-1700s. A lot of the men who helped construct it were Scots, out of work since The Clearances. The woodland you walked through last night," another apologetic smile here, "That was all that covered the ground for miles before my ancestors arrived."

When I didn't say anything, she went on. "The Highlands were razed to the ground, people forced out of their homes, their land turned over for farming, agriculture. There were people desperate for work, wandering the countryside almost. A large number came here and were employed by my great-great grandfather. A few more greats,

I'd wager." She turned to the shelves, looked behind her. "There's a book in here somewhere, a record of the house's construction. Jim, he lives in the village, he's a history enthusiast. He put together a sort of family tree I can show you."

"And eventually the house passed to your mother?"

"Yes. Her maiden name was Bassington. If you go out to the graveyard in Conger Brook there's hundreds of them. When she married, of course, my mother took Carey – my father's name."

"And what was she like, your mother?"

Miss Carey frowned slightly and looked to one side, her head cocked, contemplating.

"I couldn't really tell you, to be honest. I barely saw her as a little girl."

I let that sit a moment, wondering if she would fill the silence. When she didn't, I prodded.

"Why not?"

"It wasn't unusual in the slightest, to be frank with you." Catherine paused, looking around once more. The ladder stood propped against the shelves. I wondered how long the books had been there and when they were last read. I made a mental note to look through the collection properly later.

"Big houses like Elver required an enormous staff," she said, "and that's what we had. Cooks and chauffeurs, house-keepers, maids and butlers, stableboys and scullery girls. And nannies. Lots of nannies. I must've had at least 10."

How monotonous, how repetitive work had been all those years ago. How fixed and immutable. As teenagers, you and I had worked together at children's camps on the Lakes: sitting on hard plastic chairs, our heads snapping up when the radio crackled into life. The water was freezing, a mass grave of flies and wasps, leaves from the trees and miscellaneous plasters. We walked up and down the banks with nets to scoop up the intruders. At lunchtime we ate fat golden chips doused in ketchup and warm Coke from the hut in the car park. We'd clean the outdoor changing rooms as best we were able, sending the dirt flying with mops and buckets to settle again once we moved off. The sun dipped behind the doors of the multi-coloured wooden changing rooms and at the end of the day we'd cycle home, smelling like sun cream and algae and sweat.

Catherine made to get up and I stood too, hovering uncertainly for a moment as she made her way to the bookshelves. "Do you know why these houses need so many people?" she asked, hooking her finger under the spine of one book and pulling it free. It came away in a cloud of dust, and she fanned the air around her before turning back to me. "Look."

She flicked open the pages to reveal a splatter of black and green radiating from the top of the book. The spores of mold obscured the words, covering them randomly like flicked ink. And the smell: it floated up towards us both, rancid and old. Catherine closed the novel and put it back carefully on the shelf.

"That's why." She moved back towards the sofa and settled herself again. "There's so much to do. People think it's a luxury, having staff like that. But without them, a house of this size becomes unwieldy very quickly. The elements have a habit of gaining a rather rapid foothold."

I nodded, remembering Ireland. The hours we'd spent walking along lanes and roads roughly churned by the wheels of tractors, the houses we'd passed along the way. So many abandoned homes, their occupants long gone. We'd pulled long tops and trousers from our bags and braved the nettles to the front doors, edging our way round curled circles of barbed wire, discarded bricks and rotting pieces of timber. The bedrooms still had scraps of curtain hanging in windows, which were themselves smashed by rocks; they looked like they'd been shot at. On the floor of one, we'd found newspapers from the early 2000s, the print still legible. Out the back of one such house we'd found a patch of garden, wild and unkempt, full of sunflowers arching their backs towards the sky, and we'd pitched our tent there. I wondered if you ever thought about those times, as I was now, or whether it felt like another lifetime ago entirely.

"Ellen?" Miss Carey's voice was mild, almost concerned. I blinked and stared back at her.

"Sorry," I said. "What you said reminded me of something."

She nodded, a brief flash of that shy smile once more, and we continued.

"Elver must have been very busy then," I said, and she nodded again.

"Once upon a time, yes, it was. You were never alone: that's what I remember most. In the mornings you'd be woken by the maid tiptoeing into the nursery, drawing the curtains. As you walked to the bathroom she'd be there, wiping down the banisters, and as you passed the other bedrooms there'd be more girls inside, beating the rugs out of the windows, arranging fires in the grates. If you looked out the window, you'd see the groomsmen taking the horses for a run, or the gardeners pruning roses. My parents' bedroom was on the top floor of the house, just below the attic, but I wasn't allowed in there until I was much older – in fact I didn't know what it looked like until then. The nannies and I kept to the nursery and the schoolroom on the second floor. The room you're sleeping in, in fact. And my mother was very busy – there was so much to do."

We'd rushed ahead, as so often happened. I needed to guide her back to the start.

"You were born in 1936, then?"

"Exactly. They'd no idea what was coming, I imagine, when I was conceived." Catherine looked at her hands, traced the shape of her nails. "When war did break out, my father was exempt from service: his vision was appalling, but there was also a farm here, back in those days. So even if he'd been able to see, he would have remained behind to work the land. My mother threw herself into the war effort. I don't begrudge either of them for that."

She paused. "If it weren't for the war they'd probably have had other children. Things were so busy during those years, and then by the time it was over, maybe they'd lost the energy. I don't remember the earliest days of the fighting, of course. I was too young."

"What's your earliest memory, then, Miss Carey?"

"Catherine. My earliest memory." She paused again. "Ah, now that would be the hospital."

"Were you unwell?"

"No, not at all. The hospital was here, you see. Wait a moment." She got up once more and went slowly to the cupboards standing at the opposite ends of the room – the doors were opened to reveal a number of thick black folders. She took down the first, examined a couple of pages and replaced it. "Here," she said, taking another. "Come and have a look."

I brought the laptop with me, still recording, and balanced it on the edge of a small stool to the right of the cupboards. Miss Carey held the folder open in her hands and I saw that it was a photograph album.

"See?" she said, pointing to the first picture. "The drawing room." I peered closer and saw, with astonishment, a sepia-toned row of beds where the L-shaped sofas now stood, in the room across the hall, the room with the boot-print. All the beds were occupied. The men's faces were ghostly pale; some were smiling, but almost all were heavily covered over with bandages. Heads were wrapped in thick swathes of gauze, arms in slings. A boy with his leg in a cast gave a thumbs-up.

The picture below it showed the kitchen, as nurses in starched white caps lifted a pan of water onto the table. Catherine's hands were almost translucent, the skin stretched taut between thumb and pointer finger like webbing.

"The house was used as a hospital, a respite centre," she said. "Elver was requisitioned by the government, as were many country houses. There simply wasn't enough space for the wounded in the cities, and so the nation's mansions opened their doors. And this," she gestured at the page, "was my first memory. One day the furniture was carried upstairs and the house was transformed."

"Were you frightened? What did you think was happening?"

"I don't think I thought very much at all. I was too young. You just accept things at that age, don't you? There's no precedent, no experience. You're unquestioning, really." She paused. "What's the first thing you remember? Do you know?"

"I do, actually," I said, smiling at her. "Well, one of the first. It's more a feeling than a memory though. There were adults everywhere, all of them talking. Friends of my parents, I think. The room was white. They were chattering and I couldn't really understand them, I just remember them all being so much larger. Then one of them picked me up and showed me a sort of bucket with a pair of babies inside. The memory stops there. It's more like a snapshot. I suppose it was the day the twins were born, my siblings. I'd have been almost four."

She nodded and turned the pages slowly. "Always so hard to tell what's a memory and what's a photograph. What you actually remember and what's been recorded."

Another page, and here was a group of women with sheaves of paper and pens held aloft, sorting through a huge basket of what looked like towels and blankets.

"My mother organised a great deal of this," said Miss Carey, tapping the picture. "Old clothes, scraps of fabric, curtains, anything we could use. The attic was entirely raided: dresses and overcoats, bedsheets nobody had used for years. Mother gathered it all together and asked the locals to do the same. The items would be bleached and washed and used at the hospital. You can imagine how quickly the nurses ran out of bandages, tourniquets, that sort of thing."

She turned the page again to reveal a large cart, four horses at its front. The old man standing beside them was in the process of doffing his cap to the photographer. His arm was blurred, the time it had taken to capture him exposing the mid-air movement. On the cart sat more baskets, barrels, boxes.

"I remember my nanny at the time – I think her name was Penny, or Jenny – she took me downstairs one morning and I watched as they all came through. The men, I mean. Some were walking unaided, but many were stretchered in. The beds made the most awful racket, all metal springs clanging, and when they ran out of them, my father pulled down two of the outhouses on the land for timber to build more. As soon as we'd finally found someone a bed, another cartload of men would arrive needing them."

Miss Carey tucked the album under her arm and made her way back to the sofa. "I'd never seen so many people. I was only three or four, mind, and all of my life had been here. I'd always been surrounded by people, but I knew every one of them by name. And suddenly we were inundated with strangers. I sat in the nursery and heard the trucks as they approached the driveway. It was never-ending, all these men spilling off the vehicles. And when I went downstairs later to join my parents for dinner, the hallway was a mess of mud and blood."

I realised, then, just how intently I was listening to her. Miss Carey's voice had become stronger as she spoke, and far from the reticence I'd noted earlier, here was a story unfolding that was as fascinating as any I'd heard. All the more so, I felt, because she was warming to the theme. I got the sense she'd rarely discussed these early experiences, and was pleased to notice she appeared to be enjoying the conversation.

I perched beside her on the sofa. Her eyes met mine and I was struck by the intensity of her gaze, though it wasn't directed at me. That focused yet faraway look was one I'd encountered often, as people reached back into the past for snapshots they'd long since forgotten.

"I didn't know how badly they were injured," she continued. "And while some of them walked out after a few weeks in the san, as we called it, quite a few never left." She turned the page of the album again. The third picture down showed another room, one I'd not yet seen. It walls were lined with thick blocks of stone and it was dimly lit by several large candles.

"The crypt in the chapel," she said softly. "I had no idea where they took the men who died, but it appeared we had a ready-made morgue. The bodies were taken there until the Reserves came to collect them and return them to their families. Of course I wasn't allowed anywhere near the chapel once they started using it for that purpose."

She looked at me under her eyelashes, alert and focused. It was as though the image was right there, caught in that midnight iris, developing in bromide.

"But you went in anyway?"

"Well, it was hard to shake Jenny – or Penny," she said with a small laugh. "But yes, I wanted to know where they were taking the stretchers I'd seen. The ones covered with a sheet or blanket. I don't think I understood the men were dead, not at that age. I managed, just the once, to reach the door and find it unlocked. The chapel was by far the coolest part of the whole estate, and I remember the relief of getting inside. It was summer and we were all sweltering. I can recall thinking to myself that if I was caught, that's what I would say: I'd just wanted to get out of the sun."

"And what did you find in the chapel?"

"Nothing at first. Everything looked much the same, although the pews were covered in crates, bits of old rope. Gauze and bottles of iodine. It wasn't until I went a bit further in that the smell first hit me."

She stopped talking and her eyes travelled to the window. "It was just over there, beside the brook. The chapel, I mean."

I said nothing, waiting for her to go on.

"They knocked it down after the war. Pity. It was a beautiful little building. Stained-glass windows that turned the light into rainbows across the floor."

"And so you went down into the crypt?"

"Oh yes. I was revolted. Every part of my body seemed to be telling me to go backwards, to get out of there. Something pushed me on, though, and I went down the steps, holding onto the handrail as my mother had taught me to do in the house . . ."

Her face slackened suddenly, the colour draining from her cheeks.

Her hands shook. She looked as though she was about to be sick.

"Miss Carey?"

I didn't know what to do. The transition was so fast and so unexpected that for one terrible moment I thought she was having a stroke. She turned to me and her voice rasped, a deep guttural sound.

"What did you say?"

I shook my head. "Nothing. You were just talking about going down into the crypt. Is everything alright?"

She stood up slowly and pulled her cardigan more tightly round her shoulders. "Enough," she muttered.

I paused the recording. "Do you want to take a break?"

She reached the door and turned to stare at me, a look of such distress on her face that I almost moved toward her. "Yes. We'll take a break. Enough for today. All these questions . . . To be honest I've no desire to go raking around in the past. It's too much. Let's leave it there."

I was stunned by the change, too stunned to say anything more. She slipped through the door and closed it behind her with a snap.

I sat back and wondered what to do next.

I'd had clients become upset during interviews before, and sometimes painful memories made people cantankerous, rude even. I'd never had someone walk out like this, though. I wondered if I'd said something, or if the memory of the crypt had overwhelmed her. It must have been a hideous experience for a child – that natural curiosity suddenly morphed into incomprehensible horror. Nonetheless, the reaction had been so instantaneous, so visceral. Should I go after her? She was in her 80s, after all. There was no one else here. Was it not, somehow, up to me?

Leaving the library and my laptop on the table, I walked into the hallway. There was no sign of her, and I knew – given our earlier encounters – that I'd not hear her anyway. She moved through the house so silently, knowing where every board creaked, every stair groaned. "Miss Carey?" I called out. I didn't expect a reply and didn't get one.

"Are you alright?" I tried again. "I'm sorry if something upset you." Another pause, and still nothing. Well, I'd tried. It wasn't my house, and following her upstairs, if that was indeed where she'd gone, seemed wrong. She wanted to be alone. I turned to the front door and remembered she'd unlocked it. Small mercies.

I pulled on my boots, checked my phone was in my back pocket. And then, at last, I left Elver House.

CHAPTER THIRTEEN

T HE WALK INTO the village felt good, and the fresh air helped to clear the morning's cobwebs. The rain had stopped, thankfully, and as I walked a plan started to form, as I'd known it would. I'd find some lunch and make some calls, take an hour or so, and then start back to the house. Catherine Carey was old – she wasn't accustomed to strangers and the whole concept of talking about herself and her life was alien. We'd covered some decent ground, in a preliminary sort of way. And I was here for a pre-arranged number of days: how she chose to use the limited hours we had was up to her. She'd made that abundantly clear.

As I passed the ruined fountain and made for the totter-down gates, a small hut caught my eye to the left. Too dark, last night, to have noticed it. I strode towards what appeared to be an old summerhouse, its door slightly ajar, the faded curtains a wash of 70s orange and brown. The rotten wooden boards provided only a partial entrance and I stepped carefully inside, inhaling the familiar smell of long-settled dust, wet leaves, soaked fabric.

An old dressing table jutted out at an angle, its circular mirrors cracked and smeared with grime. I pulled open one of the drawers to find delicate ivory powder brushes, more cold cream, several dead wasps. I unscrewed a tube of old lipstick, the shocking pink worn almost to the bottom. Even after all these years, the scent of musk and wax was tantalising.

I turned slowly and surveyed the remainder of the shed. Tools stood jumbled against the far wall, pitchforks and hoes, spades and trowels, their once-sharp prongs blunted and rusted with age. The curtains flapped in the breeze from a broken window, and a pair of spiders fled from the material to the safety of webs festooning the corners. A steady dripping noise punctuated the silence: a soft, slow but inexorable beat like the rain on the windows of the house, like the determined course of the brook. I thought of the elvers again and shivered.

Another low table held a stack of old calendars. I flicked through the bottom pair and my eyes widened as the yellowing paper showed 1964 in bright relief: appointments and reminders peppered the page in curling script. The idea that Miss Carey herself could have added these entries, recorded everyday administrative tasks in this self-same calendar, was dizzying. She'd have been 28 years old at the time. The year after the Kennedy assassination. Five years before the Moon Landings. The sheer length of time between then and now, and the fact she lived here at Elver, to this day, made me feel slightly faint.

I backed out of the summer house, pulling the screen door closed behind me, and heading back to the gates.

I passed quickly through the lane, the woods less intimidating in the morning light. I avoided glancing to left or right, just as before. The path was scattered with fallen branches, pine needles, detritus scattered by the weather. I continued onto the road where Steve had dropped me just the night before. It felt like weeks ago.

The track led me back to the main road, and I pulled out my phone to check the direction of the village before remembering the lack of signal. A couple of hundred metres along the deserted track, however, there was a road-sign. If I walked quickly, I could cover the mile and a half to Conger Brook in twenty minutes.

In daylight, the countryside revealed its full wilderness. It looked as though these roads hadn't been traversed in years, decades even. Nettles obscured most of the path. I soon came to a bridge and leaned over it to watch the water gushing past. I recalled the elvers this morning in the brook, and tried to spot them, though it was impossible from this distance. Every time I thought I'd spotted one, it turned out to be nothing more than a twist of sunlight peeking through the clouds. Their translucent bodies made them almost invisible, I realised: half here and half not.

All around me the wasteland stretched on: flat, thick expanses of green. The trees obscured a full view of the horizon. It felt peculiar to be here, in this place that had existed and would exist long after I left it. How untouched it felt, how remote. How desolate, really.

I followed the bend of the stream to the left and saw the path thinning out ahead. My phone, at last, registered some bars of signal and I opened the map to find I was, indeed, just a few hundred metres from the village centre. That was something, at least. A flurry of messages came in, one after the other. It was hardly any time since I'd left the city, but I felt a wrench as I saw the bones of a plan emerging: the pub at eight, our favourite, old and smelly and apparently washed each night with Pritt Stick.

Lanterns hung there from the branches in the beer garden. There was a juke box we'd shove coins into. You'd stopped coming to the pub, to anything really. But we'd all gone together since we were teenagers, when it was the only place that let us in. Everyone has somewhere like this and that was ours. Inside we'd shout above each other to be heard. Sometimes we'd be drinking, sometimes not. Faux-fur coats and scarves knitted by our mums, for each other, would fall onto benches covered in scratchy 70s velvet. Tights would get laddered and slops of Snakebite would fall onto jeans. There were eight of us, normally, and 12 different conversations going on, all at once. Some of us would be laughing, some more serious. The door would bang open and there'd be more: wild whooping and men on bar stools staring. We jump into each other's arms, high-pitched and swaying. Someone would drop someone else.

The floor would get stickier as the song reached its pitch. There'd be a label sticking out of one dress; lipstick was passed around, plasters exchanged for heels tired from dancing. Everyone would be watching and we'd never notice. I sighed, following the blue dot of the map towards the cluster of houses that spelled civilisation.

Conger Brook wasn't quite what I'd expected. From the deserted country lanes and the battered old road signs, I'd anticipated something run-down, unkempt and forgotten – a smattering of houses and a shop that looked like it'd seen better days. This was different. A row of squat little cottages, each painted a different colour, gave the place a jaunty, relaxed sort of air. Creeping vines curled round the gate posts and geraniums lined the garden paths.

There were around 20 houses in total, huddled round the village green, with its war memorial in the centre and a few poppy wreaths already in place for Remembrance Day. There wasn't a scrap of litter on the ground, no broken bottles, no yellowing newspapers; it was immaculately kept, homely, self-contained. Conger Brook seemed a happy, peaceful sort of place.

"Out for a walk?" came a voice behind me. "Nice day for it."

I turned and smiled, recognising Steve. In the driveway of the house directly behind us stood his car, the taxi from last night. It was a relief to see the familiar face, and my own voice was giddy and high. "Saw a break in the weather and thought I'd chance it." He grinned back.

"So, how was Elver?"

"It was . . ." How to sum up the events of last night, the empty house, the hideous rain drumming on the windows, falling asleep then meeting Miss Carey, the morning by the brook, the library, the interview.

"It was good, thanks." Keep it simple, I thought. "The house is beautiful, isn't it?"

"Haven't been inside for many, many years," said Steve. "Find everything you needed in there?"

"Starting to," I laughed. "It might take a bit of time." I grimaced, laughing.

Steve beckoned me over.

"Come and have a pint – bit of conversation'll do you good."

As I crossed the green, following him, I saw to my right a flash of gold; the unmistakable font and lettering of a pub. It was tucked behind one of the houses, its entrance down a short, paved side street. I ducked down the passage after Steve, who pulled open the door and beckoned me inside. The silence of the village green was broken by a chorus of greeting and loud, contented-sounding voices.

A gaggle of people sat grouped around the bar, chatting, reading; a television was playing the news above the racks of bottles. Most were dusty, though the hand-pump for ale was currently in use, and there were several empty pint glasses scattered across the bar top. On every available surface pumpkins leered out, their faces carved into grotesque grins, their teeth sharp.

"Alright Steve?" called the barman, lifting a glass down from a shelf. "Busy evening?"

"It was, quite," said Steve, ushering me inside. "Didn't get in til gone three. Few divvies from the city getting lost on the way back to halls. You'd think they'd be fine by now. Freshers' week was ages ago."

He gave a thumbs-up to the barman, who poured him a pint, his eyes fixed on me.

I smiled as the others, too, stared at me with frank curiosity. "This is Ellen," said Steve, pulling out a stool for me and another for himself. "She's here on business."

"What'll it be, Ellen?" said the barman. "I've got some local ales, a few Devon ciders, the normal spirity bits and bobs . . . Take ye pick."

"A Coke would be great," I said. I didn't much fancy the thought of stumbling back along those quiet lanes even slightly tipsy. It would've been all too easy to relax into the autumnal warmth of the pub and wile away the hours talking, but it would make whatever issue I needed to resolve with Catherine harder when I did get back.

"So what brings you to the village?" said a woman sitting to Steve's left. She wore thick, mud-splattered dungarees and Wellington boots; her eyes were friendly. "What do you do?"

I hesitated, not for the first time. It was hard to express, and even more so since I wasn't sure how much Miss Carey would want anyone to know about the memoirs. She struck me as a proud sort of person, not the sort who'd readily admit to hiring someone for a job like this.

"It's . . . well, I suppose it's a sort of legacy project," I said vaguely. "Archiving, that sort of thing."

"Fascinating stories from round here," said the woman. "My husband runs the Historical Society. He's obsessed with the area, the legends and whatnot." She reached into her handbag and pulled out a flyer. "Anything you need, Jim's your man. And I know a fair bit myself too – I'm Lucy. Lived here all my life."

I took the leaflet and recognised the coat of arms. "I saw one of these yesterday," I said. "At the train station."

"He tries to get the tourists involved, during the summer," said Lucy. She downed the remainder of her pint in one and stood up. I liked her immediately – her no-nonsense, unguarded openness reminded me of you. The old you, I should say. You were less frank these days: protecting me, perhaps. Or you were just choosing your words carefully, treading on eggshells ever since it happened.

"Not that we get too many of those anymore," said Steve, grinning at me wickedly. "Present company excluded."

I was brought back to the present moment. "Tourists, you mean?"

"Exactly," said Steve.

"And where are you staying, Ellen, while you complete the research?" Lucy was preparing to leave, pulling on a thin overcoat. Its elbows were patched. I wondered what she and Jim did for work – what anyone did in Conger Brook, come to that. I hadn't even seen a shop on the way into the village, a post office, a school.

"I'm up at Elver House," I said, wondering what Miss Carey was doing, and wishing I'd thought to take my laptop up to my room. I'd left in such a hurry and yes, it was password-protected, but I shouldn't have simply left it there. Not that I anticipated she'd want to snoop through anything, even if she could. Still.

As I took in the changed faces of the people sitting before me, I realised just how glad I was to be gone from the place, even temporarily. The library with its mildewed books, their fraying covers, the echoing flagstones of the hallway, the freezing bedroom and the fireplace with its latex hands folded over one another as though in prayer. Here there was light and the gentle rumble of chatter, the smell of stale beer, BBC News, normality.

"Elver?" said Lucy. Her face was shocked. "Your project's about Elver?"

"Well, in a way," I said. There was no way around it. And I wanted to understand, I wanted the sort of background Laura and the agency, and indeed Catherine herself, had seemed unable to give me. "I'm working on behalf of the owner."

There was a silence. "It's an incredible house, isn't it?" I said, aiming for breeziness, for a nonchalance I could sense was anything but reciprocated.

"It is that," said Lucy. She sat back down. I couldn't judge her tone. "And, sorry Ellen, but did you say you're staying at the house?"

"Dropped her off there myself last night," said Steve. "I didn't go in, mind," he said hastily.

The barman shot me a glance, then went back to wiping glasses. Lucy frowned, shaking her head.

"I haven't been inside that house since I was a girl . . ." she said sadly. "I've always found it incredible, the way it's just sat there, all this time, not two miles away. It must be 30 years or more since I set foot there."

She shook her head again, her forehead creased. "Inside the house, I mean. Obviously we've all been onto the grounds more recently than that." She sighed.

"Don't, Lucy," said the barman. He glared at her uneasily. "Just don't. Not summat to plodge about in."

There was a fresh disquiet etched across Lucy's face, an abandonment of the ease and conviviality of just moments before. "Fine," she said shrugging. She turned back to me. "What's it like now?"

"It's . . ." I thought of the house as I'd entered it the night before, the open door, the piles of unopened post, the disarray of the upstairs study, the footprint on the sofa. And then, just as quickly, I recalled the softness of the bed, the towels arranged perfectly in the bathroom, waiting to be used. The immaculate state of the kitchen, with all its hanging pans and stacks of crockery. The library, and Catherine's father within it reading his books in the lamplight.

"It's lovely. Huge, obviously. And there's lots to do, but I've everything I need." I decided to leave it at that.

"She used to pop into the village quite often," said Lucy. "She'd come in here from time to time. Lovely woman. Very prim and proper, very polite, but never lorded it."

The barman sighed, placing our drinks on the counter before us. "Nice woman. Good company." There was an air of finality in his tone.

"She kept more and more to herself," said Lucy, by way of explanation, "and then she just stopped coming. The walk was too much for her, I suppose, and her eyesight got worse so she couldn't drive either. But if it was friendship she wanted, she had only to ask. We'd gladly have popped along to Elver for a bit of tea."

Steve nodded. "People can become a bit funny when they get older," he said, sipping his pint. "She seemed . . . I don't know how to describe it. She seemed scared, almost." He looked around at no one in particular and traced a circle around the beer mat. The barman grimaced.

"Just leave it, all of you," he muttered. "Doesn't feel right to talk about her like this."

"I'd be terrified, Steve," said Lucy, ignoring him. "All alone in that enormous house. And the woods for what seems like miles around." She picked at the sleeve of her jacket.

"Was she always alone?" I asked. If anyone was to know the sort of person I was dealing with, her life, her background, village gossip, it was Steve, Lucy and the others.

The question was met with vigorous nods. "Well, at least since the death of her mother. And that must have been . . . Well, around the last time I visited the house," said Lucy. "Not much of a parent, from what I could gather. Didn't seem the least bit interested in her own child, let alone the rest of us." She frowned.

"She wasn't the maternal type," said Steve delicately. "My parents loved her, though. She was a great friend of theirs; they were devastated when she passed."

"Yes, she much preferred the company of adults," said Lucy. I was surprised by the strength of feeling, the clear disapproval. "She used to invite the village over once or twice a year, when we were kids. You know, for a summer fête," We'd have barbecues and play on the estate, that sort of thing."

"Eel-babbing competitions," chuckled Steve. "You remember those?"

"You can do it from anywhere along the brook," said Lucy, "but the water was best at Elver. We always caught the most there."

"What's eel babbing?" I asked, and the barman laughed, clearly more comfortable now.

"Ignore them," he said. "Old pastime. Very provincial."

"Babbing's a fine tradition, Tom," said Steve, feigning outrage. He turned to me. "First you find some decent worms. We had the best compost round here, and the worms were thick as your finger. We'd take a bit of yarn, something strong and decent, and a bodkin needle. You know, the ones with the giant holes at the top. You thread the worms onto the yarn and then pop it onto another bit of string attached to a stick."

Lucy made a face. "It's barbaric," she said apologetically. She leaned against the bar stool, the anxiety of moments before replaced with an approximation of calm. "But we all did it. Down by the creek we'd set up a big bucket to collect the elvers in. Once we'd let the babs – that's the yarn with the worms attached – into the reeds and leaves, we'd sit there and wait."

"Sometimes you'd be there for what felt like ages," said Steve. "But then you'd have a wrench and you'd have a battle on your hands pulling the bab up again. Some of them were over three feet long. If you were lucky enough to haul it out you plopped the bab into the bucket." He shivered. "Rolling and roiling they'd be, especially the more you caught. When we had enough we'd get one of our fathers down."

"And they'd still be alive at this point?"

"Oh yes," said Lucy briskly. "Well, some of them were. I used to hate the next bit. The decapitations."

"Yes, the heads were all chopped off and then they were skinned."

I felt nauseous and nodded faintly.

"So thick, those skins," said Steve. "We'd dry them and make ropes out of them."

The barman nodded. "My father once ate an entire pint," he said. "There were competitions for that too. It's banned now of course. They use some kind of sustainable white fish instead."

I sipped my drink and tried to put the image out of my mind. Long, coiled bodies twisted round each other, spirals of skin. I was reminded again of the mildewed pages of the books in Miss Carey's library, the parchment-like paper spotted with fungus.

"It seems a horrific thing to do," said Lucy. "But at the end of the day, it was only fishing. And after the war we all had to get used to eating things we mightn't have wanted to before. Food was scarce."

"It's gone out of practice, now, the babbing," said Steve. "A relief to you, Ellen. You're white as a sheet."

I laughed, though there wasn't much humour in it. "But you said the best eels were down at the house, at Miss Carey's?"

"The water's deeper there," said Steve. "At least it was back then. We didn't do too badly for ourselves, given the time of day. Eels are best caught at night. Years ago there'd have been little dots of lantern-light all along the brook for miles around. Each man had his 'stump', the patch of stream that was his alone to fish."

"I saw some this morning," I said, and I told them about the elvers in the brook.

"Forget the eels a moment," said Lucy, laughing. "I'd love to go inside the house again. Tell us more."

"Well," I paused and thought about it. "It's very elegant. It looks frightening from the outside, but it's quite cosy once you're in. I've never been anywhere quite so big, though. There's no way one person could ever run a house like that on their own, especially not one as old as Miss Carey."

"She managed pretty well after the death of her mam," said Steve. "And then, I don't know . . . I suppose things changed a bit, the last few years. As I say, we didn't see her as much. She wasn't often down in the village, and when she did pop in for whatever reason she seemed different . . ." He drained his pint and motioned for another. "Such a shame. It would have been good for her, walking or driving down, just once or twice a week."

I thought back to Catherine's quick-fire, inexplicable changes in behaviour. The way she seemed at one moment energetic, enthusiastic, polite, and the next she was stalking away from me, letting me know I was dismissed, hurrying off to some distant corner of Elver.

"You said she looked scared?" I wondered how the question would land, whether they'd all clam up. But Steve nodded. I remembered her mention of the chapel on the estate. The fear in her eyes; the fact it'd been knocked down. That had seemed to upset her. I asked Lucy about it.

"Yes, it was demolished years ago," she said. "But the crypt was left as it was – a sort of private graveyard I suppose. You can't access it now. I don't think that would have been the thing, though. When we saw her scared, I mean. It just wasn't my place to ask her about that, and we'd no reason to think there was anything *really* wrong."

"Was it just the once, she seemed frightened?" I asked.

"A few times . . ." said Steve, and Lucy nodded.

"There were several break-ins," she said softly. "They really shook her up."

"Break-ins?" I thought of the house, so isolated behind its moat of trees, so removed from the village, from people, from life. How awful to think of the many doors and windows of Elver, the entry points, the once-grand house pillaged, its treasures pilfered. I thought of a line of ants each carrying a small portion of seed, trailing in a line towards their hill, hauling their cargo over the soil.

"A while back, but then they started again around a year ago," said Steve. "I think she was in London at the time, thank goodness. But she came back to find the place in a right mess. Her mother's jewels, her father's watches, some really decent artworks gone . . . They'd not taken everything, mind. Maybe they were disturbed. But they took a good haul all right. It must have been a terrible thing to come home to."

It came to me with a jolt, the image of Miss Carey framed in the doorway to the guest bedroom. *I'm warning you*, she'd said. *The police have been called.* Her suspicion and fear made a dreadful sense.

"My husband's good friends with the constable here," said Lucy. "He kept watch on the house for a few nights afterwards, and I think Miss Carey was able to claim some of the items on insurance. It's not the point, though, is it." It wasn't a question.

"Big house like that, all on its own . . . There aren't many of them left, are there?" said Steve. "Most are National Trust now, I suppose. But whoever those little shits were, the ones that broke in, they must have planned it. No way you'd just happen across the house, now, would you?"

I shook my head. There was something so unsettling, so disturbing about a pre-planned hit, a methodically assembled group of thieves. I was glad to know that Miss Carey hadn't been there, that she'd escaped whatever terrors might have awaited if the robbers had found her at Elver. But the thought of her, so old and frail, returning home to a decimated shell of a house was almost painful in its sadness. I thought again of her reaction to finding me in the house, how distressing that must have been for her.

"But . . ." I swallowed the last of my drink, wanting to get back to the house but torn with curiosity. "What I don't understand is the lack of help. Wasn't there a housekeeper, someone like that? The garden looks quite well-maintained."

"Not anymore," said Lucy darkly. "When we were children there was a whole staff. They dwindled away over the years."

She looked over at Steve, who made a shushing gesture, and rolled her eyes. "Oh come on. They deserted the Careys and we all know it." She turned to me.

"Cassie Ferrier lived in the next village over. She'd pop in a couple of times a week, do the laundry, change the bedsheets, chop firewood, and I think a bit of cooking too. Just to keep things ticking over. From what I understand, Catherine did everything else. I'm not sure how much Cassie's been over the past few weeks. But I'm sure she'll turn up soon enough. There's all sorts needs doing to that house. You're right, Ellen, it's a lot of work. Too much for one old lady, however determined that old lady might be."

"Amen," said Steve. "And especially an old lady with dementia."

I stared at him. Tom, the barman, had turned his back on us all and was noisily depositing coins into the cash register.

"We never heard she'd a formal diagnosis, but it figures, doesn't it?" Steve looked at Tom apologetically, but continued nonetheless. "She came down here less and less and she lost her confidence. My auntie went the same way, started putting her slippers in the fridge towards the end. Wandering off in the middle of the night, that sort of thing."

I remembered the soft tread of Miss Carey's feet on the stairs; the tap of her stick. Her evasive answers to my queries about her midnight walk on a rainy evening. And I felt guilty, too, in that moment. If Miss Carey was struggling with the early stages of dementia, it was going to make the task of extracting her story much more challenging. Not impossible: I'd done this before. But I remembered the pain and confusion of those past clients, the frustration as they couldn't remember the answer to a question but knew, in their bones, that it was glimmering just out of reach. The sometimes violent outbursts when I asked a particular question or raised a particular subject.

I glanced at my watch. I'd been gone a good hour, and it felt like long enough. I wanted to stay here, of course, but while I could legitimately claim an hour's walk and a brief introduction to the village as a short break, taking any longer was pushing it. Whether Catherine would agree to continue with the interviews was another matter. But she couldn't very well agree to anything if I wasn't there.

"Thanks for the drink," I said, and stood up. Lucy looked troubled. Tom barely turned as I made for the door. Steve gave a salute.

"Good luck, Ellen," he said. "You kept my number, did you? Got it in your phone?"

I nodded. "Not much reception up there, but yes, I've got it. And there's Wi-Fi at least."

"Elver's got its own telephone," said Lucy kindly. "I used to try and give her a ring every few weeks, see how she was doing. If you need anything and you've no reception, just give me a buzz on that." She scribbled her number down on a bar-mat and passed it over. I tapped it into my phone.

"Thanks," I said. "I will do. And thanks for the drink – and the chat. It's been useful." And waving to them all, I pushed open the door and was back on the village green.

As if on autocue, the rain started again.

CHAPTER FOURTEEN

Y EARS LATER, LONG after I'd unpicked the days spent at
Elver House, the hours spent with Catherine Carey, long after
I'd unravelled our interactions, pulled at their threads, strained to
remember the tone of her voice, the set of her hair, the shape of her
eyes, I would realise that time, as always, was everything.

Timing had brought me to Elver and timing kept me there long
after I had left. In the immediate aftermath of what happened I
wandered the corridors through countless sleepless nights. I spent
long stretches in front of my keyboard, staring at the screen as the
cursor flashed. I felt the shape of its wide banisters under my hands
and the sweep of the staircase to the first floor.

I tried to concentrate on other things: on work, new clients, on
fresh stories. I went on long walks to the heart of the city where
every passing person bustled along on their own trajectory. I spent
the evenings tidying the flat, packing up old books, carting clothes
to charity shops. I scrubbed the windows until they gleamed. In the
mornings I swam, 64 lengths each day, back and forth, tumble-turn-
ing at each end and pushing straight off again like an arrow. Even
in the depths of the pool the image of her, slightly hunched, dressed
for an audience of one, with her neatly brushed hair and piercing
gaze, clung to me unrelentingly like toothache.

Just two years previously, I probably wouldn't have agreed to the
assignment in the first place. That stretch of late-twenties chaos had
fuelled me, seen me grasp, always, for the next adventure. We had,
you and I, danced our way through so many countries, so many
stupid situations, late nights and cigarettes, declarations of enduring

love and devotion. We'd part the mist in early-morning trips to Hampstead Ponds, pulling on caps and strapping on goggles. The temperature board read nine degrees in January: chalk was smeared across from the rubbed-off reading of the day before, and the day before that. Long weeds tangled the bottom, just visible, swaying in gentle currents. A clump of nettles skirted the edges like hair pulled from a brush. There were wide trees and narrow ones, elbowing each other for space.

We shuddered; we regretted deciding to come when our phones pushed noise through wherever we were and woke us. I was sore and prickly, heat spreading out across my arms to the edges of my fingernails. Soon the cold would rip a breath from my chest, would cause an involuntary gasp. It became my new favourite sound, one I never knew was possible before I came to the city.

I trudged back up the lane to Elver, my boots disturbing each quickly forming puddle, and I thought of your smile, its mischief; I wondered whether the life you had created would give rise to more smiles, more mischief, or stop it altogether. You had seemed so sure, so certain, and that invincible confidence was something I both admired and feared. I wanted you to be happy, of course. I just didn't understand why one new way of life had to bring about the end of another. Surely, perhaps, we could be both.

It all felt very lofty and I was aware, that day, of feeling sorry for myself, checking my phone in the moments signal allowed. There was a long, convoluted message about an upcoming hen party, and an email asking for all bridesmaids to please wear mauve. I wasn't sure I knew what mauve was, and the thought of spending a weekend wandering around a shopping centre trying on tent-like dresses made me want to lie down, right there in the mud, and never get up.

Conger Brook's borders were hard to define; I wasn't sure where the village stopped and the next one started. Where, for instance, did the housekeeper live – Miss Ferrier, they'd said? It could be moments or miles away. From the village green there had been several smaller paths leading off in different directions, each of which must lead to more houses, even shops. The track I had taken, to return to the house, was by far the most overgrown – its width so slight and indistinct I assumed it must lead only to Elver. The rain had already filled the impressions made by my boots earlier, and I followed their reassuring tread as the trail curved to the left, past the gnarled roots of overhanging trees.

Here, unfolding around me, was life in all its messy glory. The bark of starlings, the way they took flight as one when I approached the tree in which they perched; the wheeze of a chaffinch, the swoop of a gull off in the distance, over the unkempt fields. Nettles brushed my legs, the leaves stroking soaked denim. I bent down to examine their thick, white flowers, the soft sombreros hanging delicately from stalks. Here too were the splayed open trumpets of marigolds, sturdy and resolute despite the onslaught of rain, their wet-hay scent drifting unseen beside me. Around the world, the petals were brought to altars of the Virgin Mary, a substitute for coins. Mary's gold.

The phone buzzed. *You've not lived until someone's thrown up down the back of your shirt.* You followed it up with a picture. Your face, pale and round and hopeful, smiled back. I could see the deep purple under your eyes and the thin crow's feet at their edges. It seemed impossible that the picture of cosiness before me had once climbed mountains, had once jumped onto a moving boat as it left the harbour. *Hope your day's as exciting as mine.* There in the background I could see a mat, tiny and colourful, and a selection of black-and-white books.

"Did you know that newborns can't see colour?" you'd asked, months ago. "All these stories we've stockpiled and they won't even be able to see the pictures until they're six months."

And so we'd gone out. You'd been big back then and you only got bigger. I knew it was happening but it was like, in those intermediate months, before everything changed, I wasn't prepared to accept it. We filled a shopping basket with little hardboard stories of dogs and cats, baskets of fruit, shapes and spirals. Their monochrome beginnings, middles and ends seemed, as we stood waiting to pay, like a warning.

In the far distance, just above the branches of an oak tree to my right, I saw the top of a chimney; tall and proud, brushing the clouds. The twisted cones of the roof's small spires came next. The house began to unfurl itself like a banner, glimpses of dark stained brick and the peeling paint of white window sashes. I took a picture between the branches, and sent it off to you. *Absolute middle of nowhere. Strangest work trip ever.* I carried on walking, imagining you balancing the phone as you funnelled dirty clothes into the washing machine. We spoke to each other differently now, more formally. It had taken me a while to realise. The change wasn't immediate or sudden; like a slowly cooling bath, the steam had gently evaporated, the bubbles had dispersed.

A few paces ahead I heard the lapping of the brook; the gentle movement of water over pebbles sounded like the background noise I played through my laptop, sometimes, when I wanted to drown out the racket of the road in the city. I was lucky to be here, I knew that. This was like home, proper home, not the tinny speakers I used to recreate it when traffic was bad. And when else would I ever have come to a place like Conger Brook, met a woman like Catherine Carey?

The path thinned still further. I'd been following it without much thought, the route clearly defined. As I rounded another bend and the house came into full view, I looked down for the first time in minutes and stopped short. The boot prints that had marked the way to the village, my own prints, were now pools of mud, the imprints of the soles still visible. But there, in the thick sludge, and just behind the impressions of my own shoes, there was something else. I peered, frowning, and bent down. A lighter impression, a smaller foot, but it was unmistakable. There was a second set of tracks, as fresh as my own. They'd followed mine exactly along the path.

I spun around on the spot, rain flecking off my hair and trickling down my neck. Suddenly, I was gripped by a cold, deep fear that seemed irrational, uncalled for, even as it settled on my chest and sat there unmoving.

"Hello?" I called out. The brook continued its faint babble. I thought of the elvers moving in silent succession along the flow of water. I remembered Steve and Lucy, the sticks they had fashioned to catch the fish and take off their heads. I traced the outline of the prints, trying to find some explanation. Re-tracing my steps I followed the two distinct sets of tracks some hundred metres, back round the bend, until the second pair stopped abruptly, leaving my own to continue on to the village.

I stared around wildly, pushing aside the thick leaves of a bush for any sign of further tracks, though I knew there could be none. The vegetation here was thick, fed by the rich, irrigated soil near the brook. There was no sign of any disturbance, no indication that the person who had so carefully traced my own tread had deviated from the path. I forced myself to breathe. In the distance, a flash of pink broke the horizon with startling intensity: the hydrangeas by the far-eastern border of the estate bobbed their heads.

There had to be an explanation. Miss Carey might have come looking for me – noticing that my coat and shoes were gone, she would have assumed I'd gone for a walk. Perhaps she'd been trying to find me. She'd noticed the boot prints and followed them. But I hadn't heard her, and surely she would have called out. The prints of the smaller shoe were as waterlogged as my own had been. She must have been moments behind me.

"Catherine?" I called again, and as I did so I turned and started back for the house. She wasn't on the path, that much was clear. I would go indoors, towel my hair dry, and wait for her in the library. All she had wanted, I reasoned, was to apologise for the abrupt ending to our first interview. She'd come looking for me, that was all.

So why, then, did the prints stop so suddenly? If she was so determined to find me, why not go further, walk to the village? There was no doubt, according to the villagers, that she had been inclined to do just this until very recently. Why did she stop, having come so far along the path, and turn back? And if she had turned back, where were the shoe impressions to prove it?

I passed the fountain quickly. The front door was closed, but thankfully unlocked. I stood on the threshold and steeled myself, realising with a jolt that I did not want to go inside. A creeping dread, a strange, unsettling knot had twisted itself around my stomach even as I pushed the heavy door, unzipped my jacket and hung it up. I found my eyes darting to left and right, just as I'd done outside. I heard nothing, and looked upstairs, past the dusty chandelier and the lopsided paintings. Had they been at angles like that before? I couldn't remember.

She was nowhere to be seen, and the house had a stillness to it, an air of having been undisturbed for hours. The flagstones leading to the kitchen were bare and clean, cleaner than when I'd left, certainly. There were brush-marks across the rug leading to the library, like a vacuum cleaner had been passed over it.

"Miss Carey?" I called. "Catherine?" As expected, there was no reply. The stillness was unnerving, deep and impenetrable. The library was at I'd left it, however, and I retrieved my laptop, gathered my diary and pencils. I trod my way heavily upstairs, glad of the noise of my feet on the boards, and trying to put the image of the other feet out of mind: the tiny, tail-gating other pair, imprinted in mud.

CHAPTER FIFTEEN

T HE FIRST INDICATION that someone had been inside the room was the bedside table. My glasses and book were no longer where I'd left them – on the windowsill, along with the toiletries bag – but on the small glass stand beside the bed. I stared at them, the polished lens of the spectacles far cleaner and less smudged than they had been.

At some point that morning or early afternoon, when I'd been down at the brook, perhaps, or walking to and from the village, Miss Carey had come into the room and cleaned it. The covers were turned down more neatly on the bed than I'd left them, the coverlet tucked under the pillows in a way I'd never do myself. Under the pillow, folded delicately, was the old t-shirt I'd brought to sleep in.

It was her house, I reasoned. She seemed a proud woman: someone who recalled the one-time grandeur of the place and sought, I felt, to preserve it even now. I tried not to feel uncomfortable about it, but it struck me as odd that she wouldn't simply ask, or that she'd assume I would want her to tidy up after me.

The rain continued its droplet races down the pane. I plugged the laptop in to charge and sat back on the wicker chair, cursing myself for not bringing my running shoes. Just to be outdoors, exercising in the wet and encroaching cold, would have been heaven. Instead I felt stuck here: the work I'd been sent to do wasn't being done, and I couldn't face any more of Mr Phillips' interviews right now. I started on emails: easy admin tasks, sending out invoices and logging those that had been paid. It was dull, mindless. By three o'clock the rain was still hammering down.

I missed the city like I always did, the moment I left it. Centuries ago, London would have been much like Conger Brook was now. Miles of fields where bars now stood, where we spilled out onto pavements and caught buses. It wasn't really a city at all but a series of country villages, always preparing for a summer fair. Despite the pints of concrete, centuried layers of thick foundation and flicks of steel, it was a forest of wildlife.

Last week I spotted a frog hopping leisurely past a puddle in Soho Square. A young group of bankers watched him too, eating large baguettes that dripped mayonnaise onto their freshly pressed shirts. There was a picnic atmosphere, though the summer had long faded. Later, seagulls soared over Trafalgar Square. I walked home past the old cemetery, filled with 13th-century plague victims, as a dog lolloped along; something larger than a rat but smaller than a cat streaked into deeper brushland. In St James' Park the pelicans strutted down the asphalt, their pouchy beaks stretched and taut as dried leaves.

One morning, recently, in Denmark Hill I woke to the sound of parakeets; a man was making me French toast in his tiny kitchen and said there was a roost right outside the bedroom window. He placed cornflower seeds on the sill and three of them dove down, green as acid pops, and we watched them through the glass.

I wondered if I should text him. Just as soon as the thought occurred, I turned the phone over, its black screen facing downwards, and carried on working. Outside, a rumble of thunder, so distant I barely heard it, coincided with a gust of wind and a fresh spasm of rainwater coursing down the window.

The soft tapping of the keyboard was comforting, an instantly recognisable, homely sound. After another half hour I yawned, stretched, and went to the fireplace, finding a box of matches on the mantelpiece and making another small tepee from the scraps of wood and kindling in the basket beside the grate. I blew on the flames until the wind helped them leap into life, and slowly, tentatively, I blew on the little tent and then added a log. The crackling was soft and the heady smell of wood smoke filled the air. I held my hands before the growing flames and waited to warm up.

Downstairs, the front door opened, swung wide and closed. I heard slow footsteps on the flagstones and jumped up, smoothing my hair back, rubbing some colour into my cheeks.

"Hello?" I called down. "Miss Carey?"

She stood frozen at the bottom of the stairs, looking up at me with a mixture of irritation and fear. "What do you want?" she said evenly. The bottoms of her long galoshes were splattered with mud, and the sleeves of her coat dripped steadily onto the floor.

"I- " What was I supposed to say? "Did you . . . did you have a good walk?"

She took a step back, her hand now on the doorknob, and though she tried to hide the tremor in her voice, it was there. "I'm warning you," she said. "I will call the police. You've no right barging in here. I will ask you again," she raised a trembling hand. "You'd better tell me right now. What do you want?"

Without realising what I was doing, I moved forward, into the light of the still-open front door, and began to descend the stairs. "Miss Carey," I said, keeping my voice as light as I could. "Catherine. It's me, it's Ellen. We met last night? And we spoke earlier today. We sat in the library." I gestured with my hands to the room on the right.

Her face crumpled suddenly, and for one terrible moment I thought she might cry. "Ellen," she said flatly. "Come a little closer, would you?"

I did as she'd asked and moved, still achingly slowly so as not to startle her further, until I was at the bottom of the stairs. She gazed at my face and then nodded, just once. Her eyes bored into me, rooting me to the spot. She was at once so majestic, so regal in her upright stance, and yet so frail. Her hands were lined and creased as a dress that needed ironing, and her knuckles startlingly white. The pearls at her neck clinked together slightly as she moved forward.

"Would you like me to help you with your coat?" I asked, not moving. "I've just been catching up on some work. I heard the thunder. Sounds like a storm's coming . . . I'm not sure we should go out again today, at this rate." Feigning normality, I thought, was the best option. How awful it must be to forget a person so quickly, to have the mind convince you that someone you'd spoken with, just hours before, was an unknown, a threat.

She hesitated, then nodded. I came toward her very gradually, smiling all the while, and gently undid the buttons of her jacket. Her face, in profile, was not that of an old woman's but someone much younger – the hard, straight nose, sharp eyes, the alabaster cheeks pale as milk.

No sooner had I hung the jacket up, Miss Carey clapped her hands and started for the kitchen. "I do apologise, Ellen," she said shakily over her shoulder. "You must think I'm barmy. Let me make us a cup of coffee and then we can get back to work." I waited for her slowly retreating shuffle to round the corner and then pulled out my phone and went into the library.

"Laura, it's me," I said, closing the door.

"Hi, love. How's it going over there? Did you manage to get a bit done with her?"

"We made a good start," I said evenly. "Listen, Laura, the thing is . . ." I glanced at the library doors and lowered my voice. "I think she's not well, Miss Carey. She got a bit cross earlier, when we were talking. She sort of . . . stormed off."

I described the walk to the village, the conversations with Lucy and Steve and the others. Without realising I was doing it, I omitted the part about the footprints. "And now she's come back to the house. I've no idea where she's been, though I suppose it's none of my business really. It's just she's soaking wet. And she didn't seem to know who I was."

There was silence down the line. "Laura?"

"Give me a moment, love, I'm thinking."

The door handle of the library turned weakly and I started, moving back to the bookcases.

"You still there?" said Laura. "Ok, so I think what's best—"

I walked forwards and opened the door. Catherine stood, smiling, holding a tray heaped with crockery, spoons, a cafetière, the old tin of biscuits. Her face, in that moment, was so utterly changed from the fear of moments earlier that she looked, very briefly, like someone else entirely. *Just on the phone*, I mouthed, and held the door open. She nodded and walked into the room, each step careful and measured.

"We're just about to have a coffee, Laura," I said meaningfully.

"Ok. Can you pop me on speaker?"

I did so nervously, turning to Miss Carey as she laid the cups out on the table. "Miss Carey, this is Laura – she's my editor, you know, at the agency. She just wanted to say hello."

Catherine made a face at me and shook her head.

"Hello, Miss Carey? It's Laura. We spoke last night, when Ellen arrived."

Again Miss Carey grimaced. "Ellen, am I on speaker-phone, love?"

"Yes," I said evenly. "Miss Carey can hear you."

"Wonderful," said Laura breezily. "Well, I just wanted to check in with you, see how things were going, hear how you found the first interview today."

Miss Carey looked at the phone, back down to the cafetière, and then out of the window.

I held the phone toward her but knew it was no good. For whatever reason, the older woman was refusing to talk.

"Just so you're aware, Laura, Miss Carey's nodding." I grinned up at her, and a small smile crept to her lips.

"Well that's great news," said Laura. She was so charming, so professional. Lord knows that between us, over the years, we'd dealt with all manner of strange and occasionally rude clients. Miss Carey was 87. She had lived on her own for a long time. She was clearly mistrustful by default, though I wasn't exactly surprised, given what Steve and Lucy had said about the break-ins. "So I just wanted to let you know that Ellen will be with you until Monday evening, as agreed. She's hoping to do around five hours with you each day, Miss Carey. Does that sound ok?"

I looked at Miss Carey, who started fiddling with the pearls around her neck.

"Four hours of what?" she asked.

"Of interviews, Miss Carey," I said. "For the book."

"What book?"

"Ellen, what's going on?" said Laura.

In order to save both her, Laura and myself any further embarrassment, I took the phone off speaker and placed it back against my ear.

"It's just me. I think the time-frame might be a bit optimistic, Laura . . . I'm not sure I'll be finished by Monday."

Laura sighed. I heard the jangle of keys in the background and could just see her, handbag slung over one shoulder, heading to her car. Her suits were always impeccable: sleek cuts, killer heels and a smile that radiated confidence, reassurance. She'd worked in PR for years and it shone through at moments like this.

"Look, El," and then she paused. "I'm off speaker, right?" I reassured her. "She's booked the works. A full-length manuscript, start-to-finish autobiography. The deal was a big one, and she paid through the nose to have someone there in person with her, talking it through." My stomach churned. I knew what was coming, and Laura knew I knew it too.

"Ok. If push comes to shove . . . would you stay a bit? Could you do that? I'll bump the fee. I'll double it. But we have to get this over the line. I've looked through the initial notes when she spoke to Sam, and she's paid premium for everything. We have to get it right."

I thought of you, at home with the baby. I thought of the man with the parakeets in his garden, and of my flat. I thought of the piles of books waiting to be read on the night-stand, the reassuringly chipped coffee cups, the light bulbs that needed replacing. The soft weight of my pillows, the hum of the bread machine, the dishwasher. So safe, so reassuring. But for better or worse there was little I had planned this week that couldn't wait. A few more days, a bit less pressure, and Catherine and I could wrap this, I was sure of it. The thought didn't fill me with dread, I noticed, but with a calm kind of detachment. Just last night I'd have been appalled at the idea of spending a single second longer than necessary here. I made a mental note to question myself about why that might be. Later.

"And of course I can't ask Henry to schlep out there – you remember how much of a pain he was when I sent him to bloody Margate, for heaven's sake. Lydia's on leave until August, and Sarah's not taking on any more clients right now. Plus they wouldn't do as good a job anyway . . ."

"It's fine, Laura," I interrupted her. Miss Carey had settled herself on the sofa and I wondered, briefly, if we couldn't grab the time now to chat a little more, to finish what we'd started that morning. The bottoms of her trousers were still damp with mud, but she'd slung a cardigan about her shoulders. I noticed the brooch pinned to its front, a tiny golden thistle. "If it comes to that, and if Miss Carey's happy to have me a bit longer, then of course I'll stay."

"I'm wiring half the fee over now," said Laura. I could hear the relief in her voice. "Just hang tight. Keep working at her – it's only been a day, after all. She's not used to having you around yet. It takes time. It's great you were able to get an hour in the bag this morning. I have to go, I'm doing the school run. But call me tomorrow, ok? I have total faith in you."

"Thanks, Laura," I said, and I sat down opposite Miss Carey, opened my laptop, and clicked record. "I'll keep you updated. Speak tomorrow."

"Well done, love," she said. "Keep going. I'll bet you anything you'll be finished earlier."

CHAPTER SIXTEEN

WE WEREN'T, OF course. If the first day was difficult, it was nothing to those that followed: slowly, sluggishly, with sporadic conversations I rushed to record and others I wasn't quick enough to capture. I was certainly, looking back on it, a more patient person back then. Nowadays this sort of delay, the endless hours mooching around waiting for a client to be ready, would drive me insane. But most of the time it felt like a break. Elver House was so far removed from my normality, so at odds with the rushing to and fro of city life. I had to remind myself that work, and indeed clients, would not always march to the tune I'd set out. And there was a stillness here that I forced myself to enjoy. Perhaps, I reasoned, this sort of pause, in all its total strangeness, was exactly what I needed.

And yet there was an air of something else, I realise now. A sense of waiting, an apprehension, a hiatus; uneasiness like something, though I could not have said what, was going to happen.

On the second morning of my stay I'd gone downstairs and waited for Miss Carey in the library. When nine o'clock came and went with no sign of her, I went into the kitchen to put the kettle on. Opening the cupboards revealed a jumble of boxes and half-eaten packets of crackers, old cereals; tins covered in dust advertised Fray Bentos corned beef, Nestlé's condensed milk, fruit salad, something called Smash.

The fridge was no better – a couple of cling-wrapped dishes, their contents reeking of mold, milk so thick I held my nose to pour it down the sink, and a canister of coffee granules. I made the coffee black and strong and carried it back to the library to wait.

I'd stopped feeling any guilt, by this point: if Miss Carey wasn't here, we couldn't speak. I updated Laura via text and then, seeing it hadn't sent, by email. *She has until Friday, and that's her lot*, she'd written that morning, and I carried on with other projects until, at half past three, I called Steve.

We met at the end of the drive, where he'd dropped me. I returned to Elver some hours later, my arms heavy with the weight of groceries. There was nothing for it, after all – no café to surreptitiously feed myself at during Miss Carey's long absences, and no way any takeaway driver would bother coming out this far; I did check. I hoped, when she saw the bags, that Catherine wouldn't be too offended. I'd feign an allergy, an intolerance, and claim fussiness: make out that it was my fault the cupboards were now full. We'd driven, Steve and I, along the winding country roads for eight miles to reach the market town, where for the first time in days I saw life: other cars, pedestrians, the babble of conversation.

I needn't have worried: she barely seemed to notice. She stopped short on entering the kitchen to find me frying onions and garlic. It was the first time we'd seen each other all day, and I noticed her sky-blue shirt, the long black trousers and the emerald slippers. It was like she'd just dressed for the day: the shirt was creaseless, starched and clean. As usual, her hair was immaculate, swept back and seeming to hold itself up behind her neck. She looked surprised as she took in the scene, then appeared to check herself; giving a little shake she settled her face into a smile. "I'm . . . making dinner," I said, unnecessarily. "I hope that's ok. You were out and—"

She waved away my explanations and stood beside me as I chopped carrots, tomatoes, boiled water for pasta. She mentioned the weather, and how it must be the wettest October on record. She wasn't wrong there – it hadn't stopped pouring since I'd returned to the house the previous day.

"Would you like some?" I gestured to the hob.

"Oh, not for me dear." She moved to the table and pulled out a chair. The scrape of wood on tiles set my teeth on edge. I wondered at her slight frame and the way her clothes seemed to hang off her, smart as they were.

"When you get to my age, your appetite pretty well evaporates entirely," she said. "As a girl, I'd have eaten all of that and then some."

I imagined her as a child, as a teenager. I didn't suppose she had been a carefree sort of girl. The only child on the estate, it seemed from what she'd said so far. I fancied there must have been something unmistakeably grown-up in the concern etched on her face, the way she tugged at a hangnail. I saw her at 21, her hair chopped short, a man's shirt hanging off her narrow shoulders, smoking a cigarette perhaps, a smudge of dark brown circling her eyes like a horizon. I wondered, as I stood in the kitchen and Miss Carey sat, what she would have been like at 33, 45, whether she could have lived elsewhere, abroad, how many children she might have had, how many dogs and cats. The restless autumn sky outside rumbled, briefly.

"What did you used to eat, as a child?" I said, casually. I flicked the recorder app open on my phone, dimmed the screen and set it down between us.

"Oh, everything," she said. "Even after the war, when we still had rationing . . . there was nothing we wanted for, really. We grew so much, don't forget."

"In the gardens?"

"Yes, the gardens were full to the brim year round. No space was left uncultivated. My father spent most of his time out there, worrying at the runner beans or digging up potatoes. It was a simpler diet," she said, staring pointedly at the aubergine I was halving. "None of this processed nonsense everyone seems so keen to consume these days. We had plenty of cheese and cream from the dairy farms, all the fruit we could eat, bread we made ourselves . . ." She stared at the spaghetti spiralling around the pan. "And at Christmas we always received walnuts, you know, and chocolate oranges. Peppermint creams, that sort of thing. But only as a very special treat. Children nowadays would be appalled, no doubt."

"Do you remember any toys you used to play with? Books you read?"

"Not especially. I believe I had a rocking horse. It's probably still in the attic to this day. I read whatever was in the library: we didn't have many children's books."

I nodded, not wanting to interrupt her. I thought of the thick tubes of paint, reams of creamy paper and coloured pencils we'd had at our fingertips, the Game Boys, the basket-ball hoop in the garden. I'd read endless books mostly filched from the library and never returned, books I knew I ought not to be reading.

At the age of 12, I moved all my comics and books inside a giant cardboard box that my parents' shed arrived in, dismantled. I lugged cushions and blankets from the sofa across the front garden and borrowed the torch on the tool rack. I'd pass hours in the upturned box, where it was cool and dark. I read *Black Beauty* and *Anne of Green Gables*, *The Hobbit* and *The Chronicles of Narnia*. At night, I'd lie awake fantasising about the taste and texture of Turkish Delight.

Miss Carey rested her chin on her hand. I was struck, once again, by the aquiline features, the straight nose and deep-water blue of her eyes. "After the war was over, my father continued to farm the land. I was only nine but I could tell that something had changed. The adults seemed less preoccupied, less stressed I suppose. The urgency and whispers began to fade and the wireless was switched over from the Home Service to *Housewives' Choice*, which I much preferred."

She smiled to herself, her eyes searching into the past, contemplating a scene she might not have looked upon for decades. "I'd hear that little jingle if I was downstairs and come running, even though dashing about the corridors here was strictly forbidden. It seemed incredible to me that people could telephone in to request music they wanted to hear."

I made a mental note to listen to the programme later, if I could find archive audio online. "A couple of years after the war finished, I remember my father telling me about a new programme, *Gardeners' Question Time*, and I thought it sounded frightfully boring. So many people had become self-sufficient, pretty much, through the war. All that 'Dig For Victory' malarkey. It created quite a community. I sat through a few broadcasts with him and what I remember finding the strangest was the accents."

I stirred the tomatoes again and smiled back at her, encouragingly I hoped. "The people phoning in were from all over the country, you see. I had to ask my dad what half of them were actually saying. He told me, then, that different counties often had their own distinct way of speaking, and the idea appalled me, I have to say."

"Why?"

"Because by that point I was almost 11 years old . . . The notion that there were other areas, other people with other lives and other forms of speech . . . It just hadn't occurred to me. I realised, I suppose, just how small my world was, and I think my father realised it too. I can remember the look of pity he gave me to this day. When I asked the question."

She looked directly at me and said more quietly, "I was so ashamed, really. I'd always thought of the world as Elver, and the gardens around it. The farm, the brook, the village, the woods. I spent hours in the forest, making dens and getting lost. Sometimes I went so far in I'd be gone for hours at a time. But it had barely crossed my mind that here, not so many miles away, there might be others living far more exciting, interesting sorts of lives. Other children, too. I felt that quite keenly, I remember. And I think, if it hadn't happened, my father would have persuaded Mother to send me away for school, when the time came."

Outside in the hallway, the chime of the grandfather clock began. I counted the gongs and realised, with surprise, that it was already seven. Strange, how time seemed to warp here: contracting and elongating at will.

"What I'm saying, I suppose, is that we were happy, for a time. Despite my ignorance of the world. I was perfectly content." Miss Carey paused again. "I was 12 when it happened," she said. I busied myself with the olives, slicing them thinly and adding them slowly to the bubbling stew. She sighed. "I suppose I'd better tell you about it – there are moments in every life where . . . I don't know how to describe it."

"Take your time," I said. I knew what she meant. Everyone I spoke to, either professionally or otherwise, said the same. We all had them: the sliding-doors moments. And Miss Carey was, at last, about to tell me her first.

"I told you my father had terrible vision," she said.

I nodded, waiting. The pasta was boiled but I waited, my face turned away from her, though I knew she was watching me.

"It was the summer. He'd been down at the brook, fishing I believe, and he must have slipped, or thought the path was wider than it was. We'll never know: there was no such thing as forensics, as we might understand them now. No analysis of what really happened. I was in the nursery with the governess: she was teaching me French, I remember. I hated it. It was a bright, warm day and I was staring out of the window, right at the top of the house, when I noticed Mr Simmons, that was our gardener, come running toward the front door. He was bright red, sweating and shouting."

She paused again, and it seemed now that the words were being pulled from her, little by little. Her voice was faint, and I edged the phone closer to catch the story. "We heard the most dreadful commotion downstairs, and then my mother was screaming. I stood up, I remember the chair falling backwards behind me, and I ran for the stairs. All the way to the front door, where I found her lying there in a heap. I'd never seen anyone behave like this, so utterly changed from how they had been before." Miss Carey looked up, past me and to the windows. I imagined her at the age of 12, probably metres from where we now sat.

"One of the ribbons of my plaits had come loose, I remember, and I found myself wondering where on earth it could have got to. Mr Simmons removed his cap, helped my mother to her feet, and then explained to me that my father was beside the brook. Simmons had managed to get him out, but it was too late. He'd hit his head, and by the time the poor man found him, he'd taken in too much water."

I turned, unable to stop myself, and stared at her. Her face was utterly still, her eyes still glassy, gazing off into the distance in that way I was becoming so accustomed to. "I ran, before either of them could stop me. I ran through the cabbage beds, over the roses, my feet plastered in mud. I ran until I thought my sides would burst and then, there he was."

It felt disrespectful to try to do anything else while she spoke. I kept my face in profile, not wanting to interrupt. There was a thick silence, weighty and impassable. The tap dripped suddenly though I hadn't touched it: a small spurt of pressure falling into the basin.

"His face looked just the same, exactly as it had done that morning. But he didn't move, his eyes were closed, his mouth slightly agape as though he was preparing to speak. I just stood there, looking down at him, willing him to wake up. It didn't seem real. It wasn't real at all to me then. When Simmons said he'd found him, that was all I heard, I think. In fact as I ran outside, I cursed him, leaving my father in whatever state he was in."

"I'm so sorry," I said, after a moment's delay. "How shocking it must have been. What a thing to have witnessed." Miss Carey's eyes found mine and she nodded, slowly.

"Yes," she said quietly. "It *was* awful. Mr Simmons arrived a few minutes later and ushered me away. I've no memory of the days that followed. Where I slept, what I ate, what I said. No memory at all."

"And they were never able to say exactly what had happened?"

"They might have done," she said simply. I took the water off the boil and moved to the sink to drain the spaghetti. "I was never told. The next thing I remember was the funeral, though I couldn't tell you exactly when it was. What I do know is that my nanny picked out the most awful scratchy dress from an outfitters in town, and I could feel the material scraping along my arms and back as we filed into the chapel."

Steam brushed my face as I busied myself with a plate, tossing the pasta into the pot of bubbling sauce. "I hadn't been back inside since the war. I had refused to go. And now I had no choice: it was his funeral, after all. I could never have missed it. My mother wore a veil over her face, though I knew she was watching me. I tried to avoid looking to the right, where the steps led down to the crypt, where all those men had been laid out. And where I knew my father would be, too."

I turned the pasta over and over, coating the long thin ropes in red. I hoped the audio didn't pick up too many of these background noises. I might have to use the amplifier when it came to transcribing. I could already feel the words forming, the images I would take from what she had said, and the moment of realisation on the part of this woman, once a girl, as the truth hit home.

Even as the sentences appeared, as though I was writing them now, I couldn't extrapolate: I had to write it faithfully, and so we needed to stay here, digging down a little more. When had she known he wasn't coming back? I asked the question and watched as her face, so soft and placid, so sad, set into its familiar frown.

"I never accepted his death," she said, haltingly. "And you wouldn't have either."

I waited.

"His eyesight might have been diminishing, but he knew the whole estate like the back of his hand. And he was sure-footed, not clumsy in the way I seem to be. It didn't make any sense to me. And there was no mark on him, no bloom of a bruise on his temple, no indication of how he came to hit his head. But he must have done, because the brook was only waist-deep. He must have sustained some sort of blow, or he'd have simply climbed right out of the water, no matter its temperature. This was summer, after all. It would have been warm enough."

In the distance, I heard another faint rumble of thunder. A gust of wind shook the windows in their frames and we both turned to look at the door to the pantry, creaking on its hinges.

I sat before her now: it felt odd to eat like this, while she spoke, but beggars couldn't be choosers at this point. If she was prepared to talk, who was I to stop her?

"More than anything, Ellen," said Miss Carey, with some effort, "more than anything, I didn't believe he was really gone because, not three months after his death, I saw him."

I nodded at her, but had she glanced down at my hands, she'd have noticed the tight, knuckle-white grip of my fingers on the fork. She held my gaze directly, almost daring me to contradict her. I asked the only question I could. "Where?"

"In the library, where we sat yesterday. I walked into the room on the instructions of my governess, looking for something to read, and there he was. Just standing at the shelves, his back towards me." Something in her face darkened. "I stood still, rooted to the spot. There was nothing I could do or say. I was scared to speak unless he disappeared. But he remained there, perfectly still, his arms hanging down by his sides."

"Could it . . ." I asked tentatively, "Well, is there any chance it could have been somebody else? Another man? A family friend perhaps, an uncle?"

"I can see you've never experienced anything like it," she said quickly, with an air of irritation. "If you had, you wouldn't doubt it. I was standing not three metres from the man. There was no mistaking him. And he was wearing the same clothes: the thick walking boots, the same plaid shirt as he had been when he went into the brook. It was my father, Ellen."

I wouldn't say I believed her, but I was certain that she believed it to be true. Sometimes that was all that mattered, in the end. I could well imagine her shock, her terror, her intrigue. Perhaps a denial, in the days and weeks following the vision, or whatever it had been, that her father had died at all.

It wasn't uncommon: on the contrary, a client just last month had told me much the same thing. Her son was killed in a car accident at the age of 18. For the next two years she saw him everywhere, from the shops to the bank, the post office, walking in the park. I knew the strength of the mind's power, the ability to trick the grieving into seeing what they so desperately wanted to see.

Catherine leaned across the table, tapping it lightly with her fingers as though to get my attention. "I was terrified the first few times it happened. Terrified. But gradually I grew to expect it, and then to welcome it." She fiddled with the pearls at her throat. "It didn't feel malicious. I wasn't threatened when he appeared. It was like a reminder, a way of ensuring he was always with me. It gave me comfort."

"Do you remember actively thinking that he, your father, I mean, was haunting the house?"

"Well, yes, I suppose so. But I'd read about hauntings," she gestured toward the hallway, in the direction of the library. "So many books, so many stories. Geography and history, fiction and biography, tales of derring-do up mountains and people lost in the jungle. But the family had collected a number of old penny-dreadfuls, too. The Victorian-style horror novels, you know. And in those stories, ghosts and ghouls and whatnot were always so frightening, so unwelcome."

She smiled sadly at me. "I knew my father was dead, make no mistake. I wasn't mad. But after I'd got over the shock of seeing him in the library, or here in the kitchen, or walking calmly from room to room upstairs, I got used to it. Where else was he supposed to go? This was his home."

Miss Carey pulled a tissue from the sleeve of her cardigan. I watched her closely, ready to adopt a gentler tone as we continued. But her blue eyes remained clear, and she gathered herself in a sharp intake of breath.

"Much later, with my second governess, I spent some time looking at word roots. You know, etymologies. That sort of thing." She sniffed, half-smiling. "In medieval times, the word 'haunt' simply meant 'to go', or 'to reside'. In Old French it meant 'to visit' or 'to frequent'. But its roots are likely far older, dating right back to the Vikings. In its most ancient form, a haunting is a return, a homecoming. A cohabitation. It helped me to learn the meaning, the idea of homecoming. After all, what was more natural than my father doing just that, even in death?"

I nodded. "And so it became less frightening as time went on. You wanted to see him, and he was there. It must have helped."

"I'm guessing you've never experienced anything like it," she said. There was a real curiosity in her voice, an eagerness to find common ground.

"I haven't," I said honestly. "Not yet, at least. But I've also been very lucky. No one close to me has died; my grandparents were gone before I was born."

"There are other kinds of grief," she said, appraising me. "You've never felt as though . . . I don't know . . . As though you've lost someone?"

I stared back at her. "Well, yes, I suppose so," I said, lightly. "Yes, there have certainly been friends."

Like the release of a coiled spring you were there, a flash of memory. We were boarding a night bus in north London – laughing and spluttering. You'd given your number to someone and he was ringing you; you thrust the phone into my hand like it was burning you. Later, we arrived at my flat and made toast, settling down on the sofa, necking pints of water to sober up. Hot butter trickled down my chin. We were both due in the office in four hours' time.

"I thought so," said Miss Carey. She gestured at the untouched plate before me. "You'd better finish your supper, my dear. I'm feeling quite tired, all of a sudden."

I nodded mutely and she steadied her hands on the table before standing up, stretching, and making her way across the room. "We'll speak more tomorrow, shall we?" I nodded once more, and she passed through into the hallway. "Goodnight, Ellen," she said, and closed the door softly behind her.

CHAPTER SEVENTEEN

T HE HOUSE WAS its usual sullen self as I ate, more slowly than usual, and washed the dishes at the sink. Every now and then a fresh gust of wind kicked at the door leading out to the garden. The rush of water coursing through the pipes came and went quite suddenly: at once fierce and strong, then feeble and trickling. I was fairly certain Catherine wasn't running a bath: I had come to understand her habits a little more by now, and she retired early. She was, by this point, probably asleep, though it was only just gone eight.

I left the kitchen and stepped out into the cool, dark corridor, flicking on the side table's lamp. On my way past the library I paused, looking instinctively left and right as I scanned the room. There, on the table, sat the discarded coffee cups, the milk jug, the biscuit tin from the day before. The rain threw itself with abandon across the windows. I shivered and closed the doors before heading upstairs to my own room.

The day felt far longer than it ought to have done. I'd not been back upstairs since the early morning, when the prospect of coffee and porridge had lured me downstairs – under, it soon became clear, false hope. What had Steve said, as he leaned across the seat to open the passenger door?

Glad you called. There isn't a decent grocery shop round here for miles.

Thank god for him. He'd waved away the twenty-pound note I'd immediately offered him, and started the engine. *I'm surprised the gas hob is even working at the house, to be honest. You did check them, right?*

I'd cursed myself, but nodded anyway. I'd sort something out.

It felt like days ago. And it had been good, so good, to be pushing a trolley around the supermarket: people going about ordinary, routine sorts of days, filling their baskets with lemons and peppers, bacon and soft loaves of bread. I'd bought a small camping stove, just in case, and a canister of gas.

Must get lonely for you, at the house, he said on the drive home. The bags of shopping sat reassuringly between my feet.

I guess it's a pretty solitary sort of job, to be honest, I'd said. *I'm used to it. And it doesn't feel lonely – though there is, of course, a lot of time alone.*

Bit like driving a cab, he said, nodding as we approached the turning to Elver. *Come on down to the pub, when you next get a chance. Though I know you've plenty to be getting on with here.* He shook his head. *Lord knows I don't envy you the task.*

We drove in silence for a few moments until we reached the track leading up the path, through the trees and on to the house.

You know, he said, switching off the engine and rubbing his nose, *I never did ask you. This project of yours – for Miss Carey, I mean. Who's asked you to do it? Are you writing a book about the area, or the house? Or is it more, like, a family thing?*

I liked Steve. He tried to feign nonchalance but it was clear, from the way he peered out of the window while speaking, and from the would-be relaxed tone of his voice, that he was curious. I could well imagine him recounting the conversation the following day, at the pub perhaps. Like hairdressers, maybe local cabbies were equal fonts of village gossip.

I suppose it's more a family project – or at least it's more focused on Miss Carey herself.

Steve nodded, staring down at his hands.

Lonely for her, too, he said. *She never married. Living all alone up there without anyone to talk to, not even a dog or cat. It'd drive me mad.*

He stared out of the window again and sighed. *Perhaps it drove her mad too.*

The tinkling sound of the brook dropped into the silence between us, like pebbles thrown from a great height. How strong the water must be, I thought, for the sound to reach us here.

And who's asked for it? Steve said again. *Who actually . . . I don't know what you say, commissioned it? The story of Miss Carey? The history of Elver, and all that?*

Well, she did, I said. He looked at me, his eyes unblinking. *A few months ago, I think. She got in touch with the company I work for – we mostly do legacy memoirs, though from time to time you get the odd celebrity too—*

Steve gripped the wheel, now; his breath, when he finally let it out, came in a ragged sort of whoosh.

And now you're here, he eventually managed. I nodded unnecessarily. Where was he going with this? The vein in his throat seemed to throb as I watched him. *Just doesn't strike me as the sort of thing she'd want,* he said. *So . . . private. Not one to make a fuss or put herself in the limelight.*

People have all sorts of reasons for doing something like this, I said. *And they often feel it's especially important towards, you know, towards the end of their lives. Sometimes the desire to leave something behind is stronger than the guarding of oneself . . . if that doesn't sound too haughty.* I tried to muster a half-hearted laugh, but it sounded as forced as it was.

Hmmm, said Steve. *I suppose so. And now you've got a lot of digging to do, eh? Unearthing the skeletons in the closet.* He smiled sadly. *Right. I've to go and fetch someone's great aunt something from the station. Good luck to you, Ellen.*

The corridor was in full darkness upstairs, and I felt my way along the walls until, fumbling slightly, I found the doorknob and turned it. The room was freezing. I switched on the bedside lamp and crouched down before the grate, coaxing a small fire into life, not feeling my fingers anymore. The basket of roughly chopped logs sat beside it, and within a few minutes, the dance of flames made shadows on the wallpaper. I sat back, watching them. *Living all alone up there without anyone to talk to . . . It'd drive me mad.* I couldn't imagine what life must have been like for Miss Carey – all these years, the changing seasons, the long winters and harsh frosts. How did she stand it?

It made still less sense given all she had said. Hers was a childhood that sounded, above all else, isolated and forlorn. A sibling might have helped ease those endless hours, the tedium of lessons with governesses keen to do their hours' work and be gone. And a sibling, or even a friend, would certainly have helped her after her father's death. At least the pain would have been shared. Though perhaps it had been, with her mother, though everything Miss Carey had told me about her made me doubt this somehow. I made a mental note to ask the next day.

How hideous to spend one's teenage years cooped up here, without any sense of the world outside, pining for the first debs' ball, the choosing of material for a dress, the hope that must have accompanied the first season out. Or maybe not. Perhaps Catherine had simply remained here, hopeful for a change. She'd said this had once been the nursery: perhaps she had slept in this very bed, waiting for life to happen.

I remembered your childhood bedroom then: a cultivated thing, a terrarium of tights and discarded comics, a typical hybrid of the space your parents had created for you and the older space you had grown for yourself. On the floor beside the open door sat the model of Noah's Ark you used to love, its chipped wooden animals spilling down the blue gang plank. On the wall hung a tacked-up poster of a band I knew for a fact you'd never listened to. It was the exact mirror of your sister's bedroom: the bed at a right angle to the desk, which was cluttered where hers was neat and ordered. Newspapers were piled into the furthest corner, yellowing now on the bottom. Shirts hung limply on the open wardrobe rail, a black hoodie draped across the back of your chair and socks littered the floor.

It was a desperately identifiable adolescent room, replicated up and down the country, but it was as though you had studied the manual on creating a convincing domain and simply stuck to it. It felt different, this mess, to the rooms of other girls our age: an organised, carefully curated sense of dishevelment. Only the desk escaped this cluttered performance. The dead flowers you insisted on keeping in vases contained the once-yellow husks of chrysanthemums from the garden. Rows of jam jars held the stationary we all hoarded like addicts. There were the fountain pens, HB pencils sharpened to a point, the multi-coloured gel pens that smelled of years-old bubble-gum, felt tips, a battered protractor and thin tubes of purple ink. Postcards tacked above the desk jostled with little notes sent from girls in our class.

I thought of myself at Catherine's age, the endless hours we'd spend hidden in the shed at the end of the garden, sitting among the tools and the smell of grease and leather and earth and telling one another ghost stories. How, at 14, we'd made our own Ouija board and summoned the spirits of men we'd heard about in history lessons. And here at Elver, in another time, was a girl convinced the man she'd witnessed, dead on the bank of the brook, was wandering the hallways, pacing among the library shelves. Our games had been Miss Carey's reality. There was no giggling through the horror for her, no ability to end the playtime.

I crossed to the window and began to brush my hair. There seemed little else for it but to go to bed, though I'd no idea how I'd sleep with the howling of the wind, the way it whipped the smoke, whistling, up the chimney. I turned to face the garden and my hand slowed on the comb, pausing to hover in mid-air as I squinted.

There was a figure on the lawn: small, hunched, dressed in a long night-gown.

I moved quickly to the bedside table and switched off the lamp, plunging the room into semi-darkness the better to see. It was clear the rain had soaked right through the cotton of the dress: it clung to her thin, spindly legs.

For a moment I found myself marvelling at the presence of another person at Elver House: a friend, a housekeeper, anyone. But no – it was Miss Carey moving away, her feet bare. I recognised the silver streaks of her short hair, the delicate frame of her shoulders. I felt a cold settle on my chest as I watched her, the weaving, almost drunken way she walked, but what made the hairs on my arm stand up was the *speed* with which she moved, the impossible pace, the lurching motion. She had the gait and rapidity of a woman 30, 40 years younger. Her stick was nowhere to be seen.

I rushed to the door and flung it wide open, hearing it smack back against the wall as I careered along the corridor and threw myself down the stairs two at a time. I clumsily pulled on my boots and slung an anorak over my shoulders, yanking at the front-door handle, finding with a fresh wave of dread that, just as before, it was locked. I wheeled about, suddenly terrified, and heard the gushing of the pipes somewhere above.

There was no one here to turn the taps, no one to run a bath or flush a toilet and yet, clearly audible, the water poured along its route, petering to a thin trickle.

I wrenched open the door of the living room, empty save for the shadows of pictures on the walls, and the still-present outline of the shoe-print on the sofa, and checked the windows. All were locked. With a cry of frustration I crossed the hallway, my feet echoing on the flagstones, and rushed into the library. The doors leading out to the garden stood wide open: the wooden boards before them soaked and shining. I lurched forward once more, half-jumping over the steadily forming puddle, keen to be gone from the shadowy shelves standing sentry behind me.

The courtyard directly beneath my bedroom window was empty. I stared around wildly, cursing under my breath. Within moments my hair was plastered to my scalp, and I pulled my arms through the thin covering of the jacket. I called her name, moving forward, scanning the few metres before me like the beam of a lighthouse, first this way, then that. She was nowhere to be seen.

The grass became thicker, the weeds higher as I moved forward, my hand shielding my eyes. Long tendrils of drenched vegetation snagged on the laces of my boots like they were trying to pull me back.

"Miss Carey?" I called again, and the rain seemed to swallow up the sound. As I walked on, though, I heard it. Perhaps, subconsciously, I'd known I would have to.

The brook.

I pressed on, panting, placing my feet as carefully as I could on the uneven ground. The sound of the water became much louder. It was closer, certainly, but there was something else. The rain had slowed its onslaught for a moment, seeming to pause, and then stop entirely. Great trees came into view above me, their leaves shaking and shuddering as the final drops tumbled from the browning leaves.

"Catherine?" I cried, and I heard my voice echo as it hadn't before.

A figure, crouched by the water.

She ignored me utterly as I beat through the bushes spilling across the path to the brook.

"Miss Carey!"

There was no bridge, no crossing to the other side, not even a smattering of larger rocks on which to place one's feet. The water was coursing by with an intensity I could never have imagined yesterday morning, as I watched the little elvers darting through the gentle stream like ropes of grey and green. As I observed her, she continued to sit and stare with an intensity that was at once unsettling and upsetting in equal measure.

"Miss Carey?" I tried one last time, and then, not really knowing why even as I said it, I called again: "Catherine?"

She was so small, so slight, her body hunched over itself. And she was staring, utterly transfixed, into the water. But not the sight of her from my window, nor the creeping terror I'd felt as I crossed the garden, and not even the terrible, twisted shape of her, were anything to the fright I felt now, as I looked at the swollen brook and took in the fact that Miss Carey, inexplicably, was on the other side of it.

Her head snapped up and she was suddenly alert, regarding at me with shocked surprise. "Are you alright?" I called over the water.

Her face was streaked with mud, her arms covered in small cuts and scratches. She was so different, so changed from the woman who'd sat with me over dinner, so pitiful. This was another person entirely, though her features jibed the same, like a person wearing a mask of their own likeness.

"Perhaps . . . perhaps we should go back inside?"

Her lips formed a cold, thin smile that broadened to show her teeth. Her hair had soaked through to reveal several patches on her scalp. It was impossible to look away.

I held out my arm and beckoned. "Let's go inside, Catherine. Is there a crossing somewhere? How did you get over?"

I waited.

I felt helpless, standing there as my legs smarted from the streaks of nettles. She would either come or she would not, and a large part of me did not want her to. The physical barrier separating us felt, for a moment, like a form of protection. There, on the other side of the bank, was something I was never intended to witness, a letting-go, a possession almost.

"We could come out tomorrow, if you like?"

She said nothing, and I waited, my arm extended. The water churned below us, a roiling, hissing churn. And then, without giving any indication of what she was about to do, Miss Carey stepped down, onto the slope of the bank, and descended until she was just inches above the water. The trees, several hundred metres away, were still audible above the din of the storm; they tossed their emptying branches in the wind. I couldn't make out the hydrangeas but knew they would be there: standing guard, drinking in the water as it hurled itself against the ground like an invader demanding entry.

I shouted out, scrambling down myself, but she was too fast. Within seconds she had entered the brook and her night-dress billowed out around her, past her knees and up her thighs. She remained steady. As I watched, my hands outstretched, she took great, wide steps through the current, her eyes dazed and fixed on a point over my shoulder. I crouched like a diver about to spring forward on the starting gun, waiting for the loss of balance, for the moment I would almost certainly need to haul her out.

She ignored me completely, and stepped, her feet cracked and bleeding, onto the opposite bank, my bank. She dug white fingers into the mud to haul herself up. And then she stood before me, her teeth chattering, her once-coiffed hair plastered to her forehead and along the back of her neck. There was a glassiness to her eyes, something foggy and vague, almost like cataracts. For the first time she looked not only her age but far older. I found myself wondering, crazily, how she had ever been a child, a girl.

"Are you alright?" I said, not knowing what else there was to say. She focused on me then, and nodded slowly in a distracted sort of way.

"Why am I here?" she whispered. She stared down at her sodden legs, the drenched nightgown. She wrung her hands slightly, looking behind her at the brook, shivering. "Ellen?"

I took off my jacket and helped her push her arms through the sleeves. She took my arm when I offered it, her small hand slipping into the crook of my elbow. My shock was so deep, so profound, that it was all I could do to walk beside her, helping her along, all the way back across the damp grass and into the house.

She said nothing more, and I found that even if I'd wanted to, I couldn't.

I didn't tell Laura about what had happened, and to this day I'm not sure why. I should have. Without doubt, she would have told me to leave. To call Steve, take a cab, go to the station and come home. She'd have rung the council, social services; she'd have stepped in, raised the alarm and tried to find Catherine the help she clearly needed.

And if she had done so, if I'd returned home to the flat and the friends, the ease and comfort of my life in the city, what then? What might the dedicated officers, nurses, whoever, found when they arrived at Elver House? Would she be dressed in her smart skirt and pearls, or located somewhere near the water's edge in her nightclothes?

I don't know. The outcome, in the end, might well have been the same. Would the project have continued with the material I'd gathered so far? Might it not be abandoned, the tapes deleted? In all likelihood I'd have been moved onto the next client, thinking of Catherine Carey and the house and the brook less and less as the weeks went by until, eventually, I forgot all about it.

There was always so much to do in the city, so much to see, and sometimes the choice was exhausting. I'd wake up itching to get going. I loved my jobs and I wanted more. I enjoyed doing whatever I liked, the steady stream of income, the feeling of independence. I'd send flowers and presents back home, write to friends on thick, cream paper which scratched as I filled it with news, week after week. Anything I had done or owned was inconsequential in the grand scheme of things, but it felt like so much and it was mine.

When I first arrived a decade ago, I'd buy halter-neck tops and experiment with not wearing a bra. I cooked duck and the flat stank; I'd mash cranberries and grapes with a fork and drizzle it over the scorched meat. I ate at burger restaurants where the music was achingly hip, a thick bumping grind. I smeared Vaseline across my eyelids and covered them in sparkling shadow, all colour and electric and teeth flashing. I developed a monthly mascara fund and found nothing so pleasurable as putting it on in the morning, nothing so wretched as taking it off at night. I wanted everything I can possibly have, and dashed about the city looking for it. Almost always, I found it.

CHAPTER EIGHTEEN

T HE FOLLOWING MORNING was Sunday. The first day
of November. I woke to a room flooded with light. It was gone
ten, and I scrambled to get dressed, opening the window to see the
grass sodden and glistening from the night before. In the distance
the grey clouds gathered but, for now at least, the garden was bathed
in a soft, tentative glow. As I opened the bedroom door and made
for the stairs, I resolved to discuss what had happened, and readied
myself for whatever reaction this elicited from Miss Carey. Would
she even remember? Would she be embarrassed?

I'd two texts, both sent within half an hour of each other; the
first at 3am. *Sorry to message now,* you'd written, *but I think she
just smiled?!* The second was a photo, and it certainly looked that
way to me. Her face was familiar, yours and yet not, her eyes darker
and her cheeks rosier. I'd respond properly later: for now a series of
kisses would have to suffice.

The soft runner on the stairs concealed my footfalls and I paused
in the hallway, listening for a moment.

"In here, Ellen," came a voice. I turned in surprise to the library.
From the doorway I made out one green-slippered foot; she was
sitting on the sofa. I hesitated on the threshold, caught momentarily
between autopilot and some deeper, more primitive part of my brain.
The part that pulled at my shirt, as if from behind, warning me
not to go inside. I thought of the man, drenched from the brook,
standing with his back to the door, facing the shelves. Of the woman
dashing with hideous speed across the wet grass. I didn't want to
enter that room, but there was no choice.

"Good morning," I said, as breezily as I could manage. I avoided her eyes but noticed, as I crossed the room to the desk in the corner, that she was neatly dressed once more – tailored slacks and a simple turtle-neck jumper. The image was so at odds, so far removed from the drenched, huddled figure of the night before that for a moment I doubted myself. As I sat down I turned to look at her and she smiled: nothing but the pallor of her cheeks and the purple beneath her eyes suggested anything out of the ordinary.

"A bit of respite, at last," she said, motioning to the window. "I thought it would never end, that storm." She sounded almost chirpy: relaxed, certainly more at ease in my company than I was in hers.

A ripple of anxiety settled on my chest. It *had* happened, of that I was sure. On the way into the library I'd spotted my boots, their leather fronts soaked through, the laces still tied from when I'd slid them off as quickly as possible the night before. Desperate to be upstairs, away from her. I stared down at the dried mud embedded deep under my fingernails, and opened the laptop. It *had* happened.

"Did you sleep well?" Her voice interrupted my reverie and I blinked up at her, shielding the light from my eyes. It seemed so unnatural, after the past days, to feel the sun on my face, to squint through the shadows.

"Not brilliantly, actually." I couldn't see her properly through the glare, but I could tell she was watching me. The sofa creaked as she moved towards its end, into the shade, and crossed one foot over the other. I could see her more clearly now, at least, and marvelled at the difference between night and day. By rights she ought to be in bed with a hot-water bottle: there was a part of me that wondered, as I moved files around the desktop on the computer, if I was being irresponsible by not tackling the issue head-on. But there was a brisk energy about her that seemed to resist questioning, probing. If she didn't appear so capable, so completely ordinary this morning, it would have been easier to broach what had happened during the night.

"I'd go for a longer walk today, while the weather's turned a bit," she said. "I imagine you need to work off some more energy. You're unused to an old woman's pace."

With a shudder I fought to suppress, I recalled the speed of her movements just hours before, the way I'd struggled to keep up with her. But there was nothing except innocence in her suggestion.

"Not at all," I said, adopting the same no-nonsense tone. "I was exhausted when I went to bed yesterday. Must have been something else. But I'm sure it'll be better this evening." Inadvertently, I yawned.

"Let me get us some coffee," she said, and she rose unsteadily to her feet, picked up the stick propped against the arm of the sofa, and began to shuffle towards the door.

"I can do it—" I said quickly, but she waved me away.

"Five minutes," she called as she left the room. "And then we can make a start."

On the screen, I moved the previous recordings into a new folder, dragging and dropping, dragging and dropping. There were several, but I knew most were under an hour. I wondered how much more we'd realistically be able to do – it was now three days since I'd arrived and we had so much more to discuss. I avoided looking into the corner of the room at all costs, my eyes focused on the screen with an almost manic intensity.

When I heard her tread and the tap of the stick on the hallway flagstones I rose to help her with the tray, and soon we were both seated once more. The cup she passed me was so delicate I resisted holding it by the handle, and gripped it tightly between two fingers instead. Like everything else at Elver it was fragile, primed to be broken or snapped or to malfunction in some way. But the coffee was hot and good and Miss Carey gave a contented sigh on the sofa. I was bone-tired, and yet we were here, and I needed to grab the opportunity.

"I thought it might be useful to focus on your mother, today, Catherine." No point beating around the bush. "We were discussing the impact on her. Of the time immediately following your father's death."

She nodded, sipping. "Of course. It wasn't easy for her. It wasn't easy for any of us."

The grandfather clock chimed in the hallway, but otherwise the silence hung between us. I continued to avoid looking toward the shelves opposite the door. At all costs, this morning, I'd wanted to dodge a return to the topic of her father and his death. The plaid shirt and boots she'd described him wearing, his back facing his daughter as she stood rooted to the spot – these were images I felt we could both do without right now. But there was no way of extracting the information about her mother without at least skirting around the fact.

"She was a complicated woman," said Miss Carey. Her eyes narrowed not, I felt, in anger or resentment but as though she was searching for the right words. "She would have felt enormous pressure to have children, I believe, if only to produce an heir to Elver. If that hadn't been a factor, I'm certain she would have chosen not to. I sense she'd have been better off without." She seemed surprised at herself, momentarily, and then went on.

"She adored my father, and he worshipped her. After his death she never spoke about him, and she forbade me from going anywhere near the brook. People underestimate how important it is to discuss these things with children, or at least they did then. And I so wanted to go to the water's edge, where he had been found. I felt a pull towards it, towards him. I never regarded the crypt as his resting place. I'd never have gone down there willingly, to sit by the carved stone or lay flowers. The brook would have made most sense to me, but she expressly instructed me not to."

We were back: to the shouting, the running, the shock, the soaked and bloated horror of it.

"When you say you think she'd have been better off without children," I said, "what do you mean?"

"She was a private person. She kept her thoughts and feelings to herself, though I believed she had shared as much as she could with my father. And I think she always regarded me as his, rather than as her own." She paused. "I'm not saying she was unkind to me, Ellen. Not at all. She did her best. But she was distant. She didn't want to spend her time reading to me, or playing, or chatting. When my first governess left shortly after my father's death, she was bereft: beside herself with worry. It took her just a week or two to find a replacement."

Her face darkened and now the narrowing of her eyes was altogether darker, angrier. "If my mother felt indifferent to children, Miss Ferrier actively disliked them."

The name rang a bell. "Was Miss Ferrier the new governess, then?"

"She was employed just after my 13th birthday. She only lived a few miles away, so I suppose my mother saw her as the best fit, the most convenient. She'd been out of work for several months when she came to us, though her references were good. She set to teaching me everything I needed to know – a bit of French, the history of kings and queens, needlework and singing and whatnot. But she made herself indispensable to my mother very quickly: when she wasn't teaching she took on the role of housekeeper, occasional cook, gardener, you name it."

I remembered, then. Steve, or one of the others, had mentioned Miss Ferrier in the pub.

"What made her so unpleasant, then?" I asked.

"She never allowed me to speak," said Miss Carey. I stared at her. She looked right back, unblinking. "In the schoolroom, she said, I was to listen. To write things down. If I had a question, I was to raise my hand and scribble it onto the chalk board. There'd be hours every day when I never said a single word."

"And did you tell your mother about it?"

"I didn't want to upset her. She was so busy herself: there was always so much to do here. She'd taken on all the duties my father once did, and then some. Money was becoming tighter and tighter:

the west side of the house was flooded shortly after my father's death. They never found the cause, but the damage was indescribable. I'd never been allowed in there before, since it was my parents' own private space. After the accident, though, the doors and windows were all opened to air it. I loved the chaos . . . isn't that awful?"

I smiled, shook my head. "Not to a child. There's something exhilarating about that kind of commotion . . ."

She nodded, a fleeting mischief playing on her face. "The floorboards were all at odd angles, warped from the water, and the wallpaper peeled off in great damp sheets. The first time I stood in the doorway of their room, staring at the pool spreading out like a deluge, I was thrilled."

She continued. "Over time Miss Ferrier taught me less and less, until soon enough our lessons were abandoned entirely, and I was pretty much left to my own devices. By this point I knew there were examinations I could take: ways to prove myself, to gain a place to study somewhere more traditional. But I also knew I hadn't a hope in hell. My education was so sporadic, so patchy."

"Do you regret that?" I asked, knowing the answer.

She surprised me. "Not particularly. It was a different sort of education, I suppose. I planted carrot seeds and collected raspberries, dug the potato drills, watered rows and rows of cabbages. I'd grind eggshells into a thin powder and spread them across the soil. And I'd no interest in attending any of the debs parties. By that point, when I was seventeen or so, I was more than happy to remain here. I couldn't actually have imagined living anywhere else."

"And your mother?"

"What about her?"

"When did she start to recover, do you think, from the shock?"

"I don't know that she ever did," said Miss Carey thoughtfully. "As I say, she was far more interested in my father than me, when I was small. And then afterwards, I think she regarded us more like sisters than anything else. A team of two overseeing the running of Elver, its maintenance, all the million things that needed doing.

She would've been happy for me to go to debs balls, if only to meet someone I could marry. Someone who could come and live here with us, dedicate themselves to the same task, provide those much-needed extra hands. And, of course, to provide an heir myself."

"It sounds like there wasn't a great deal of parenting."

"No, not from her. She didn't know how to do it. I never held it against her – perhaps because I had nothing to compare it to where mothers were concerned. Her own mum, my grandmother, was very absent. She was largely raised by nannies and governesses, like me. Not everyone is cut out for children. And especially back then, there was a sense that the commitment to one's offspring extended to food, clothing, a scant education of sorts. Nowadays people are so knowledgeable about the whole thing. About enrichment, progress, you name it. And it feels like there's more of a choice, generally. Less of an expectation."

"To have children, you mean."

"Exactly." Miss Carey regarded me for a moment then, almost shyly, "I never even asked you, but I suppose you don't have any? Yet?"

I was momentarily taken aback, but clients did often enquire, and I was prepared at some point for Catherine to dig a little. It was only fair; there was a reciprocity to these interviews, I'd found: it helped the client telling their story to know the other person, the listener, was a human. Someone with thoughts and opinions of their own, a back story, a set of values, vulnerabilities. Ordinarily, I'd tell them what they wanted to hear – not lying as such, but offering up something I knew they would appreciate or understand. *Of course,* I might say. *Just waiting for the right time. Maybe one day. I hope so!*

"I don't, no," I said simply. Would she leave it there?

"And would you like to?"

I thought of the picture sent through in the early hours of the morning: the smile, the scrunched-up eyes, the tiny stripe of a mouth.

"No, I don't think so."

Now it was Miss Carey's turn to wait. Perhaps it was the

way she hadn't reacted, hadn't frowned or smiled sadly. Hadn't pressed. Whatever her reasons, I uncrossed my arms on the table and decided to be honest. "Or perhaps it's not so much an active reluctance," I said, "And more a lack of desire? If that makes sense."

"Go on," she said, taking another sip of her coffee.

"Well, it's like appetite. When you're hungry, all you can think about is food. You imagine the smells as you cook. Or you wake up starving and that first spoonful of porridge, first bite of toast or whatever, is like a rebirth. I just don't ever feel that same pull, that same sense of necessity. When you're not hungry, you don't think about food."

"I suppose that's as good an analogy as any," said Miss Carey. She nodded slowly.

"Of course it's all anyone asks you about, at my age," I said. "And however you frame it, the result's always the same. *You'll change your mind. It's the greatest joy you'll ever know, you'll never feel a love like it. Don't you worry about what'll happen when you're older?* Even now I feel like I'm encouraged to see it as this enormous taboo. Or people suspect you're bluffing, flaunting some kind of Peter Pan complex, clinging to selfish freedom . . ."

"I would've hoped things were different now," said Miss Carey. "It sounds much the same as it did when I was your age."

"I wouldn't say it's the same," I said carefully. "Superficially, at least, there are improvements. Laws. Statutory rights. But you get the strangest comments, still, sometimes from people your own age. Recently someone said that maybe I'd just not met the right person. Which felt particularly odd given that her partner never cooks for them . . . She literally puts his lunch for work in a Tupperware every evening. When I went for dinner, it embarrassed me so much that she cleared the table after she'd laid it, cooked and breastfed in between. I stood up to help and felt mortified doing it while he sat there. I wanted to help my friend, but it also felt like giving in to something."

"So you felt that her comment about finding the right person was ridiculous."

"In a word, yes." I laughed. "And people often tell me I'll change my mind. I find it baffling." I paused, suddenly embarrassed, wondering if I'd said too much, but Catherine seemed genuinely interested. "I mean, we all change our minds about everything, all the time. They say it as though that expected mind change will be the *right* change. That I'm just too immature or irresponsible to know it yet. I'd never dream of telling someone who wanted a child, or who was trying to conceive, that they'll change their mind, or they just need to give it time. Can you imagine."

"I believe my mother felt much the same, really. If she'd been born in a different era, had different role models, I think she'd have decided against it."

"And you?"

"Oh, I'd have loved to," she said. "I'm not sure I'd have been any good at it, but I'd have liked to try. I love children, I love their energy. It just didn't happen. I barely attended the coming-out balls and the years seemed to pass so quickly . . . Suddenly my mother was old and I realised, with complete shock, that I was, too."

I thought of the girl transforming into a teenager, becoming an adult. The straightening of the back, the loss of an awkward adolescent posture, the slow and steady march toward maturity.

A deep thud, metallic and clanging, made us both start. The ground shook. I gripped the sides of the desk, hard, and stared wildly at Catherine.

"What was that?"

Her expression was stricken, the colour drained from her cheeks. She picked up her stick and got to her feet, though with none of the speed of the night before.

"What *was* that?" I said again.

Another boom sounded out, far louder this time. I stood, closed the laptop screen and followed Miss Carey as she moved slowly through the library and onwards to the front door. A heavy, sporadic thudding, like pipes crashing together, was coming from the front lawn.

Her face etched with trepidation, Miss Carey pulled the door wide and we both stood, looking out at the scene before us.

A two-tonne truck was parked on the forecourt, surrounded by men in neon-yellow vests. Some stood atop the lorry, their gloved hands passing long poles to those waiting beside it. A large pile was forming next to them, the clang of each dropped tube ringing out. The engine was idling, a low thrum, and the men were calling, laughing, their backs mostly to us. One, standing by the door to the cab, raised his hand and waved. I stared back.

"What on earth are they doing?" said Miss Carey. "Who are they?"

I'd no idea of course. Several others turned too, raising their hands or smiling. I waved weakly back.

Miss Carey's breath became shaky and her fingers tightened on the stick grasped in her right hand. "They've no right," she breathed. "What is this? The council? Why are they here?"

I realised, and of this I was becoming increasingly aware, that I'd need to do something. Miss Carey was clearly too shocked to act, to demand answers, and I could see that the men frightened her. Placing a hand on her arm, I asked her to go and make us some more coffee.

"Or a cup of tea," I said gently.

"More?" she looked at me. "Why now?"

"Let me go and speak to them. I'll find out what's happening. It's probably nothing. Just leave it with me a moment, Miss Carey. Catherine."

She turned without a word and I heard the sound of the stick as she made her way along the hallway. The man, possibly the one in charge, was still smiling and waving as I hurriedly pulled on my soaked boots and went out to where the group was working. They'd parked close to the edge of the estate, just beside the crumbling brick wall of its perimeter. As I drew closer I saw, once again, the flash of pink: the shock of flowers, an isolated patch of colour to the east.

"Morning," he said, as I approached. He was tall, mid-forties I guessed, with a thick brown beard and a boyish energy. "Sorry, we did plan to start yesterday. Bit delayed on everything at present."

"I'm Ellen," I said, and then wondered why. A couple of the men closest to us murmured a greeting. I waited for some kind of explanation, but the man by the lorry simply smiled back at me.

"Sorry for the noise," he said. "Shouldn't be too much longer with the unloading." He stared up at the house. "Lots to be getting on with. We'll need to bring the lorry up later, to the walls I mean, to unload the heavier beams."

"Sorry," I said, "you've lost me. What's going on?"

"Just unloading the scaffold for now. We can't get started without it all in place—"

"No, I mean, why is the scaffold going up?"

He frowned at me and pulled a packet of cigarettes slowly from his trouser pocket. "For the repointing. The brickwork. But first, the roof. Up that side particularly." He pointed to Elver's left side, where the gabled roofs reached up into the sky. "Full of holes and leaks, apparently."

"It's just—" I frowned, trying to understand. "Well, it's just the owner of the house didn't seem to know you were coming. She's quite elderly so perhaps it's my mistake—"

"Hold on a mo," said the man, balancing his cigarette in the corner of his mouth, and pulling out his phone. He scrolled briefly, clicking and tapping, and then nodded. "Mr Walsh. Elver House, roof and repointing?"

"Mr Walsh? Who's that?"

The man spread his hands. "The guy who asked us to do the job. It was all booked in," he said. "We came round to give a quote a couple of weeks back."

"For Miss Carey?"

"Miss Carey? No, it wasn't a woman. Couple of blokes took

us round. I guess one of them was this Mr Walsh." He smiled. "Beautiful old house. Falling to pieces, though."

I shook my head, distracted. "What d'you mean, a couple of blokes?"

"Suits, you know. Business types. Flash-looking. They were very nice. They wanted us to start then, but we were booked up. Everyone wants things done in the summer, so we were up to our necks. I had to push the date back a bit," he said, looking at me with some concern. "They were quite happy with that, the guys. We would've come yesterday, but there's no point in rain that heavy. One of us would have slipped and fallen, no question. So here we are. I know it's not ideal on a Sunday." He spread his hands out at the sky, trailing smoke. "No rest for the wicked. But, yeah, we agreed end of October, or thereabouts."

I nodded, though I'd no idea what to say. "I'm just here working . . . for Miss Carey, I mean. And, like I said, she wasn't expecting . . . I mean she seemed quite surprised to see you here."

"I don't know what to tell you," he said, not unkindly. "It's been partly paid for – deposit came through almost immediately. I'd suggest you or the lady takes it up with Mr Walsh directly."

I nodded slowly. "I suppose I'd better go back inside," I said. "Leave you to it."

"No chance of a cup of tea, is there?" he asked. "Sorry to ask."

I said I'd see what I could do, and stomped back to the house. Perhaps it was tiredness, perhaps I'd just had enough, but in that moment I truly wanted to pack my case and leave. It wasn't the myriad strange things that kept throwing themselves at me here, at the house and within the grounds. It wasn't the jarring metallic thuds of the scaffold poles as they were dumped onto the lawn. It wasn't the patchy phone reception, the bizarre behaviour of Miss Carey. None of that, or not in that moment. I was more incensed by the interruption than anything else. The whole project, the whole interview stage was just taking so long, and every time we got somewhere, another incident, noise, intrusion would throw us off course.

"Miss Carey?"

I heard an answering voice from the kitchen and closed the front door behind me. I found her sitting at the scrubbed table, her head in her hands.

"What did they want?" she said, to the table. "Did you get rid of them?"

"Well, not quite," I said quietly. I resisted the urge to sigh. "They're here to do repair work."

"What repairs?" she said, and the seriousness of her voice almost made me laugh. "Repairs where?"

"On the roof, I think."

I explained what the man in charge had said about his initial meeting.

"I don't understand." She looked terrified now.

"You didn't know about any of this?" She shook her head. "It's just that . . . well, they seemed to have been hired to do the work . . ."

"Not by me."

Her face was defiant, her lip jutting out like a child's. "They've no right to turn up here. Unannounced like this."

I agreed, though it wouldn't help to stoke the fire. "Miss Carey, they mentioned a Mr Walsh. Does the name ring a bell? He's hired them."

"Mr Walsh?" Her eyes moved to the ceiling as she considered, clearly flustered. "I don't think I've heard of him."

"The man outside said Mr Walsh had given them a quote. In person. About two weeks ago or so."

She stared at me. "Two weeks ago?" She paused, fiddling with the clasp of her necklace. "That would have been . . . well, I must have been away then. Perhaps I've got the dates wrong."

I remembered her lack of response to Laura's phone calls and emails, and nodded. "Where did you go?"

She ignored the question and continued turning the pearls over, her fingers moving quickly.

"Do you want to go outside and speak to them? We can get to the bottom of this. You're sure you don't know anyone by that name?"

"Absolutely sure," she said, fixing me with that deep-blue stare. I believed her.

"Well let's go and speak to them, then. It might help." I wondered if seeing the men, face to face, might help jog her memory.

"You go," she said. "I need to have a walk." And with that she stood, shuffled over to the door leading off from the kitchen and let herself out, towards the rear side of the garden and grounds, towards the brook.

As soon as she was out of earshot I allowed myself a groan. Who knew when she might be back – and now I was here, once again, alone to deal with whatever this was. After last night I'd a good mind to go after her, to follow at a distance at least, but another clatter of metal on earth reminded me of the tea. And if Miss Carey couldn't remember anything about their presence, or had never been told, I reasoned I'd have more chance of getting to the bottom of things with the men outside.

Five minutes later I strode back across the forecourt, balancing a tray complete with mugs, a teapot, a bowl of sugar I hadn't looked too closely at, and a small jug containing the milk I'd bought with Steve.

"Wonderful. Thanks so much," said the man overseeing the others. They quickly huddled round and I stood apart from them, gesturing to the one in charge. He collected a cup, splashed milk into it and walked over to me.

"I've just spoken with Miss Carey," I said, craning my neck to see if I could spot her round the side of the house. "She doesn't know of any Mr Walsh."

The man frowned. "This is the owner, right? Miss Carey."

"Yes, she's lived here all her life. I just wonder if there's been some mistake."

The man sighed and reached once more for his phone. He found what he was looking for more quickly this time and held it up for me to see. "Here. This is the confirmation. Not to me, mind. It was forwarded from my boss." I squinted at the screen, and there it was in black and white. *Schedule of works*, I read aloud. *Elver House, Conger Brook, commencing 27th October. Client: Mr J Walsh.* A telephone number appeared in brackets beside his name. *Balance paid: £25,500 (receipt attached below and received with thanks). Remainder to be confirmed upon completion.*

There followed a lengthy list of things to be done, from roofing to gutter-replacements. I scanned it quickly and asked if I could take the phone number down; the man nodded, clearly as perplexed as I was. "Makes sense to give him a ring," he said. "But you agree, it looks like we're booked in?"

"It definitely looks like it," I said, as I tapped the number into my own phone. "I don't get it, but I've only been here a few days. I've no idea how Miss Carey runs the place or who else is involved here. What I do know is that she's the owner. And she lives here alone."

"And you said she was an older woman? How old?"

"Mid-to-late eighties."

"Ah," said the man thoughtfully. He took a long gulp of tea and inclined his head to one side. "Well, you know her better than I do. But I wouldn't be surprised if she'd hired a management firm to organise the repairs. It's quite common. This Mr Walsh could well be a client of hers, someone she's instructed to see to the upkeep. It's far too much for one person to do on their own. Lots of people outsource it, you see, especially with these big houses."

"But she says she's never heard of him."

"Listen," he said. "My dad's the same. I bring him toast and a boiled egg in the morning, he eats it all up, and then half an hour later he shouts down to me that no one's given him any breakfast. Sometimes I've even filmed him bloody eating it, you know, on my phone. Just to show him."

"You think she does know Mr Walsh, but she's just forgotten?"

"Could well be. I don't know, I'm not an expert. Where was she when we came over, anyway? I didn't see her, I don't think. Just him and his mate."

"She was away. I don't know where."

The man shrugged and smiled helplessly. "What is it they say . . . the simplest explanation is the right one? This Miss Carey, she lives here alone, right? But she asks someone else to run this side of things –" He gestured behind him to the men drinking their tea. "She has a sinking fund ready to pay for it all." He tapped the screen again. "Honestly, if you ask me, we're here because she's hired someone to get it done, but she can't remember doing it."

I thought back to Miss Carey's distant stares. To the very first night, and her confusion at my presence. To the events of yesterday at the brook, and the fact she had not so much as hinted at what happened this morning. To the lack of food, the comments of the villagers at the pub, at her increasingly fragile grasp, it seemed, on reality.

"You're probably right," I said to the man. "Thanks for the number. I'm going to go and find her now, but let me know if you need anything. I'll be indoors."

As I walked back to the house, and despite my better judgement, I dialled Mr Walsh's number and waited. Of course it didn't connect. Back inside, mercifully, the Wi-Fi allowed an online call and I waited as it started to ring. *You've reached the voicemail of Patrick Walsh*, said a bright, cheery voice down the line. *Please leave me a message and I'll get back to you as soon as possible.*

There was nothing for it. "Hello Mr Walsh, my name's Ellen. I'm currently working at Elver House, and the builders have arrived this morning. I just wondered if you were free for a quick chat. Could you ring me back when you get this?"

I gave my number, ended the call and scanned the grounds for any sign of Catherine Carey. I strode over to the brook, checking as far as I could see, but she wasn't there.

Inside, I started chopping carrots for a soup. Once again, the interviews would have to wait.

CHAPTER NINETEEN

A S THE WEEKEND drew to a close I noticed, with surprise, that I felt better. Calmer. I had arrived at Elver House with an agenda, a role, and I'd expected to find a certain type of client: fussy, perhaps, formal and proper. Somebody unused to talking about themselves, most likely, but slowly willing to do so. Miss Carey had revealed herself not so much an unreliable narrator as an intermittent one. I would need to keep taking her as I found her – not because she was rude, necessarily, or unwilling, but because she was clearly unwell.

I felt a sense of protection toward her, a need to shield her. It didn't seem right that she should experience such sorrow, such perplexity. The fear of the past days slowly receded like waves on the turn, and though I wished things were easier for Catherine, I was filled with a determination to do what I could, and write something she'd be proud of, something that would brighten her days, give her a sense of her own chronology, a mooring.

I'd spent the afternoon working, as the builders continued to construct their scaffold. The metallic beams clanged and clashed against one another, and the buzzing sound of drills filled the air. The slow chime of the grandfather clock, quarter-hourly, was the only marker of time and mostly I missed it entirely. It felt good to be immersed in admin, responding to queries from other clients, scheduling phone calls and meetings for when I was home. To my surprise, despite the interruption I was glad of the noise of other humans, their conversations reaching me in fits and starts as the afternoon wore on. Their laughter, jokes, calls to one another all combined to loosen something in me that, I realised, had been coiled for days.

It's going well, I messaged Laura the following day. *We've not done enough, obviously, but we're getting there. And I can definitely write the first chapters based on what she's told me so far.*

I realised even as I typed the words that it was true, to my surprise. The interviews had been far from ordinary, far from the hours and hours I was used to before starting books like this from scratch. But there was a sufficient skeleton.

Laura wrote back almost immediately. *So glad to hear it. You're doing really well. Has she settled down a bit?*

I think she's more used to my being here, I wrote. *It's hit and miss every day, but she's telling me the things I need to know.*

Where have you got up to?

Childhood, mostly. Adolescence. The death of her father. I avoided looking into the corner of the library as I wrote the words. *Her relationship with her mother. Governesses. That sort of thing. The first 15/20 years or so basically.*

And what happens next? she asked.

No idea, I wrote. *I get the sense she hasn't travelled much. She's certainly not lived anywhere else, or that's the impression I get.*

Husband? Kids? She didn't mention any when we spoke.

I don't think so. There's a lot of interesting history about the house, though – stuff I can dig into more when I'm back. The locals know a lot too. I have some of their contact details. They can fill in the gaps. I wonder if she just wanted a sort of heritage document about the estate, the area, the farming. That sort of thing.

But you don't get the sense she's building to something?

The word brought me back into the room and I lifted my head, trying to catch the sounds of the men at work, but they were silent. I peered through the long library windows and saw, to my dismay, that the truck was gone. A trio of poles erected just outside cast thin shadows across the carpet. They stopped before they hit the bookshelves, and the lamp from the desk did not reach quite far enough to illuminate the furthest corners of the room. I looked down quickly, determined to hold my nerve.

We'll see, I said. *To be honest, she may have had something specific in mind when she got in touch. But whatever it is, she's either not ready to share it, or things have changed . . . There were builders here today and she doesn't recall hiring anyone. I think she outsources that sort of thing, but she didn't recognise the name of the guy who manages the property.*

Wow. It's not ideal, Laura wrote. *Must be scary for her. I do wish she'd told us, though.*

Told us what?

About her Alzheimer's. I mean, that's what you're getting at, right?

I thought about this. It was true I knew Miss Carey was struggling. But my limited understanding of the disease was further clouded by the memories she described, and the way she described them. There'd been a linear structure to the interviews we'd had, a clear understanding of time. Her behaviour was bizarre, and Saturday night had been downright frightening. But the speed with which she recovered from the episodes, and the fact she clearly managed to live fairly independently didn't fit with my scant knowledge of Alzheimer's.

I mean, she forgets things, for sure, I typed. *But everyday things. She has no problem with the past. It's things like the shopping, or getting my name wrong, or just seeming a bit confused.*

Those are classic symptoms, El, said Laura. *Poor thing. Obviously we don't know exactly what's going on, but dementia would be my best bet.*

I pulled my laptop across the desk and opened the screen. For the next 20 minutes I researched, checking off Miss Carey's symptoms one by one. How much easier this would all have been if we'd been briefed beforehand: Laura was right. She could have sent a more experienced writer. A pair of writers, in fact, if one had more luck than the other when it came to collecting the information.

As it was, I was here and it had taken me days to fully appreciate the extent of her illness. My phone vibrated again. Laura.

Not long now, she wrote. *You're ok to leave the day after tomorrow, right? The 10.04? Just a day later than planned.*

Yep, all booked, I wrote back. *Just two more nights.*

The shadows elongated and I stood up, stretched and went out into the hallway, glad to be away from the library. I didn't expect to see Miss Carey again today. Staring up through the banisters I waited, watching, but heard nothing.

The kitchen was dark and gloomy, made darker by the overhang of the new pipes and poles standing sentry outside. I switched on the light, opened the larder door and selected a baking potato, its skin crusted in dirt. I inhaled its rich, earthy scent and watched as the small clumps fell away under the warm tap-water; soon enough it was marked with a cross, dabbed with oil and salt and pepper and inside the Aga on a baking tray far too large for it.

I sat at the kitchen table and wondered what you were up to. It was past six. You'd probably be doing bath-time, the room a mess of bubbles and soft soaps, no-tears shampoo and plastic toys. I knew that you'd be alone, singing or patting dry or changing while the clock ticked. I remembered our conversations as we ordered pints before a pub quiz, the disgust on your face: *So after all that, he said he was going back to work at the end of paternity leave.*

A fortnight. I'd shaken my head. *Two weeks after she's had the baby?*

She says they need the money – and fair enough, they probably do. Kids are expensive. But these are, like, long days he does. Leaves before seven and he's never home before nine. By that point the kid's asleep, she's exhausted and he's no better, all grumpy and smelling of the tube.

But he'd still rather be at the office than there, with them?

Well, yeah. You'd marched the glasses back to our table and sloshed a good third across its sticky surface in your agitation. *He says it feels like being stuck in limbo. The day revolves around feeding, changing, laundry, tidying up, cleaning, whatever. He can't take it. I don't blame him. But the plan was that they'd split the parental leave. Now she's off work for a year, totally isolated, going mad. That's after nine bloody months of pregnancy, getting up every hour to pee from the third month, sickness, not to mention actually giving birth. Now she's sore from the stitches and fed up with being trapped inside the same house. It's like* Big Brother *but without the cameras and where the only other housemate is a 12-week-old.*

We'd fumed about it for the rest of the night, circling back and round, letting out the frustration. Another friend with a rum deal and a situation they'd never expected to find themselves in. *I'm going tomorrow to stay for two nights,* you'd said, as we fluffed our way through the general-knowledge round, *and Olivia's there from Monday.*

How's Olivia going to do that? She can't exactly work from home. Olivia was a doctor.

No, she's taken three days off. She's taken unpaid *leave to go and help care for our friend and her baby, while the baby's dad sticks his stupid head in the sand. Can you imagine the embarrassment of knowing your friends are round trying to help clear up the mess you'd promised to deal with?*

Two months later we'd sat in the same pub, same table. A pint for me, a lemonade for you. So much hope, so much expectation and nervousness, fear and jubilation on your face. It was early days but you'd taken three tests and you were late. *I've no idea how it'll all work out,* you'd said, *and there's no point getting excited just yet. I know that. But Ben's so happy. So, so happy. I've never seen him like this.* I clasped your hands and felt my selfish heart break, wanting this for you and yet wishing there'd been just a bit more time, a little longer. *If everything runs smoothly, I'll do the first six months and he'll take the second. We'll both have our own time with the baby, you know, we'll both be experts. Actual co-parents. Doing it together. And I'll go nuts after all that time off anyway.*

Four months after that, we'd been there again. Your hair was sleek and thick, your belly just starting to show. We'd barely discussed the pregnancy for the first hour. And then—

Ben's work have turned down his request for the shared leave.

I'd stared at her. *Can they do that?*

Apparently. You smiled sadly. *I'm gutted, obviously.*

But . . . aren't there other options?

Not really, you'd said. *We need the money.* A chill ran down my spine.

Why can't Ben quit his job, if they won't allow it? You earn more anyway.

You'd shrugged. *Honestly Ellen, it didn't even occur to me.* I could tell, now that you'd spilled the beans, that you wanted the conversation over. *I'll just have to make do.*

And here you were, making do. The promotion you'd been promised had melted away: your boss couldn't wait a full year, that was never the deal. I knew better than to mention it. And next year, as you'd already intimated, you'd be pregnant again. We both acted like this was the most normal thing in the world, this set-up, and the depressing thing was that – clearly – it was. When we spoke, in those earliest days, your face was pale and taut. But at least he was there, someone else, a presence with two free hands and a willingness to help. When he returned to work, you behaved as though nothing had changed, like everything was manageable.

Your world had shrunk to such a pinpoint even while your heart expanded with love. It was a strange dichotomy. I was in awe of what you'd done, amazed by the steps your body seemed to have known without being taught, from conception right through to the day you went into hospital. I was proud of you for the tentatively excited, measured way you'd approached pregnancy.

It was only now that the tug of loss made itself so startlingly apparent, when you remembered so little of our friends' lives beyond odd half-snippets. Our lives seemed irrelevant besides the task of keeping a tiny infant alive, fed and bathed, dressed, entertained, educated. Perhaps they were irrelevant. Now someone else depended on you for everything: I understood that, but the change, the shift, was like nothing I'd experienced before.

I knew that to a certain degree this was unavoidable. I knew my irritation was selfish. You were inflexible now, with good reason. And yet the wall remained. It had been erected between us as I texted you frantically from the tube, from the office, from the high street, from the airport. As you wrote back when time allowed from the sofa, the park, the rocking chair. And yet neither of us had consciously built this barricade: bricks were simply added, day by day.

It was different in Miss Carey's infancy: a different century, different expectations, different roles. The sons and daughters of houses like this were barely ever cared for directly by their own parents, and she was no exception.

I wondered, had her own father been more involved in her day-to-day life, her first steps and picture books, bedtime stories and pats on the head, whether her memory of him would be stronger, perhaps less idealised. He had died before she had a chance to know the man behind the parent. Her images of him – as a figure of authority, a problem-solver, a fixer, a farmer, but not necessarily as someone who looked after her – were rose-tinted and pretty. I wondered what he had been like, and why he had returned to Elver House after his death.

Returned? I checked myself.

Well, Catherine had said as much. But it was an illusion: a mechanism for dealing with the sudden bereavement. There was no point wondering why he'd returned to Elver because he hadn't done so in the first place. I rubbed my arms, noticing the chill, suppressing a shiver. I needed to get a grip.

I crossed the kitchen and tried the back door. It was unlocked, and I stepped out into the garden. A soft breeze pulled gently at the grass, moving it to left and right as though an invisible hand was passing over it. I peered through the gathering dusk in the direction of the brook, and recalled the sure-footed way Miss Carey had walked across it.

No doubt she'd done the same thing a thousand times before, all through her childhood and beyond. Muscle memory would come into play, even though her body was older now, more fragile, more susceptible to losing its balance. And I thought too of the elvers, wending their way in silvery streaks through the clear, cold water. I'd never seen one before, alive or dead. I'd probably have felt the same revulsion if I'd never seen a tadpole before. To the people of Conger Brook, the eels had been their bread and butter, quite literally. People had come from miles around to fish this stream. In London, eel and mash houses were all the rage, and then they just . . . disappeared. Did people get sick of them, or did the eel population just decline and fall until it wasn't lucrative enough anymore?

In the dwindling light the grounds were beautiful. A smattering of wildflowers to my left danced in the breeze, the dying heads of cornflowers in startling blue, faded purple campions with hands outstretched, marigolds a gaudy swatch of brightest yellow. In the thick tufts of overlong vegetation a grasshopper leapt from stalk to stalk, its antennae feeling the way ahead like a cat kneading at a blanket.

Some flowers are pretty to look at and some are grown because they smell nice. Some don't flower at all but bear seeds that can be used for other things. Others are sown naturally, on the wind, and are so numerous that we consider them less special. They achieve, in their ubiquity, an almost weed-like status, like the dandelion. We grew up amongst flowers, amongst bags of sod that seemed so incongruous with the carefully co-ordinated perimeters of our northern town. We knew how to identify a common from a garden lily, a tulip from a begonia. We knew why Japanese knotweed was such an insidious phenomenon.

We knew about vegetables and growing patterns and when to sow and reap. We chewed on still-green raspberries, daring ourselves to eat another and trying to keep a straight face as the sour juice ripped at our taste-buds. We knew about tomatoes and pea-shoots, potatoes and aubergines. We knew what a nightshade was and how it liked to grow to full term: in the gloom, in the dark, without interference.

I walked briskly towards the brook, keen to stretch my legs. The sun would soon be gone. I wondered what the winters were like at Elver. I imagined the ice, the puddles across the lawn frosted over and waiting patiently for a careless foot to shatter their surfaces. I pressed on, walking parallel to the brook but keeping my distance. Something about it both intrigued and repelled me, and I did not want to be reminded of Saturday night. Instead I continued for a few minutes more until, shaded by a waist-high sweep of brambles, I made out a brick wall – the perimeter of the grounds. Behind it, far away in the distance, was the road I'd travelled down with Steve on my first evening at the house. It felt like weeks ago.

Turning to my right I followed the wall as it arched round and completed the circle, with the house at its top-most centre point. And through it all ran the brook. I followed the edge of the estate until I reached the water, noticing how the flow was thinner here, the banks closer together. It was, in fact, easy enough to step or hop across – at least it was for me. I bent down, peering into its gentle coursing, and then dipped my fingers into the current and brushed them against the flow.

From the banks came sharp movement, and I pulled my hand back like it had been scorched. There were just three that I could see, but they churned and roiled, twisting this way and that like they were connected. I stared down at them, their translucent bodies rebelling against the current and remaining just below where I perched. Beside me on the bank lay leaves of burnt orange and I cracked one in my palm, scattering the pieces on the water. The elvers rose up, nudging the fragments and then scattering once more. Their movements were at once random and balletic: there was a synchronicity, a practised routine to the way they jerked and folded, flipped and weaved.

I lifted my head and stared at Elver House, at the hulk of scaffold now covering its exterior. The little turrets were untouched, lining the roof like meringue peaks. How odd to think we had lived here together, she and I, for days and nights at a time, here in the midst of all this activity, this wildlife, a bubbling beneath the surface and in the long blades of grass, the brambles, the softly whispering branches of trees. I imagined the bustle and excitement of the open-house days described in the pub, the bunting strung up around the forecourt, the noise of boots on gravel and children's enthusiastic cries. From here, the house looked unoccupied, its windows dark and fathomless, its doors closed, its corridors empty. Almost empty.

The vines along the right-hand side seemed to tumble and fall like a bottle of ink tipped over, like liquid ascending, defying gravity along the brickwork. I wondered how long they had been making their steady way, climbing laboriously through the years, watching Miss Carey as she grew from the child with plaits loosening from their ribbons. As she became a young woman, adrift and isolated from the world, as she marched across the lawn in the mornings and returned in the evenings, muddy and tired. As she nursed her mother, perhaps pushing the older woman in a wheelchair across the forecourt, pointing out the potato beds, the courgettes thickening on long ropes of green, the blackberries ripening from fuchsia to twilight purple. And how in the middle of the night, herself now old and tired, unwell and confused, she moved from the house through the rain to the brook and returned again.

Behind me, the sun finally dipped below the horizon and dusk settled over the grounds of Elver. I trudged back, to the still-open kitchen door, and laid the table for one. The potato fell open as I slid it from the Aga, and yielded like butter to my knife.

CHAPTER TWENTY

"HI, ELLEN. IT'S Tuesday 3rd, about . . . 1 p.m. This is Patrick Walsh returning your call." His voice – cheerful, posh, a Southerner. London, probably.

My phone had alerted me to the voicemail; irritating, since I'd had it on me all afternoon, deliberately placed on the loudest volume. It seemed the signal was strongest in the library, so I ducked inside after dinner and listened. "I tried to phone you back. I'm free for the next hour, so do try me again."

I hit return, flicking open the laptop screen and hitting record – just to be sure. I could use it later to help Catherine remember, I reasoned. She might not recall his name, but voices had a peculiar power. To my relief, the call connected after three rings.

"Patrick speaking."

"Hi, Patrick. This is Ellen. I'm staying at Elver House at the moment."

"Ah, Ellen. Hi." His voice was relaxed, at ease, friendly even. "How can I help?"

I hesitated. "Well, I thought I'd better give you a call. Like I said, I asked the contractors here on Sunday for your number."

"I'm sorry – I do hope you weren't disturbed. What is it that you do?"

"I'm writing Miss Carey's memoirs. I've been here since Thursday evening."

"Goodness," he said, sounding genuinely surprised. "I'd no idea. Was it terribly noisy? I know the early days can be a bit intense—"

I frowned, confused. "Oh no, nothing like that. It was all fine. I just wanted to check who . . . well, who asked them to come . . ." I trailed off.

"That would have been me."

I waited, not understanding.

"I manage the estate," he said. "The boys are in for a couple of weeks, though they were late starting."

I breathed out slowly. "You manage the estate?"

"Yep," he said. "There's just such a lot to do. And the place was falling to pieces. Well, not falling to pieces. It's a sturdy old beast, but it needs a little taking care of. Catherine understood the need for development of the site. I can't say she was thrilled by it initially, but she was absolutely on board. She knew that without some kind of renovation Elver wouldn't survive another 10 years, let alone 100."

I'd thought Miss Carey had kept Elver in fairly good condition. "Is it really that bad?"

"God no. I mean, it's not a wreck. Otherwise we'd just knock the whole thing down and start again, you know? But there are some serious repairs needed on the roof, which is leaking in places, and the repointing will stop the subsidence gaining more traction . . . The windows need double-glazing – you must have noticed how arctic it gets." I thought of my bedroom upstairs, the way I'd had to wrap the duvet around me just to collect my dressing gown and slippers. The constant, bone-deep cold. The peeling paint of the library's walls.

"Yes, I suppose so."

There was a pause. "I suppose that's it, really. I just wanted to make sure, you know—"

"Oh, totally, totally. I get it. I'd do the same. A bunch of guys you hadn't expected just turning up and interrupting . . . What was it you said you were doing?"

"It's a legacy project. A book about Miss Carey's family, the history of Elver, the village. That sort of thing."

"Lot of material there, I imagine," said Patrick. "But look, you have my number now – any issues, any noise you could do without, just give me a bell. We'll work around you."

"I'm only here another day or so," I said. "Don't worry about it." I glanced to the library doors and lowered my voice. "Anyway, I'm glad we've spoken – I know Miss Carey will be relieved to hear it. I get the sense her memory's not quite what it was."

There was a silence down the line. I pulled the phone away and checked the screen – we were still connected, but the bars on the top-right corner had dropped.

"Hello?"

"I'm here, but you're breaking up. I didn't catch that."

"I was just saying Miss Carey will be relieved. I'm sure it'll come back to her. She hadn't mentioned an estate manager so I thought it'd be wise to speak to you. On her behalf, I mean."

Another silence. "Mr Walsh?"

". . . Could . . . repeat . . . not sure I understood?"

The line was cutting in and out until, as I moved to the library doors, it ended with three quick beeps. I considered phoning him back, but there seemed little point. I'd relay the information to Miss Carey at some point. It wasn't relief, as such, because it confirmed what I had suspected: but at least we had an explanation. I doubted Catherine would be happy to hear it, nonetheless.

I made my way upstairs, treading softly along the runner, and into the gloom of my bedroom. The house was silent, the grate empty. I lit a fire and sat back against the headboard, opening my laptop and reviewing the audio files from Miss Carey's interviews. There were at least 12, though I knew only three or four contained longer, more structured conversations: the rest were simply snippets of facts or information I'd leapt to record in chance moments as we'd chatted.

I clicked onto the first conversation and switched off the volume, making a note of the length of the recording in my diary. Usually, as the interviews wound to a close we were asked to calculate the time spent: most clients needed around six hours, but Miss Carey's project had been allocated 20. I clicked and scribbled for a few minutes before, with dismay, I sat back. We'd spoken for a total of seven hours – it wasn't enough. I was glad I'd kept Laura up to speed as we went along. Seven hours wasn't unmanageable, but it was no mean feat to write a standard-length book with this scant amount of actual, concrete information.

I sighed, dimmed the screen and closed the laptop. Ordinarily, at this point, I'd have transcribed at least some of the recordings, looking for gaps to fill, for questions so far unasked. But there was so little already, and I knew where the gaps were. When did Elver – this bustling, busy haven all of its own – begin to lose its lustre? When did the staff hand in their letters of resignation, when did the farmers down tools? What happened when the house went quiet, and it was just Miss Carey here, managing everything and caring for her mother?

Another text from you. A picture of the baby. She was growing fast, her eyes curious, the blue slowly darkening. I smiled, loving her but noticing the familiar ache in my chest. Your focus was entire; there had been a personality shift, a transformation not unlike the ones Catherine exhibited. I was beginning to realise the fundamental divergence in our paths: we'd had our differences before but they were minute, easily remedied fissures, not gulfs. And they had never lasted. This was not only the largest, seemingly, but the most permanent. It was a state I could only hope to achieve by joining you, but I had no wish to.

When we first moved in together we filled the flat with rubbish. We spent a Saturday in pound-shops and discount stores along the High Street. You were extravagant; it was one of the things I liked best about you. We told ourselves the mop, bleach and curtain rails were investments. We found a purple-and-white bin, printed Warhol-style with pictures of the Queen's face and we threw it into our cart. There were things we needed, now, that did not belong solely in our bedrooms: things to decorate with, things to scatter about in other rooms. The keys to the flat were resting deep in the pocket of my coat, heavy and reassuring. They were currency in a country we'd just arrived in: they were precious to us, these tiny tickets of adulthood, the paper-thin lampshades and spare batteries.

We both worked Saturdays normally, but during the summer, one weekend, we had the same day off. The street felt different to its weekday grind, like it had pulled on an old t-shirt flecked with paint. On a residential road nearby a woman stopped outside the job centre to smell the flowers in someone's front garden. They were big and blooming and strong despite the wind. Further down there was an antique shop. We were laden with bags but on the corner a shopping trolley stood, one of its wheels twisted out of shape.

The shop was cool and dark, cluttered with wood and old smells. We ran our hands along the dust, opening drawers with tiny brass handles. Inside one I found a receipt for its original purchase in 1914, somewhere in Sussex. Among the mahogany I spotted a flash of green, a tassel. There was a trunk hiding underneath a large dining table, its wicker sides bruised with brown. I bent down to look, running my fingers along the frayed edges: it was deep, when I opened the lid. I bought it for more money than I'd make that week, and we put it in the shopping trolley where it slipped and slid with the loo brushes and the Hoover bags.

I wanted you back, and not just to reminisce. I wanted you to sit and talk about now: I wanted to hear how it was, how it really was. The joy and the sadness, the frustration and the regret, the intensity. I was genuinely interested. I wanted the sort of honesty I was getting here, from an old woman I'd never heard of until a fortnight before. Perhaps, with age, the scales fell off and people cared less, masked less, came out with it. Perhaps you were too tired to talk.

And yet surely there was more, surely you wanted your child's life surrounded by difference, by variety, by a clutch of friends whose lives presented different possibilities. A melting pot. And yours was a fundamental experience, a primal experience, one I respected and wanted for you, even if it wasn't mine. I wanted to know. Here was time, I wanted to say, before you clammed up again.

The fire crackled. I huddled down into the thick duvet and closed my eyes, suddenly exhausted. Outside, the stream burbled its way along as it had done for many years and would do for many more. And if Miss Carey went out that night, alone across the wild lawns to stand at the banks of the brook, I was not awake to witness it.

CHAPTER TWENTY-ONE

"TELL ME ABOUT life here in the 1950s," I began. She sat before me, as smartly dressed as ever. The rain was back and the skies were a moody, thundercloud grey. The grandfather clock had just chimed 10 times, but it could have been far later. Conger Brook seemed almost to have a time zone all of its own, a place where the sun set much earlier than normal and rose, shyly, much later. I remembered the images we'd pored over of northern Norway; the seven-month winters where the polar nights sent explorers to distraction, causing insomnia and aggression, even hallucinations, madness.

Today was my last at Elver House, and the thought was so welcome, such a relief, that I found myself galvanised for this last push, this last brief stretch with Miss Carey. We'd done what we could. I was ready to leave, desperate – I realised – to cross the boundary of the estate once more and return to a world of noise, of people, of sirens and zebra crossings, streets with familiar names. A place where parents remained dead and buried in the ground, where the elderly did not live alone and confused, but met with friends and chatted about their lives, their families, their health.

Miss Carey's eyes flicked to the window briefly, grimacing at the scaffold, and she seemed to think.

"Well, the years do rather blur into one another," she said slowly. "But I remember my 21st birthday. We had a small drinks party here, at the house. I found it odd that we were celebrating at all, but my mother had asked me. I was thrilled."

"Who did you invite?"

"Oh, the sons and daughters of my mother's friends. Villagers mostly. I barely knew any of them."

"Would you say you had close friends, at that time?" I knew the answer.

"Not at all," she said. "Never have done. Acquaintances, yes. Family – well, of course. I've told you about that. But no, I never really had friends."

I remembered a pair of women I'd worked with – years ago now. They were in their sixties, having met 40 years before, as girls. Even in their older age they were remarkably similar: much of Annie's upbringing paralleled Lin's, and although this might have been an initial attraction to both, it was their differences that kept them close. There had been times, they told me, when Annie arrived to stay each week, or Lin travelled to meet her; other months they barely saw each other. Such, I learnt, was friendship, particularly among girls and women. Sometimes they needed each other more than others.

Annie was gregarious, at ease in herself and in what had happened over the course of her life. She'd once, she told me, met Monroe, she'd danced with Brando. Her legs went up to there. She smoked cigarettes from a long tube but never bought a single pack of her own. She bathed three times a week, which was considered decadent. She drank Bollinger from the navels of men who adored her. She stayed up all night. She had been the golden girl, but only Lin seemed to remember that by the time I met them.

Each brought something else out in the other, and as I watched Annie laugh I'd notice Lin, her wicked grin. What I sensed about them, and what I imagine attracted each to the other, all those years ago, is what binds many human interactions across lifetimes: that is, to have spotted something, magpie-like, in each other. They enjoyed that enormously. The recognition in another person, a quick and immediate hook – something that says, 'we like each other's company, and shall spend more of our lives within it, because this makes things better'. There was a tremendous, refreshing honesty to their interactions.

"Why do you think your mother threw the party?"

"I think she felt guilty. I think, to quite a large extent, she often forgot I was there altogether – I'd sort of blended in, become a part of the furniture. She always had this distracted sort of air to her, like she was looking at something the rest of us couldn't see . . . I expect nowadays she'd have been diagnosed with something or other." I waited.

"She wasn't a bad person," said Miss Carey. "I'm just not sure she was cut out for motherhood. She'd have been happier without me – it was my father she wanted."

The grandfather clock tolled the quarter hour.

"I often wonder, you know, if she saw him."

I felt my shoulders tense as the words left her mouth. I wished she would stop talking. There was something soft and low and cunning in her voice, something I'd never heard before.

"Saw . . . your father?"

"Yes, after his death. The way I did. Mostly here, in the library, as I told you. But sometimes outside, in the grounds. He'd walk past a window, or you'd spot him off in the distance, his back straight, his arms hanging down at his sides."

The wind gave a sudden anxious whoop. "Sometimes I wanted to see him, and yet it was in those moments I knew he would never appear. He always caught me off guard, made me start. I'd be in the middle of something else, just minding my own business, and then I'd feel him. He never looked directly at me, though there were times I did call out. He never turned or acknowledged it. I don't know if I was the only one to see him, but it seems unlikely. We never spoke of it, my mother and I."

I nodded, keen to change the subject. "On the whole, was it a good relationship?"

"I don't remember there really being much of a relationship at all, if I'm honest," Miss Carey frowned, smiling slightly. Her voice became brisker. "That sounds dreadful, doesn't it? But we just didn't have much to say to one another. She had her life, I had mine. And the house isn't exactly small, is it, so we kept largely to ourselves." She sipped her tea thoughtfully. "Do you know, I've never really given it much consideration. We simply . . . were. We existed within the same space for all these years without ever really knowing who the other was. But it worked. Do you know what I mean?"

I didn't, but I nodded slowly anyway.

"I suppose once the staff started to leave we had more to do with one another – but it was always very practical. Always related to the house, to the farming, to the open days we'd hold."

"I've heard about those," I said without thinking. She frowned, confused. "At the pub. Some of the villagers mentioned coming here as children."

Her face relaxed. "Yes, those events went on for many years. We'd organise a sort of fete every September. Can you imagine the forecourt as it once was – full of people, coconut shies, children having their faces painted. And we took tours all around, from the top to the ground floor, then outside to the brook for eel-babbing. I expect they told you about that?"

I nodded.

"Otherwise we largely kept to ourselves. The governesses left years before, of course, but then the maids quit, one by one, and the gardener, and then finally the cook. Don't forget these were all people I'd known my entire life – I never thought of them as staff. My mother was so disappointed. And it didn't help that any replacements barely stayed a year before they left, too. I suppose the isolation of the place scared them off. It was different when I was a child: you couldn't move for people, for activity, for something going on somewhere. Over time, all that melted away. And then my mother became unwell."

"How old were you?"

"I suppose I'd have been in my mid-thirties, when she was first diagnosed. I waited. "With MS. Within a few years, she needed almost constant care. Doctors came and went but it didn't seem to make much difference. Don't forget this was 50-odd years ago.

Things were different then. I suspect there's all sorts nowadays that they could do."

"It must have been very hard on you," I said. More a statement than a question, but she nodded.

"I suppose it was, but there wasn't anything I could do about it, so I didn't see the point in wishing things were different."

We sat in silence for a few moments then, the clock in the hallway marking time. The library looked beautiful in the shade; without the spotlight of mid-morning sun, none of the defects were visible. It looked homely, relaxed. The spines of the books gave no hint of the mildew between their pages, and without beams of light to reveal them, dust motes danced through the air unseen.

Miss Carey looked at me expectantly. I realised she was waiting for me to ask another question, perhaps to move away from the topic, but something was niggling at me, a sense of information lost, a hook or clue overlooked. I struggled to focus, then asked her to describe daily life with her mother.

"We'd take a lot of walks," she said, pointing to the grounds through the windows. "She loved the estate. Even when things became much more difficult, years later, she'd never have agreed to leave. You know, go into some sort of respite home. Elver was her life."

"How did she feel when the staff began to go? Did they explain why, any of them?"

"Not especially, no. Or they gave excuses. Generally, I think, the whole concept of live-in staff was becoming outdated. And rightly so, I believe. How was anybody supposed to have a life out here? The village is a good walk away, and not much fun for a young person. A hundred years ago young men and women expected to work in one house, for one family, for decades at a time. But the young had different prospects. Can't say I blamed them."

"And how did you manage the farm, the gardens, that sort of thing? Was there any help?"

"Less and less as the years went by. I spent most of the day outdoors. Before she became unwell my mother and I would spend hours out in the fields – picking, sowing, cleaning and sweeping, loading the surplus onto carts we'd then take to town on market days. But by around the 1980s, it was just me." She made to stand up and, expecting one of her customary shifts of mood, I rose too. But she beckoned me over. "Come and have a look, it might be useful for you to see these."

I followed her out of the library and across the flagstoned hallway to the drawing room. I'd not been inside properly since that first, strange evening. The door creaked on its hinges as Miss Carey pushed it open with her stick.

She crossed to a bureau beside the fireplace and lifted its lid. I stood, watching, the laptop balanced across one arm. "Sit, sit," she said distractedly as she rifled through the papers inside. I glanced down at the canary-yellow sofa, and recognised the faint outline of a boot-print on the end cushions. It looked as though it had been scrubbed with water, though some of the imprint remained indented on the fabric.

"Did the have builders come inside when they visited before?" I asked lightly.

"Which builders?" she said, flicking through paper.

"The ones Mr Walsh organised."

She turned to face me, a clutch of envelopes and ring binders in her arms, and grimaced. It was hard to make out what she was feeling: whether she remembered the contractors, the mentions of Mr Walsh or not. I gestured to the boot-print and she shrugged.

"They must have done, I suppose," she said. She was either unconcerned or pretending to be: I couldn't tell which. "Lord knows why they'd need to walk on the furniture." We both looked up at the ceiling, its paintwork cracked in places. "And if they did, one would hope they'd clean up after themselves."

"Somebody has," I said, pointing at the watermark surrounding the print.

She shuffled closer, placing the papers and folders onto the seat beside me, and traced the outline of the stain with her finger. I watched her, waiting, wondering. Then, as if deciding something, she shrugged and walked slowly to the chair, lifting the documents to sit down. She flicked through the first pages and handed them over to me.

The first showed a faded colour photograph of the house. The vines were half their current height, the stone carving bearing the year of Elver's construction seemed cleaner somehow, more pronounced, and most windows were open, the curtains pulled back. The tiles on the roof, now visibly gaping in places, were intact, a clean sweep of slate. There was an air of life about the place, a sense of welcome even though there was nobody in the photograph. It no longer looked imposing, an interloper in a wild landscape, a husk. Here was a house used and lived in, a place where one could imagine the bustle and noise of people talking, working, tapping across the corridors, playing and sleeping.

Three sets of faded Wellington boots were placed at jaunty angles beside the front door. Neat rows of hydrangeas stood upright and proud in front of the library, where we'd just been sitting; a startling, iridescent blue. I traced a finger across the row and Miss Carey chuckled from beside me.

"Gorgeous, weren't they? My pride and joy." She sighed. "They were so tall, so healthy. You probably already know this, but the colour of the flowers depends on the soil. In hydrangeas, I mean."

I continued to stare at them, their open petals brushing the window-frames. "I didn't know," I said.

"In fact, if you place nails under the ground they'll change colour. It's all about the acid and the alkaline," she said. "The content of the soil. I could only ever grow the blue. The ground is very acidic, you see. But some people have pink flowers one summer, blue the next. You just have to put the work in, change the chemical composition of the soil."

I imagined the attempts she might have made, over the years: the interaction between earth and human, the trial and error of altering the panorama and watching her creations flourish in new robes. How across one season the flowers might outgrow their girlishness and step into lilac, then deepest berry-blue. I remembered as children how we'd attempted to spot the exact moment that autumn arrived, one cool September night. How we'd tried to document the precise second the trees and plants threw off one hat and pulled on another.

We sat before the bushes and trees in your garden, sharing crisps and plucking the summer's final daisies from the lawn. The sky moved from hazy afternoon yellow to quiet Babar-grey and nothing happened. The soles of your socks were blackened, one toe poking through the cotton. You drummed her hands on the ground, "It's taking too long," you said. Eventually we got bored and went inside. It was obviously going to take longer, the transformation, than we were prepared to wait for.

"They're beautiful," I said. I was cautious of over-complimenting the rest of the house; it felt wrong, somehow, to draw attention to the sharp differences between then and now.

But I needn't have been coy – Miss Carey pursed her lips slightly and shook her head. "This was the image we used for the brochure. We had to wait weeks for the right evening, the right light. The photographers were wonderful."

I turned to the next page and saw the hallway, resplendent with the soft glow of a chandelier above, the doors closed against the polished grey stone, and a paragraph of text below it:

Designed and constructed by the Bassington family, this impressive stately home has stood the test of time across three centuries. For many years the land was leased by the Bassingtons to a monastery before the family returned to the house and made it their permanent residence at the turn of the 18th century.

Since that time, seven successive generations have served as custodians of its fascinating legacy, farming the land and playing host to the area's eel-farming industries into the 19th century and beyond. During the Second World War, Elver opened its doors once more to sick and wounded servicemen returning from battle.

Elver is a historian's dream, an architect's delight; art-lovers will appreciate the multitude of rare oil paintings, while bibliophiles can browse the first-edition copies of classics in the library. Outside the ancient Conger Brook wends it way across the estate, replete with the elvers which gave the house its name. Intrepid explorers will enjoy locating the remains of the ruined chapel, with the Bassington family crypt undisturbed beneath. Boasting 11 bedrooms as well as two large reception rooms set within 14 acres of land, Elver is a haven from the outside world, a space of calm and contemplation.

For the first time, visitors are invited to explore this stunning country house, to find out more about its long and illustrious past, and to contribute to the continued upkeep of one of England's finest hidden treasures.

I finished reading; surprised, I turned to Miss Carey, who watched me expectantly.

"You opened it up?"

"I did," she said simply. "For a time, a few years, and it worked quite well. We advertised locally, at first, and soon enough a few of the national newspapers picked up the story. Elver was full again."

I glanced back down at the text, reading it aloud this time for the recording. Miss Carey waited patiently.

"It's a good idea," I said. "Did it help?"

"Financially speaking, it was a god-send," she said, smiling. Her eyes creased at the corners. "It was a blessing. Of course my mother wasn't best pleased, not at first, but she grew used to the idea. And we weren't open often – a couple of Saturdays a month, perhaps, and during the long summer holidays."

"What did it mean to you, to have the house accessible like this, to the public?"

"I enjoyed it. I loved seeing people's reactions to the place, to the house and to the grounds. They were able to see what I saw in Elver, I think. They could appreciate it for what it was." She fiddled with the pearls around her neck. "It gave me something to focus on, too – something besides caring for my mother and overseeing the crops, the plants, the flowers. A bit of a change, I suppose. And I so enjoyed speaking with the visitors, taking them around. I did all of that myself."

I picked up the ring-binder and several photos slid out the back. I held up the first to the table lamp beside us. The woman standing beside the brook was almost unrecognisable. She looked taller, more upright, her face unlined, her hair a rich chestnut brown, characteristically permed in the style of the 1980s; it tumbled down her back. She wore a smart red summer dress and matching plimsolls. She was grinning from ear to ear, mid-speech, before a group of men and women with cameras, children clinging on to the hands of their parents, a dog on a lead staring at the photographer.

"I was so proud," she said softly. "So happy."

"What were you saying here? Can you remember?"

"I expect I was telling them about the eels," she said, amused. "Such a fascinating life cycle. Incredible creatures. They're such a mystery."

She tapped the picture at the spot the brook met the bank. "We don't know much, but what's almost certain is that baby eels are born in the Sargasso Sea, miles out off the east coast of America. A dangerous stretch of ocean. Columbus mentioned it in his diaries, I believe. It's full of seaweed, thick and tangling." She looked up at me quickly, as though she required permission to continue. I smiled back at her.

"No one knows exactly where they're born," she said. "Within the seaweed somewhere, I presume. They're carried on the currents all the way to Europe. Can you imagine?"

She paused, warming to her theme, clearly enjoying the chance to tell the story as she once had. "They turn up at the coastline, here in Britain, and then the tides carry them upstream: from salt to freshwater. And it's at this point they become elvers. They'll live among our streams and brooks for up to twenty years. After that, they change colour. They change sex. Their eyes expand by ten times. They put on weight, gain muscle. And then they make their way all the way back to Sargasso."

"They return?"

"Yes. When they're ready, they go back, all the way back to the seaweed. About four thousand miles. That's where they spawn, and then they die. The eel is an organism of pure metamorphosis."

I was reminded, and not for the first time, how it was moments such as these that I loved best. The nuggets of information, the strange facts, the pictures people painted when you allowed them to speak. Miss Carey shrugged slightly and laughed, embarrassed.

"Do stop me. I'll waffle on for hours. We were talking about showing the visitors around."

"Yes. I can hear how much you loved it. Why did the open days stop?" I asked – a seemingly innocent question, but one I hoped would edge us forward, would bring us at last to the heart of the matter. The light had all but faded entirely, and the halo from the table lamp cast Miss Carey's face into shadow. There was a silence, heavy and sad somehow.

Catherine shivered audibly and I waited. "I didn't want them to," she said, "but my hand was forced on that front." Her fingers pressed against her temples. "We were always full, always busy on the days we opened. But I'd no advice about how to manage the guests. I hear other properties, National Trust houses and the like, have specific areas kept private from the public. I'd no idea, so I opened the whole house. There was nowhere they couldn't go."

Outside the first rumblings of thunder began. I was almost used to it by now, the speed with which the sky darkened completely and leaves began to spin through the air. We never had weather like this in London, though I remembered it from childhood: the warnings not to walk in the forest or through the parks, the creaking, snapped boughs of ancient oaks prone to tumble at any moment, the whirring of helicopters sent out to scour for missing walkers stuck on mountains with ancient, magical-sounding names. Skiddaw. Coniston. Catbells. Belncathra and Helvellyn.

For now, the storm sounded far away but rain began, as if following a script. Soon it was drumming an insistent retort on the windows. I edged the laptop closer to Miss Carey, beside us on the sofa, determined to pick up every word.

She sighed. "I'd no idea what to make of it, the first time guests told me what had happened. It felt like such a slap in the face. Ordinarily I led the tours upstairs, you see, and organised the groups so that people could wander around as they pleased across the ground floor and out into the grounds." She continued to turn the pages in the folder before her, one after the other. Photographs leapt out in swathes of Technicolour, poppies saturated in red, the grey of the house made bright and cheery, the vivid blue water of the brook as it ran along its path, a table laden with food outside the library windows.

"One afternoon I was showing them around, as usual, the guests I mean . . . and there was the most terrible commotion downstairs. I ran as fast as I could from the upper floor, almost tripping face-first. There was a group, huddled in the hallway, two of the children wailing. At first I thought someone must have fallen or broken something, but then I saw the faces of their parents, and knew it couldn't be."

I pushed the laptop still closer; her voice had dropped to barely more than a whisper. "They said they'd come from the kitchen. I often left out an urn of coffee inside, plates of biscuits, that sort of thing. One of the guests whispered that there had been a man there when they'd entered the room. A man in uniform."

I frowned. Why would this have upset them so much? As Miss Carey turned another page I saw a photo of a crowd, at least 50 deep, standing in the entrance hall. Men and women and children; an old man in a wheelchair, a bored teenager in a Nirvana t-shirt, his hair obscuring his face. "What was the problem? With the man in the kitchen, I mean."

"Well, he was a soldier."

I frowned, not understanding, thinking of the scrubbed table, the low ceilings, the lack of light. The way I'd sit there alone, night after night, eating and drinking and thinking.

"His head was covered in blood, they said. The left side of his skull nothing more than an open, gaping wound. He was dressed in khakis, with bandages covering most of his torso."

I nodded slowly. My chest felt suddenly tight, my ears beginning to ring. I desperately wanted Miss Carey to stop talking, to change the subject. I wanted to leave the house and walk outside, gasping in lungfuls of fresh air.

"The group scattered outside, jumping into cars or waiting far from the front door. I had no idea what they'd seen and a part of me was terrified that this man, whoever he was, had had some sort of accident while visiting the property. It wasn't inconceivable, after all." She stopped turning the pages and fixed me with the same stare I was coming to know so well.

"I was also horrified that the group's response had been to run in the first place: whoever the man was, he clearly needed help, no matter how frightening his appearance. I entered the kitchen and watched as this person, whoever he was, pulled the back door open ever so slowly and then walked jerkily over the grass. I never saw his face, I just watched as he continued along the path leading to the old crypt, what used to be the chapel."

"Who was he?" I asked. "Did you ever find out?"

"No. When he reached the crypt he simply . . . I don't know. It's like he melted away, like a photograph doused in water. It wasn't exactly sudden, more like a fading. I simply couldn't see him anymore. I went looking, of course. I followed him, straight out into the grounds, but there was nothing." She rested her hands on the files before her. I was struck again by the clarity of her skin, the straight, neat features, the slightly faded lipstick, the smart twin-set that belied a life lived outdoors, knee-deep in mud and compost, up to her elbows in buckets of weeds.

"I returned to the group, or what remained of it. I told them the man had gone. They were terrified, some were angry. One even asked if this was my idea of a joke – a way to get more people through the door . . . Hire an actor, dress them up, turn it into some sort of ghost-train." She laughed bitterly.

"They asked me who he was and I lied, Ellen: I said he must have wandered into the house. Perhaps he was a trainee from the local barracks, I said. It's not far. It could have been plausible. I apologised, though I'd no idea what for, if I'm honest."

I could imagine the chaos, the children crying, the furious parents, the strides off toward cars and the slamming of doors.

"Was that not a possibility?" I asked. "Maybe he came in through the back of the house? Could he not have been a trainee, as you'd suggested?"

"It would have made more sense – in fact it would have been the only semi-logical explanation," she responded. "But I knew that wasn't it; on his arm I'd seen a regimental banner." I waited, not understanding. She sighed. "It was old, far older than it had any right to be."

There was a tap on the window. I glanced over sharply, startled, and saw a couple of the builders waiting outside. They were smiling, thumbs-up, their hair already plastered to their heads. "We're starting on the roof," one of them mouthed. I nodded. "Is that ok?" I nodded again.

Miss Carey eyed them nervously but said nothing. We continued.

"That was just a year or so after I'd started the tours. I was shocked, of course." It seemed an understatement, and she smiled slightly as she realised it too. "Well, more than shocked. I didn't know what to make of it. I tried to come up with an explanation, some sort of reason, and I couldn't." She stopped, eyeing me expectantly. "And so I had to assume the people in that kitchen were all mad, had suffered some kind of communal delusion. Either that, or what had happened to me had happened to them."

My next question, when it came, felt wrenched. I wished more than anything that we could move onto something else, return to the opening of Elver's doors, the excitement and the independence it had given Miss Carey - possibly for the first time in her life. But these interviews were her time, not mine, and this was where she had led me.

"You mean to say, what you saw wasn't . . . well, wasn't, human?"

"I think they were both human, Ellen. The soldier and my father. I just don't think either of them were alive."

She said this with such simplicity, such accepting understanding, that I felt myself pulled along in the same current - almost. "How . . . frightening," I said weakly. The rain ceased for a moment as the wind changed direction, then continued its onslaught.

"I saw them both with my own eyes," she said carefully. "The two of them. And I wondered, then, if there hadn't been more of them all along. If opening the house had just increased the chances of guests catching sight of something. More people, more opportunity. I'd seen my father on and off for years. I'd grown accustomed to it: he was familiar, even after all that time. The soldier was a different story. Of course I didn't know him, had never seen him before. But the fact he was here, and could well have been here for years - undisturbed, unnoticed, as the house slowly emptied, well . . . I didn't like it. I wondered whether this might explain the resignations, the staff leaving."

Up ahead, in the near distance, we heard the beginnings of hammering, of knocking, of work starting.

"Nonetheless, business was good. We were doing well." Miss Carey gestured to the living room, its yellow paper untouched by damp or mould, its furnishings simple but expensive. "We'd finally been able to install central heating downstairs, for one thing. It made a huge difference to my mother's condition, as you can imagine. And for better or worse, the soldier simply fuelled speculation.

Our numbers seemed to triple overnight. The local paper got hold of the story and one of the guests was interviewed about it." She turned the page to a faded newspaper article, a grainy black-and-white photograph of the kitchen taking up most of the front page. I couldn't make out the columns underneath, but could guess at their contents.

"Soon we had to implement a ticketing system. The nationals were going to do a photo shoot, though I declined. I'd have said yes, if I thought they wanted to profile the estate, the building, its history, that sort of thing. But it was one of those 'haunted house' puff-pieces and I just . . . I couldn't do it."

I could well anticipate the sorts of offers she had received. Even as I sat there, wishing we could talk about something else, I felt my own curiosity peak in spite of myself. To have Catherine report the sightings of her father – in the midst of terrible, gnawing grief – was one thing. To have others report on the same phenomena was quite another. If I'd been safely back in London, sprawled across the sofa with a coffee one weekend morning, I'd have read the article those newspapers were so eager to scoop.

"And then it happened again."

I turned back to her, nodding.

"In the kitchen, you mean? The same soldier?"

"No, this was much later. I'd stopped the teas and coffees by that point and locked the kitchen door when guests were arriving. Partly because of what had happened, and partly to ensure there was only one entrance and exit to the house. It seemed safer."

I'd not considered this, but it made sense. "Were you concerned at all? I mean, about safety, about the security of the estate?"

"I might have been, possibly, if I'd known what was to come," she said. She sat back and closed her eyes, suddenly tired. I suspected we were almost finished for the day. "I knew that Elver was remote, but I'd always imagined, growing up, that other people knew about the house. It's a listed building, after all. The curiosity when I opened it up proved otherwise. It seemed nobody had really heard of us at all. In fact most of the first visitors were local. As the prospect of seeing the house became more popular, I was warned on several occasions not to allow guests upstairs. Not to speak so freely of the fact I lived here alone, with my mother. It probably seems foolish to you, now. But I just didn't know."

It did, I suppose, sound naïve – and yet at the same time I'd grown up similarly sheltered, protected, in a world of unlocked doors and neighbours popping by, where children were cared for en masse, given squash and biscuits by one parent, grandparent, friend or another. I could understand how Miss Carey would not have known to be cautious, would not have anticipated the sly, sinister intent that could accompany a pair of women advertising an open house. I thought of the dense forest just a few minutes' walk from the house, the myriad hiding places, the ability to blend into the blackness and wait.

"This time I was here, in this very room, when I heard the screams," she continued. "I rushed into the hallway, thinking at first that something must have happened to my mother. She was much frailer by then, and though she kept mostly to her room, there were times in the summer when I'd take her outdoors, settle her with a book under a parasol, that sort of thing. I came into the hallway and they were pointing towards the library," she said. "A much larger group, three or four adults, a whole army of children it felt like." My phone buzzed; I ignored it.

"And there he was, just as he had always been. His back was facing us, as we stood in the doorway. But this time water dripped from his hands, there was barely any flesh covering the fingers. His clothes were sodden, and there were patches where his hair had thinned across his scalp."

"Your father?" I asked, feeling ill. She nodded.

"I turned back to the families and tried to placate them. I said it was just a mirage, just a memory of sorts, and that it couldn't hurt them. Although of course, I didn't know that for sure."

I imagined them – the adults and children alike, the shock, the gasps, the fear. I wondered how it must have felt to stand there and know that everyone could see what you were seeing. This wasn't a singular event, an apparition appearing to one person while others searched in vain. How the brain must have flip-flopped, struggling for an explanation, somersaulting over possibilities each more improbable than the last. And all the while the floor grew wet as water dripped onto it from cold, dead hands.

"What did you do?" I asked.

"We just stood there and watched. There didn't seem to be anything else we could do. After a few seconds, though they felt like hours of course, I reached forward gently and closed the doors. The guests left. The following week, I decided that was enough. I closed the house, removed the website, and stopped selling tickets. We went from bustle and noise to silence again. A few magazines tried to call me – one of the guests that day was a jobbing reporter, worse luck. I ignored them. And then a few weeks later Princess Diana died, and any offers of photographs or feature pieces dried up overnight. The news cycle moved on."

The rain seemed to have worn itself out; its soft patter relenting. "We continued as we had done before, my mother and me. She declined rapidly after that, and within a year she had died."

Silence hung in the air. The phone buzzed again, vibrating against my leg. I cursed it silently, hoping the noise wouldn't distract Catherine.

"It must have been so painful for you, her death," I said.

"I just didn't know what to do with myself. It was *time* that felt so unusual: I had so much of it, all of a sudden. Time I'd spent caring, washing and cooking, changing sheets, pushing her around the grounds. It all evaporated in a day. I was lost, for a few months." She placed the ring-binders, folders and loose sheets on the table and stood, shakily, as I knew she would.

"Enough for today?" I asked.

She smiled, nodding.

"If you don't mind, Ellen. I'm sorry I can't be more forthcoming

. . . It must be frustrating for you. I just get so tired. And talking about all this . . . it's exhausting."

I smiled back. It was a genuine moment – both of us acknowledging the other.

"It's not a problem, of course," I told her. "Miss Carey, Catherine. I just wanted to mention . . . I'm going back to London tomorrow. To write the book." This was often the moment clients galvanised themselves, realising the time was coming to an end. Final interviews were usually the most focused, the most urgent as a result.

She seemed prepared for this. I wondered if she'd remembered what Laura had told us on the phone; it didn't appear to come as a complete surprise.

"Of course," she said. "You have to get back to your life, Ellen. And I have to get back to mine." She smiled sadly. "I've not given you all the time you needed, I know, but perhaps you could spin something out of what we've discussed."

I gestured to the laptop. "There's always more than we think, to be honest. And I can do some research, add in sections about the house, its history, your parents. There's plenty to work with. Don't worry."

She smiled again and, using her stick to guide her, crossed the room. At the doorway she paused and turned back. There was something hesitant about her, like she was willing herself to speak, as I had done moments before.

"All these things I've told you . . ." she said. "About the house. About what was seen. Does any of it surprise you?"

I wondered what she meant. Surprise wasn't quite the right word. I thought about it. Before I could answer, though, she spoke again. Her voice was questioning, almost pleading. Our roles reversed.

"I mean to say, have you seen anything, while you've been here?"

I stared at her. "You mean . . . like the things you've seen? Like the guests saw?"

"Yes," she said simply. "Anything like that."

"I haven't, no," I said. My mind left the room and wandered across the hallway, to the library doors, the long shadows on the carpet, the skeletal frame of the scaffold. "No, nothing at all."

She nodded, seeming satisfied. "I'm glad," she said, and she left the room.

CHAPTER TWENTY-TWO

"SORRY," SAID LAURA. "Didn't mean to interrupt." I pulled my phone out of my pocket once the living room door had closed. A text and two missed calls.

"No worries," I said. "We've just finished. I think that's probably it now."

I heard Laura tapping away, the whoosh of a sent email. "You've done what you can." She sounded tired. "How are you feeling about coming back?"

"I'm looking forward to it," I said. "It'll be good to come home." I kept my voice low, just in case Miss Carey was still in earshot beyond the door. "How're you?"

"Honestly not great today," she muttered. "I was up most of the night with Isla. Just couldn't get her fever down. And my mum had a fall, so I've been liaising with the care-home team on that."

"I'm sorry," I said. I felt, suddenly, as weary as she did. "Where's Oliver?"

"In Saudi for work," she said. I could hear the gritted teeth from here. "Anyway, that wasn't why I was calling. Accounts have let me know Miss Carey hasn't paid her final invoice."

Ordinarily, our clients paid half before the interviews began and the second half a month later, when it was assumed the interviews would have taken place. If they didn't, we couldn't start writing.

"That doesn't surprise me," I said. "I can ask her, if you think that's a good idea?"

"Yes, do," Laura said. "She hasn't been very keen to chat to me so far, has she."

"Will do. I'm sure she's just forgotten."

"Probably," said Laura. "Whatever the reason, I don't want you starting on the draft until she's made the payment. You've been really patient, El, staying there longer than agreed and I know it's not been easy. Obviously we want to complete the book for her, but not until things are sorted from her end."

"Makes sense," I said. "I'll just get the transcribing done once I'm back."

"Cool," she said. "In the meantime, I've got a new project if you're free. Starting Friday. It's in London – should be fairly straight-forward. A former police detective. He wants to do a sort of warts-and-all memoir. Joined the force in the late 60s, so he's seen a fair bit. Could be interesting. I know you like that sort of thing."

I wasn't sure if I did anymore. The days spent here, with Miss Carey, had somehow removed the onetime fascination with the sombre, the macabre, the darker aspects of human nature. Here, at Elver, my morbid curiosity had been more than sated. Then again, work was work.

"Sounds good," I said. "I'll be back tomorrow evening. Thursday I'll do her transcribing, and then Friday I can start again. How's that sound?"

"Perfect, love, thanks," she said. "It should be much simpler this time round. He's in Stockwell, not far from you. Sounds nice, easy-going, relaxed."

"Sign me up," I said, my eyes wandering to the stack of papers on the coffee table, the battered folders, the photos spilling out.

"How's she been, the past couple of days?"

"We've managed to get a little bit further," I said, and it was true. "Made a bit more progress. Still far less than I was hoping, but it's been better, definitely."

"Well done."

There was a silence, then: "And you're ok?"

"I'm fine," I said. "Just tired, I suppose. Ready to get out of here and come back to the city. There's so much space, but it's claustrophobic somehow. Any longer and I'd get cabin fever. I don't know how she does it."

"Makes you realise, doesn't it," said Laura. "We're so lucky, really, aren't we."

We chatted for a couple of minutes and then rang off. I pulled the folders towards me and took pictures of the house as it once was, reading aloud from the articles for the tape. Leaflets written on a typewriter and photocopied gave a general overview of the house, its construction, the farming that had been done here. Generic, run-of-the-mill context. A second sheaf of glossier brochures featured an introduction from Miss Carey herself and a small headshot. I peered closer at the fuller face, the open smile, the image of youth combined with the practical chic of her clothing.

Each ticket sale, she said in the welcome note, contributed towards the continued upkeep and maintenance of this historic building. A cutting from a local newspaper showed a profile focused on Catherine herself, only child of Mrs Alice Carey née Bassington and Alfred Carey. I read the article aloud, again for the tape, and took a picture on my phone to be sure I'd captured it. At this point, every last scrap of information would be a help. Miss Carey described the September harvests, the early mornings, the day-to-day running of an estate like Elver. She told the reporter, as she had told me, about the makeshift hospital when the house was requisitioned by the army during the war.

Alongside these duties, the 55-year-old divides her time between village life, including local fetes and the May Day parade, organising the Christmas Appeal drive and raising funds for the Conger hospice. The house and estate, however, take up most of her time. That, and "caring for my mother, who has always loved this place, and is keen for its legacy to be enjoyed by the general public."

Mrs Carey, who welcomed us graciously into her home, has

been unwell for a number of years. As the custodian of Elver House, she is determined to maintain the land and the home to the standard it has held for so many decades – an increasingly difficult task. "The elements do tend to get a foothold here," she says, looking out over the grounds. "It's a constant battle. But it's one myself and my daughter are sure we can win. With the right mindset, anything is possible."

Mrs Carey's husband, Alfred, died almost half a century ago. "He drowned in the brook," she says, matter-of-factly. "It was a dreadful shock. We never found out the cause. He was a tremendously hard worker: he knew everything about the land and treated it as his own. My daughter suffered a terrible shock, as did we all."

Alfred Carey was just 36 years old when he was found unresponsive in the babbling brook which cuts through the Elver estate. "We simply carried on," says Catherine, soberly. "There was nothing else for it. But we're keen that Elver, which has seen so much sadness, should also remain a place of happy memories: a place for families to come and visit, to enjoy the space."

So what is it like, I ask, to live here – in a house so remote and isolated few people have ever heard of its existence? Catherine and her mother exchange a look, but I can't quite make out what it means. "We don't feel alone," said Catherine. "But I suppose, technically speaking, that's the truth of the matter: we very much are. By opening up the house, perhaps less so."

I stared down at the photograph of Mrs Carey, her clothes as well-kept and pressed as her daughter's. She smiled out from her wheelchair, the sun reflecting off ash-blonde hair by the library doors. A ripple of fear shimmered down my arms. They'd been so innocent, so brazen in their honesty. Two women, one of them severely unwell by this point, living alone in a remote house far from the nearest village, from other people, from help. Why had they advertised the fact so openly?

I thought back to the trashed study, to the papers scattered across the floor, the torn lampshade, the upended, shattered chair, to the plastic gloves in the grate, repulsive to the touch though I'd no idea why. I glanced sharply down at the footprint and shuddered. The villagers had said Miss Carey seemed frightened recently. Was this – uninvited guests, intruders, opportunistic thieves – what had caused her fear?

It was midday by now and the rain showed no sign of stopping. I watched as a group of builders shook water off their helmets and climbed inside the lorry. I wanted to invite them inside, but knew Miss Carey wouldn't like it. Given everything she'd just said – about the guests, the things they'd seen, the sense of disappointment when it hadn't, ultimately, worked out – I could partly understand why. She had turned inward since the open-house days, become gradually more reclusive: it fitted with what Steve and the others had said in the pub. As her mother's condition deteriorated, she would have found herself unable to do very much of what she enjoyed. And then her mother had died, and Miss Carey had found herself an elderly woman: friendless, abandoned, increasingly immobile. It was a depressing, pathetic thought. A life spent in service to house and parents, and what did she have, now, to show for it?

Perhaps this was her reason for the book. Perhaps she'd wanted, just once, to have somebody listen to her, ask her questions, probe a little. Somebody to whom she might tell the whole story, even if it ended sadly, with little resolution. From what I understood, she had nobody to whom she might turn if things became hard for her; nobody to see out the days with. And when she did die, Elver would have no one to take care of it. No one to nurture it and watch it grow, no one to fill the corridors with life or illness, joy or sadness, lights blaring out across the grounds in winter. And what was worse, she knew that. This house had been everything to her and now that she'd spent a lifetime here, it had also robbed her of anything else.

But did it rob her? Perhaps something could only be raided, taken away, denied if it had been present in the first place.

I traced my fingers across the raindrops following one another down the glass, remembering the evenings we'd spent tottering down six flights of stairs onto the High Street, to the newsagents that sold crisps and out-of-date sponge cakes. Amber-coloured liquids caught the overhead lights and sparkled; dark, viscous stuff in long-necked bottles sat dirtied with stickers for £8.99. We'd buy as much as we could carry and have a party. It seemed like there were 50 people crammed into the flat but it was only ever us.

Letters arrived from the council and we pushed them into a plastic tin. We blew smoke rings, or tried to. We pinned fake flowers in our hair and catwalked the hallway, blurred and overexposed all at once. The windows were grimy, thick with soot and smoke from the passing cars and our lipstick marks, scarlet imprints for the light to filter through. The walls were cream, covered in our posters, blue tack from people who'd lived here before. They were fast nights, our plans changing at the drop of a hat, from pyjamas to heavy green-velvet dresses. Our bodies were uncoiling, unfurling, straightening up.

I didn't miss that time, but I missed you. I missed the chitchat, the intimacy, the ease. I missed it even while we were living it.

I left the room, climbed the stairs, passed the shut door of the study. Inside my own room, the fire had burnt itself out, tendrils of smoke still curling up the chimney. I pulled my suitcase from the corner and opened it on the floor, piling clothes inside, slotting the unread novel beside them and closing it. It felt bizarre, impossible even that this was it: we'd finished. This time tomorrow I'd be wending my way back to the city, back to normality, far removed from stories of draughty corridors, faceless figures fading into the night.

The rest of the day passed slowly. I tidied up as much as I was able, wiped down the surfaces of the bathroom, folded the towels. I swept the hearth and emptied the shards of broken wood into the fireplace. There was no sign of Miss Carey, no noise of feet or stick on the stair. To my surprise, I found myself exhausted afterwards and climbed back into bed. When I awoke, the light outside had vanished entirely, replaced by the rising disc of a full moon. For the final time, at 6 p.m., I went downstairs to cook.

CHAPTER TWENTY-TWO

I'M HERE, READ the text, *bottom of the drive*. It had just gone nine on Thursday morning, and I stood before Miss Carey in the hallway. Steve had arrived.

She'd asked me several times if I'd got everything I needed: the "gadgets", as she described charging cables, Dictaphone, headphones. She was paler than I'd ever seen her, if that was possible. This morning, she had the same distracted air I'd come to know so well.

"Thank you, Ellen," she said. "For everything. I've so enjoyed this."

"You're welcome," I replied. "It's been a privilege." She shook my hand, kissed my cheek, her lips cool and dry. I realised it was the first physical contact we'd ever had, and would now be the last. "Thank you for having me to stay." Over breakfast that morning, I had already explained the next steps, and promised to give her a call the following week with an update. As Laura had requested, I mentioned the invoice and Miss Carey had nodded, telling me she would make a note on the calendar stuck beside the fridge.

"Safe journey, Ellen," she said. I stepped over the threshold and looked up at the house. There was no sign of the builders today, though the lawn bore the flattened streaks of their tyre-marks. "Take care of yourself."

Miss Carey clutched her cardigan around herself and crossed her arms, leaning on the door jamb. For a moment she looked almost young, a mirage of the girl in plaits and the teenager escaping her governesses, the dedicated daughter keeping watch over an ailing mother.

I set off across the forecourt, past the fountain with its shillings and pence, past the widest section of the brook, where the elvers darted backward and forward, until I was level with the patch of hydrangeas far in the distance, to the east. I reached the gate and the crumbling brickwork beside it and turned once more to Elver, where Miss Carey stood framed in the doorway, one arm raised in farewell, her face a soft white sphere against the gathering clouds. I waved. Within moments I'd crossed over onto the tree-lined path, strewn with newly fallen leaves that crunched beneath my feet. Just seven days earlier this had seemed a desolate place: terrifying in its isolation. If I'd known then what I knew now, I wondered if I'd ever have made it to the front door.

The twin beams of Steve's headlights winked in the distance, flashed once as I approached.

"You did it," he said, as I pulled open the car door. "Time served. You're free."

I laughed, buckled myself in, and watched as the trees thinned. We drove in companionable silence back to the station, my breath misting the window, Steve nodding along to the radio. I felt my shoulders relax, tension I hadn't known I'd been carrying dissipating with every mile away from Elver.

The station was deserted, but the train itself waited patiently on the platform. There was no one else on board. I was reminded of the first night, the way it had sat idling away the moments before departure. Now we were headed in the opposite direction: back to London. At 10.04 precisely, the train left the station and, six hours later, I was fishing keys from my rucksack and throwing wide the door to the flat.

The wall mirror was the first shock: I could barely recall ever looking so pale, and that was saying something. My clothes seemed to hang off me, the waistband of my jeans visibly drooping. I'd used Miss Carey's bathroom mirror at Elver, but she'd not had a full-length one, and the change was stark. I looked waxen, ill.

I dropped the bags in the kitchen, throwing piles of clothes, still-damp socks and hats into the washing machine. Soon the flat was filled with the reassuring scent of detergent.

Despite the day's travelling I felt wide awake. I pulled on my boots and set off down the street, the neon glow of kebab shops and nail bars illuminating the pavement. People hurried past without a glance; drivers in a queue at traffic lights honked and craned their necks out of car windows to shout at one another. Coats were buttoned up to chins and long scarves trailed along the ground until they were hastily gathered up and coiled once more around necks. It was bliss: the hum and propulsion of it all, the anonymity, the familiarity of over-full bins on the street, pigeons and pedestrians jostling for space, moving out of one another's way.

Inside the shop beside the tube station I filled a basket with sourdough, salted butter, eggs, three different kinds of cheese. The floor was wet and dirty from the hundreds of pairs of shoes traipsing dirt and rubbish, gum and mud from outside. Aubergines, tomatoes, jalapenos, potatoes, garlic. Milk and sugar, lemons, coffee and herbal tea. Cleaning products and sponges, dishwasher tablets, rinse aid. Comfortingly dull.

At home I fired up the stove and placed the coffee pot on the flames. I hung out the laundry, grilled some bread and had breakfast for dinner: thick slices of toast with raspberry jam. I drank the coffee and cleaned the bathroom, hoovered, flicked fresh sheets onto the bed and took a shower. I wondered, as I stepped out in a cloud of steam, what Miss Carey was doing now. It was bizarre to think of her crossing the flagstones of the hallway, dimming the lights, slowly making her way upstairs to bed.

Remembering she'd asked me to let her know when I arrived back, I pulled up Laura's initial email about the project, found the number and dialled. It rang several times, but there was no answer, and no machine to take a message. I tried again – nothing. Well, I reasoned, I'd done my best.

I tried you instead. You answered on the first ring. "Are you back?"

"Just," I said, settling myself onto the sofa and draping a blanket across my knees. "Bit of a culture shock."

"I bet. Listen, give me one minute." You turned the phone screen-upwards; the slowly turning arm of a baby's mobile appeared in the frame and then moved out again. I heard low muttering rising to irritation. "Just take her for a minute, Ben, ok? One minute. I'll be in the other room." A grumpy sigh and the phone was back in your hand again as you closed the door behind you and sat on your bed.

"Sorry about that." Your face was drained of colour, the marks beneath your eyes deep-set, purple and livid. "We're just in the middle of negotiations."

"What sort of negotiations?"

"Ben's got a stag-do next month in Portugal so he'd be away from Thursday until Monday. He's been working so hard to help me out so I was all for it – my mum'll come, it'll be nice. But now it seems his mate's also asked the groomsmen to arrive at the actual wedding two days beforehand, which is just before Christmas. So he'd be away for almost four days then too."

You sighed, a deep and slow exhalation. I didn't know what to say. You'd been on the fence about having children in the first place: it was Ben, insecure, sarcastic Ben who'd banged the drum for starting a family he barely seemed to see.

"So then I got the calendar out, right before you rang, and said it was basically fine and I'd make it work, but unless I could find someone to help me get up there with the baby I'd have to duck out of the wedding. I mean, these are his friends: the guy getting married is a colleague I've never even met."

"What do you mean, 'he's been working so hard to help me'?" I asked, before I could stop myself. It was the wrong thing to say and I knew that even before the words were out.

Your lips pursed and you tried to adopt a breezy, nonchalant voice. "He's been really great, El," you said. "That's all I meant. He's been up all night with the baby since we stopped exclusively breastfeeding. And he does a lot of babysitting when I go and see my grandma."

"Why wouldn't he? He's her dad. And you haven't had a night's sleep since about September, right?"

"Way before that," you said. "Six weeks before she arrived I'd barely slept three hours a night. The amount she turned and kicked."

"So . . . why is it such a burden for him to be up all night feeding?"

"Because he has work."

I tried to count to ten, honestly. I really tried. It didn't work. "He chose to work. He could have taken parental leave. You know this. You could have split the time."

You were silent, eyes fixating on something off camera. Unlike me, you were never outwardly irritated. Only the silence belied your fury.

I didn't want to be having the conversation. I wondered how many times we'd have it and when one or both of us would get sick of it. You had other friends now, new mums from NCT groups who barely saw their partners. A small, mean part of me wondered if they indirectly validated what was happening to you. I could either remain silent while you expressed your feelings, or I could push back. I had tried to nod, to listen. If this were an interview with a client, I'd simply have let the person speak. I wanted to do the same now, to give you the space you needed. But I had phoned to check in, hear your voice, ask how you were, and I was actively making things worse. My needling was not going to change things for you, and we both knew that. So why was I doing it?

"He could have, yeah," you said flatly. The topic was closed. "Anyway. When did you get back?"

"Just this evening," I said. We'd been here before and the subject had been changed, moved to safer territory. I knew you felt there was no point explaining. My life, as you saw it, was relatively free of compromise, sacrifice, responsibility. Maybe it was – maybe you had seen a bigger picture, and I was blind to it.

"How was it?" you asked. "What was she like? The woman you were interviewing."

I loved you for asking. You were sleepless but you had remembered I was away, had remembered Miss Carey. There was a time I might have told you everything in forensic detail, but even as I started talking your eyes flicked to something off-screen.

"She was . . ." I paused, searching for the words. "She was kind. A little absent at times. Lived in the same house all her life. She did her best."

A cry in the distance and a louder, more panicked one. The baby was bawling and Ben was calling you.

"I have to run," you said. "Let's text later. It's good to have you close by again, El."

"Definitely," I said. I was glad to be back. I'd go to yours next week, while Ben was away, and you'd sleep while I piled laundry into the drum, cleaned the fridge and changed the baby. I wanted to do these things. I wanted you to let me.

In the distance, the sound of keening fireworks broke the stillness; a rat-a-tat series of blasts like a sort of frenzied Morse code, though it was impossible to see their lights from here. I imagined the firecrackers and rockets, Catherine wheels, crossettes and sparklers. The sharp fizz of something larger, with a longer trajectory, exploded into the sky just as I felt myself falling asleep.

CHAPTER TWENTY-THREE

I SPENT THE weekend away from the laptop, out of the house. Friday's first meeting with the new clients Laura had arranged went well and we'd arranged another for a fortnight's time. Two free days beckoned, and I switched off the computer, pulled on my trainers and set off for the common. The first five minutes of the run were painful after the break at Elver, the sedentary days and the cold: my knees and calves needed warming up.

The morning's frost had all but melted, though patches of ice remained when I left the path and set off into the trees. Blackbirds shrieked and clattered away on bare branches as I plodded through the thickets and dormant, tight-knit wild raspberries. Dogs off leads raised their heads momentarily then returned to sniffing the ground, their tails alert and still. I passed the sycamores as a gust of wind sent leaves helicoptering to the ground. I listened to the far-off sounds of children in the playground, the screams and whoops, a plane flying low overhead. Within 20 minutes I was sweating, my pace quickening, and the hill was up ahead challenging me to make it in one stretch, without stopping. I wiped my forehead on my sleeve and ploughed on.

Back home I showered, towelling my hair dry before the mirror, switching on the overhead light to peer at my skin. In the kitchen the sounds of the radio, a debate of some kind, were reassuringly bland. From the fridge I took a chicken, its legs trussed, and untied the string binding it together. I slipped my knife underneath the skin of its breast, quick incisions soon to be filled with garlic and rosemary, dabs of butter, sea salt and pepper.

I boiled potatoes, chopping them roughly once the jackets began to split, and heated a pan of oil in the oven before dropping them all inside. On the top shelf the bird slid into place, a bulb of garlic resting between its legs now, carrots and onions organised haphazardly around the edges, sprinkled with sage and lemon zest and, when it was done, strewn with sprigs of thyme from the window boxes. I leaned back against the counter, content in the semi-silence and the hum of the oven.

It was dark outside but the street lights were safe, reliable orbs of amber against the shadows, and it never truly felt like night-time here, in the city. It was odd how quickly being back – the noise and activity of the place, the possibilities and potential – had pushed Elver and its occupant from my mind. But they lurked there quietly, in the background, as though I'd left the keys in the lock downstairs, waiting for a neighbour to ring the bell and remind me. I thought of the Aga at Elver House, the pantry filled with untouched, dusty glass jars full of brine and pickled vegetables. I wondered what Catherine would be doing now.

I dressed then read while the food cooked and when it was ready, I ate quickly, using the blank screen of my phone as a mirror to smear mascara across my eyes. Dishes stacked and leftovers in the fridge, I left the flat for friends, for drinks in crowded bars, for the night bus seven hours later.

The following morning we met for breakfast, just you and me and the baby. She burbled away in her pram, a thick woollen hat pulled down over her head and her eyes inquisitive, frowning slightly as we ate croissants and shared a pot of tea. You winced when you moved to wipe her nose and I wondered, again, how you managed the sheer physical demands of carrying and lifting the baby, dressing her, walking the streets with the buggy all while trying to recover from childbirth itself.

"Late night?" you asked, grinning.

I thought of the bars, the karaoke, the breakfasts in bed, and I wondered if it hurt to be reminded of a life that no longer existed.

I hoped not. I found myself focusing instead on the quiet hours, the contented cleaning of a well-loved home, the plans for a proper herb garden on the windowsill, the Wednesday evenings spent in silence listening to music, embroidering or drawing or flicking through recipe books.

You spoke of sleep schedules and your overbearing mother-in-law, a book you were trying to read, a podcast on parenting you enjoyed in the small hours as the baby fed. You thanked me for the flowers and the baby-sensory finger puppets, the maracas. You said you didn't mind, really whether she was bright or needed extra help at school, but it would be good to try and get a head-start at least.

I listened, recalling the others last night. The chats about films and music, gigs and politics. I did not, of course, tell them anything about Miss Carey beyond the bare basics: what she had said was confidential, but they'd leaned in to listen to the descriptions of the house, the grounds, the brook as it sliced through the estate and the elvers that danced within it. I was thinking of them now.

"Ben's still fuming about this wedding thing," you were saying. "But I just don't know how I'm supposed to get there without a car."

"Where's the car?"

"He's taking it," you replied, looking at the table. "It *does* make sense, I know that – he's got a load of wine to take up. You know, from that place in Camberwell. Boxes of it, and his suit, his shoes, clothes for the extra days. In a way it'll be a relief . . . Not having to go, I mean. But my parents are away, it turns out, until just before Christmas."

"I can come over, if you like," I said, scalding my tongue on the coffee. "I'm here until the 20th or so."

"It's ok, El," you said, looking down again at the table and fiddling with flakes of pastry, "I asked Martha and Pete, they'll come down." Friends from university who'd moved out of the city and whose loss was less painful being, as it was, so expected. Their children were already at primary school. "It'll be easier to just pool childcare I think. And their kids don't need as much . . . you know, they're older. It's less intense."

Within half an hour I was desperate to leave, to be away. You finally asked about plans for Christmas, then fussed over the baby while I answered, your brow furrowed. For the first time in my life I lied to you and said I'd be in the Lakes, as usual. You could picture it, I knew: family gathered and crackers merrily pulled. You seemed relieved: I hadn't the heart to tell you the truth, that flights were booked, that along with school friends I'd be in Transylvania, that we needed snowshoes and thermal jackets and there was a good chance we'd be cut off entirely in the mountainside hut we'd booked on a whim, in the pub, on a warm summer's night just after you'd had the baby. We hadn't invited you because we knew you couldn't come. It felt unkind to mention it. But you wouldn't have wanted to come. Those days were behind you.

The baby began to scream. A couple sitting at the next table along looked over, then began to talk loudly, ostentatiously so. You pulled her out of the pram and rifled through the bag beneath it for a bottle. The baby screwed up her mouth, her face darkening. You removed the bottle and she let out a shriek of fury. She balled her fists and waved them through the air like an interpretative dancer. The high, nasal whine reached a peak, or seemed to. A man working on his laptop pulled out a pair of headphones and snapped them on. You made reassuring noises at her, singsongs and half-snatches of nursery rhymes, causing the couple beside us to talk even louder.

"Sometimes it's enough to just chat to her a while," you said, cradling her, placing a muslin over your shoulder as her head bobbed by your neck. "It's the worst right now because I can't anticipate when she's going to be like this. Normally the crying's better in the morning . . ."

Your last words were drowned out by another pitiful scream, a long protracted wail, an agonised sob. The waitress shot you a pointed look as an elderly couple entered the café, heard the screams and backed out again; I was blindsided by a white-hot rage, a furious desire to yell at them louder even than the baby. "I don't think this is going to stop," you said tearfully. You dropped your voice to a whisper. "I think we're just pissing everyone off."

"It's ok," I said, and stood up, taking the baby while you pulled your arms through your coat.

We left the café. You lifted the pram with practised ease down the single step and fastened your coat, pulled the hood down. I wondered, suddenly and unexpectedly, who might once have stood the way I was now standing – a friend of my own mother's trying not to glare down at me while I bawled in a pram.

"It's always like that," you said outside. "Wherever you go it's either disapproval or comments. Advice dressed up as observations."

I nodded, incredulous. You'd never said anything like this: not since the birth. "It must be maddening."

"People tell me off for holding her incorrectly. For burping too hard, not burping enough. If she's crying like today they avoid me like I'm infected. They cross the road. Or they'll just tell me directly how her hat's too small, her gloves are too big, her skin looks sore, her bib is dirty, she looks too hot. Someone came up to me at the doctor's surgery and told me her nails were too long." You rubbed at your eyes. "Ben's mum asked what I thought was going to happen, now we've chosen not to have her christened."

I couldn't see if you were crying: your face was lowered against the wind. The baby burbled quietly now. I stroked her cheek. She was such an image of you, the almond-shaped eyes and olive skin, the messy tangle of her new hair like overcooked noodles.

"Of course when Ben takes her out nobody muscles over to tell him anything. He takes her for a solo walk on Saturday mornings and no one's ever given him a single piece of advice. She had a meltdown here," you gestured at the café, "A few weeks ago. I asked him what had happened, when he got home. He said one lady smiled at him when she kicked off, and the waitress said what a great dad he was.

Hands-on." The sky was darkening. In the shop windows beside us twinkly lights cast polka dots onto the pavement.

"Anyway, I'll take her home," you said. "I'll see you soon," you said hoarsely, and I nodded.

We said goodbye, hugging tightly on the street corner. I remembered the smell of your hair and the soap you used, overset now with something else.

I walked in the direction of the tube and, within half an hour, was at the gallery. I walked around the newly refurbished wings, staring at the portraits, the faces set in smiles or frowns or something on the cusp of both.

I met a man for lunch in Chinatown and we drank cold beers under braziers, woolly blankets stretched across our laps as we ordered more gyoza, dim sum, plates of green peppers stuffed with prawns and stir-fried broccoli, steamed fish with ginger and scallions. He asked me about the house, about Miss Carey, about the weather in Conger Brook, all with such focused attention, such interest. His eyes were kind, his beard bristly and full.

As the mid-afternoon sun dipped behind gathering clouds we left the throng of the streets festooned with lanterns, hired electric bikes at the station and raced one another back to his, where I woke on Sunday morning as wintry light spilled through a gap in the curtains, and where coffee was brewing downstairs. The man's cat, his tawny coat like a weathered pumpkin, leapt onto the bed, onto my chest, and began to purr.

Two hours and three pieces of toast later, Marmite leaking onto our fingers and sticking to the table, I returned to the flat. I sat before the windows leading out to the garden, watched a film, painted my nails. It felt warmer suddenly and I opened the windows, letting in the smell of wood smoke from a garden down the road. Lamps flickered on in flats and houses opposite and silhouetted figures moved between rooms, cooking, chatting, on the phone. We were all animals in the same jungle, scurrying about, cooking sausages and putting lunch for the week ahead into Tupperware.

I picked up my phone, idly, and dialled Elver House. Once more the rings stretched out, even as I waited the extra seconds in case she was far away from the phone. I imagined her slow, shuffling feet, the click of the stick on the flagstones in the hallway. After a minute I rang off. I hoped she was ok. Infuriating, really, to be worrying about a woman I'd known for less than two weeks. But the extended stretch of time spent living alongside her had given me more than the usual interest, care, understanding. I resolved to try her again tomorrow.

I went to bed early, looking forward to the week ahead. I'd finish Mr Phillips' memoirs, start sub-editing a book I'd been sent for review, prepare sample chapters for Catherine. I realised, just as I switched off the light, that in order to achieve this I'd need, first, to transcribe her interviews. I cursed myself for not having started at Elver House, but it wouldn't take long – no more than a day or so, considering the brevity of our conversations.

As a rule, my job had taught me one thing above all else: we never know when the turning points will arrive, when life will change overnight, when the forks in the road jar us suddenly off course or onto a new route. It came up time and time again, through myriad conversations: the young man who'd arrived home to find his father dead on the kitchen floor, the woman whose son had raided her bank accounts and fled abroad, never to be seen again. The couple with the daughter who'd died in a car accident. The sudden diagnoses, the unexpected news, the double line on a pregnancy test, the phone call in the middle of the night.

We never knew when it was coming and I was no different. Looking back, that night – in the soft glow of a Sunday evening in late autumn, as the weekend drew to a close, I'd no idea that this would be the last truly restful, dreamless night I would have for a long time to come.

Just after seven I was up and making coffee in the kitchen. While the water boiled, I rifled through the salad drawer, picking out things for later – a handful of vine tomatoes, a cucumber, a jar of green olives. In the cupboard I took down a bulb of garlic from its twisted stalk, laying it all out on the table ready for lunch. Gazpacho – thick and cold and with a good slug of olive oil, a few de-seeded chilis.

I went through to the study. One wall was given over to photographs, faces twinkling in the dim dawn light. Books and old CDs were piled on shelves by the window and I drew back the curtain, settling myself in the office chair under the desk and opening the laptop. I clicked into Miss Carey's folder and created a new document for the transcription.

It always took a few seconds for the interviews to load, and I pulled my hair back into a ponytail while the file launched on the audio player. If I worked solidly until lunch I'd go for a walk to the deli where sandwiches made from soft focaccia, brick-like, weighed heavy and warm on the stroll home.

The file launched and I increased the volume. I heard my own voice, brisk and querying, the slight rustle of papers in the background as I'd opened a notebook or moved a newspaper. I pushed the volume button to its loudest and moved closer to the screen.

I heard my own voice. *It's a beautiful room. You're very lucky. A beautiful house, in fact.*

A silence, punctuated only by faint rustling. *I suppose you've read every novel in here.*

I frowned. There was a pause, another rustle. The sound of legs – mine – being crossed and uncrossed. I remembered doing it. *Tell me about him.*

We'd been in the library. I had scanned the shelves of novels, the dusty spines of ancient books, of heavy, out-of-date encyclopaedias, ancient maps of the Americas, strange, rhomboid sky charts and almanacs.

Another pause. *How old would he be now?*

The gaps between my questions were getting longer. Miss Carey had responded: I remembered her answers, dimly. My own voice was clear, loud even, given how high I'd cranked the volume. There was no background noise, no interference save for the rustle which filled the silence left between my questions.

Yes, sorry. I just want to try and get a parallel view of life for the family here – for your father, I suppose, after the First World War.

I closed the file, opened another. The same thing happened. I scanned forwards on the tape and heard nothing but silence.

I closed the laptop screen, sat back in the chair. Outside the sun was beginning its slow ascent across a clear blue sky; in the communal garden down below, a pair of squirrels chased one another across the bare branches of a cherry tree, its wood a dark silhouette like a climbing frame. I stood, went to the kitchen and heated coffee in its silver pot on the stove.

Years later I'd reflect on this exact moment. I'd see myself pouring the coffee and taking my phone into the living room, phoning Laura to tell her about what had happened: the technical glitch that had, for reasons unknown, prevented the recording of Miss Carey's answers and, therefore, scuppered all chances of her book being completed to any sort of standard.

I highly doubted Laura would have asked me to return to Elver House – not after everything that had happened and the fragile state, we now knew, of Catherine's health. In all likelihood she'd have asked me to try and write what I could from memory, to piece together the main facts, the chronology, to the best of my ability. Recordings were, from time to time, corrupted in an irretrievable way – it had happened to me twice beforehand, when the Dictaphone malfunctioned mid-way through a conversation, or my computer system had rebooted without the good grace to save the day's work.

But it had never happened like this before, never gone wrong in such a strangely specific way. My questions were useless without Miss Carey's answers.

I waited, forcing myself to stand at the back door and drink the coffee slowly, to have a glass of water, to empty the dishwasher. I returned to the study and rebooted the laptop, prepared to sit back and for the issue to have resolved, prepared to laugh at myself for the panic and the melodrama.

I leaned forward and watched as the screen lit up, as Catherine's folder appeared. I double-clicked, then selected the second recording. A long static buzzing filled the room and I reached over to turn the volume down. I couldn't remember exactly where we'd had this particular conversation, though the time stamp on the recording showed a week ago, around six in the evening. The faint rustle was back. I felt my hands start to shake, hovering over the keyboard, desperate to turn down the volume again but caught as if in a trance.

After a few more seconds, I heard my own voice – relaxed, casual – and the hiss of the stove. I must have been cooking.

In the gardens?

There was no response.

I waited and then, again, there it was – *Why?* Still the seconds ticked on and the rustling intensified, like an animal creeping over fallen leaves. I moved the timer forward a minute and still, nothing. Then my voice, once more: *Take your time.*

I remembered the conversation now, remembered Miss Carey sitting at the table, the tomatoes browning in the pan as I stirred them, added garlic, grateful to Steve for taking me to the shops for something fresh, besides the canned goods in the pantry. She had been talking about her father.

I paused the recording and clicked on the third. The morning light was harsh now, and the normality of the street, the cries of children on their way to school felt unnatural compared to the prickling of my arms, the cold sweat at the back of my neck. The fear was unlike anything I'd felt before – a sense of dread stealing over me like one drink too many, like the tipping point between sobriety and inebriation. I waited and heard, once again, the sound of my own voice. I strained my ears, restarted the recording, raised the volume, turned the whole thing off again and rebooted it.

The same thing happened.

With a cry of frustration I almost ran to the hallway and pulled the Dictaphone from the front pocket of my rucksack. I flicked to its most recent file, hit play, and waited. *Would you say you had close friends, at that time, or now?* And, a few minutes later, *Why do you think your mother threw the party?*

It made no sense.

I went through the remainder of the files methodically, skipping ahead, playing back. They were all the same. My own voice, the gaps, the rustling. There was nothing else, not a sigh or a whisper, a cry or a laugh from Miss Carey.

I Googled it. I went on forums. I rang the tech team at the agency, who took control of the laptop remotely and tried – unsuccessfully – to work it out. At midday my phone rang.

"El?"

"I'm here," I said shakily. I tried to sound normal.

"Listen, the guys just told me there's an issue with the recordings from Catherine Carey. What's going on?"

I explained.

"Well that's totally bizarre," she said. "Christ. After all that . . ."

"I honestly don't know what's happening," I said. "It's not like I'd forgotten to hit record or whatever. My own voice is there. Clear as day."

I heard Laura exhaling, clearly thinking. "It's not ideal," she said. "But I've still not had the invoice paid. Until she does that, I don't want you working on the manuscript anyway. We might never hear from her again. You remember that client Michael worked with – the one we thought was all paid up, and two months' work later the poor thing's got the book all ready and waiting. We never heard back. God knows what happened to him."

"Did she pay the first half on time?" I asked.

"Oh yes," said Laura. "She was quite prompt. She wired it through and then phoned to confirm it had arrived. One of the sales boys spoke to her I think."

"Strange."

"It is. But the whole thing *was* strange, wasn't it?"

I nodded, staring out of the window. "It was odd, all of it. I'm glad to be back."

"And I've tried to ring her – I'm sure you have too – but she never answers."

"That sounds about right . . ."

"It seems like she really trusted you, though, Ellen. I know it wasn't easy. But you did really well. She clearly wasn't keen to speak to anyone else."

"How do you mean?"

"Just that I never spoke to her while you were there." I heard the click of a lighter and a long exhale. "Obviously we had an initial chat about the project when she first got in touch, and I proposed you. She seemed friendly, you know, excited. So I could never really understand why she didn't want to engage with me while you were at the house."

Something lunged into focus. A word, a phrase, an image – I couldn't tell which, but it swooped, like the sure knowledge that sleep was coming, that the seconds of consciousness were fading away. I couldn't grasp it.

"Ellen?"

"Sorry, yes, I'm here. But I don't understand."

"I mean, she never spoke to me. The times you phoned, the times she was on speaker-phone. Even that first night. And to be honest I think that was pretty rude . . . She had a fair bit of explaining to do."

"Wait, Laura. Hold on. You never heard her voice?"

"No, nothing."

"But she was talking to me. While you were on speaker-phone." I looked at the laptop. "She just didn't seem eager to chat, maybe she was embarrassed – I don't know. But she was talking to me. When you asked me to stay on for a few extra days."

Laura laughed. "She must have been quiet as anything. I didn't hear a peep."

"I have to go," I said hurriedly, and ended the call. I dialled

Elver House and waited, tapping my foot against the floor, while the phone rang and rang.

I'd had enough.

Within 15 minutes, I'd booked a one-way ticket leaving from Liverpool Street. Half an hour later, I locked the flat behind me, a rucksack crammed with the bare essentials, a notebook, the laptop.

On my feet the walking boots were caked with the mud of Elver's grounds; my hat was pulled down low over my ears. I'd chosen my warmest coat from the cupboard and had it zipped up below my chin. As I crossed the street a cyclist swerved to avoid me, shouting something over his shoulder. The wind was biting as I caught the bus, where steamed-up windows transported others to work, to school, to normality. The train was waiting on the platform and I hesitated, just momentarily, before pressing the button to open the doors and climbing aboard.

CHAPTER TWENTY-FOUR

I SAT, IMPATIENTLY hunched over the screen as the train trundled slowly towards its destination. I scoured the emails about Miss Carey's project, from Laura's initial briefing to this morning's, when someone from IT had copied us both in.

The first message dated back to the start of August. *I've a new project if you're interested*, Laura had written. *She doesn't want to use video conferencing and so it'd be residential. Unless I can get you a hotel nearby, which I doubt – here's the postcode.* The address followed in full. *I've spoken to the client – Catherine Carey, she's called – and she's very happy for you to come and stay at the house while you get everything you need. I sent her your profile and she sounded delighted. Let me know by the end of the day, please.*

It was dark by the time I arrived in Conger Brook. I'd already messaged Steve during the change at the Junction. He'd responded immediately: he was away for the week, he said, but passed on the number of a colleague who'd be able to help.

Back so soon??? he asked.

Forgot something, I replied. *Just a flying visit.*

I hoped it was true. And it was a relief to know I wouldn't have to try and lie to him. I wouldn't have known how to explain it, even if I'd wanted to. I just had to see. Had to ask.

Steve's friend was mercifully silent as he drew up beside the station. He was much older, with a grizzled grey beard and large, thick spectacles.

"Elver, isn't it?" he said softly when I tapped on the window, and

I nodded. "Hop in, darling." I climbed into the back seat and leaned my head against the upholstery, watching as the roads thinned.

We barely spoke until he took the turning that led to the forest. "Anywhere here's fine," I said. "Don't worry, I know the car can't manage up the track."

"No trouble, my love," said the driver. He turned in the seat and looked at me questioningly. He had the air of someone who took life as it came – a gentle, relaxed demeanour, and it put me at ease. "I can pull it around to the side road."

"What side road?"

"It's just up here on the right. Of course if you'd prefer to walk that's fine, but—"

"I didn't know," I said. "I'd no idea there was a way to drive up to the house."

"Steve drop you off down here, did he?" the old man grunted.

"That's right."

"He won't go up to Elver, I suppose." The man rolled his eyes at me in the rear-view mirror, amused. "Silly, really."

We continued. Lying on its side, sticking up from a mass of nettles encroaching upon the road, a flash of white. I peered through the gloom at the wooden board, its painted white background, and the curling script upon it. *Elver.* It had been yanked up by its post, pulled from the earth and left there, inconsequential, a white flag in the dark.

The old man clicked his tongue and drove past. "A pity," he said sadly.

I was too focused on the next steps, on the walk across the forecourt, the sound of the brook, the vines curling their way along the walls, to notice what he said, or the way he said it. We sat in silence as the man indicated, though for whom it wasn't clear, and turned to the right. We bumped and slid our way along the rocky track, ascending slightly just as the path through the trees inclined with the shape of the earth. I willed my eyes to adjust to the shaded trees, the tottering brick wall. As we slowed, I saw through a gap in the wall the tall heads of the pink hydrangeas, still and erect as guardsmen.

The driver pulled up before a second set of gates, far less ornate and grand than the ones I'd used on the other side of the estate. I thanked him and paid him.

"You'll be ok up here?" he asked, looking out anxiously as I zipped my coat up.

"I'll be grand, thanks. Listen, I don't suppose you're working tomorrow, are you?"

"Sure am," he said. "Need a lift back?"

"I think so. I'm not sure of the time, though. Maybe mid-afternoon, would that be ok?"

"Absolutely," he said, putting the car into reverse. "Just give me a bell when you're ready. I'll fetch you from the village, shall I? Where are you putting up for the night?"

"Here," I said, though I'd no idea if this was true, no idea what Miss Carey would think about my unannounced return. "I'll be here."

"You're sleeping here?" he asked, his eyes wide.

"Or the village. I'm not sure. I'll call you, shall I?"

The man gave me a puzzled look and nodded, waving as he backed the car down the drive, turned it around and returned to the lane with the toppled sign.

I reached the wooden gate and pulled it open. The squeak of its metal hinges sent a pair of blackbirds flapping away indignantly. I passed through into the furthest edge of the estate's eastern side. In the distance, some two hundred metres away, I could make out the black hulk of Elver House in profile, side-on, the bars of the scaffold jutting out at right angles against the exterior. It seemed a lot smaller from here, from this vantage point.

I set off, crunching along the frostbitten grass. There were no windows set into this side of the house, so even at a distance I wouldn't have been able to see if the lights were on. I flicked the torch open on my phone. The ground was uneven here, almost boggy. As I passed the torch in an arc around me, I noticed a flash of colour: the hydrangea bushes. They were here, at the furthest reaches of the estate, at its perimeter.

I shivered suddenly, the muscles in my arms spasming unpleasantly. I had lived here for a full week but the place felt alien somehow, inhospitable. Winter had arrived and changed its atmosphere in less than a week. I had an uncanny sense of déjà vu, though I had never walked so far to this eastern-most edge of Elver's boundary.

The sound of the brook increased with every step. I stood on the bank, shining the light over the water, and was struck by how smooth the water now appeared: nothing like the rolling mass of the weeks previous. It had slowed, not to a trickle – there was more to it than that – but to a gentle babble.

The moss-covered rocks jutted out at odd angles, and I steadied myself on a branch dipping low above. I lowered first one foot, then the other, onto a pair of stones. The water was slow, sedate almost. It coursed through the scattering of rocks leisurely. I wondered dimly if it froze over in the winter or if thin trickles carried their chill downstream toward the river, wherever it joined.

I crossed the bank and heard the slap of wind on plastic – a loose piece of tarpaulin. It cut through the silence with a crack. It wasn't until I had almost drawn level with Elver House that I saw it, and saw the need for it.

The roof was open, gaping all along the left-hand side, its timbers exposed like bones on a scan. I stared up, eyes straining to see more. The lights were all off. I moved quickly, the uneasiness that had settled upon me since that morning now rising to something new, something disquieting and heavy, something I couldn't ignore no matter how hard I'd tried all the way from London. I wondered at my own stupidity, the mad dash across the country on the slowly emptying train, the way there had seemed no other option but to return when I knew, deep down, there were several.

The forecourt was empty, the truck and the builders gone for the day. It looked different somehow, though I couldn't pinpoint what had changed.

As I neared the door I made out a large skip off to the right. Turning sharply I walked toward it, shining the thin torchlight over its contents, then immediately taking a step back. The fountain sat on a heap of rubble, its thin edges chipped and broken. I turned and stared at the space it had once occupied on the forecourt. Beside it, smeared with dust and dirt, lay the circular, porthole-like windows from the top floor. I reached out and touched one of them. Without thinking about it, I wiped my hand – the one that had grasped its splintered wood – on my coat. It felt like sandpaper, bristling and dead, cold to the touch.

The door was covered in tape, criss-crossed to the edges where it met the wall, a spider's web of red and white. I turned the handle, just as I'd done before, and pulled the plastic aside.

I had known, as the train wound its way along the tracks, that the return to Elver House might throw up obstacles. What was I hoping to achieve? To apologise in person? To offer to stay, try and run through whatever we could tomorrow morning? I'd known Catherine might be surprised, shocked even, and certainly disappointed by the error, the glitch that had forced me to return.

Forced? It was quite the opposite. Laura had expressly asked me not to write the book. For all we knew, the interviews would never amount to anything. But once again I found myself at the turning points I'd always asked my clients about: the moments of no-return, the junctures, the fulcrum. I knew, as I switched on the lights and called out for Miss Carey, that this was one of those moments. I was here now, for better or worse.

The hallway was unchanged: the coats hanging lifelessly by the door, the collection of shoes beneath them. The doors to the library, living room and kitchen, once I craned my neck, were all closed.

"Miss Carey?" I called out. I moved forward to the stairs, where my feet caused dancing plumes of dust to rise up and settle once more. "Hello?"

There was no response; I'd not expected one. From above, the thin whistles of the wind coursed along the corridors, moaning, rising and falling. I thought of the soldier in the kitchen, witnessed by the guests visiting the house all those years ago. Of Alfred Carey, the drowned man standing still against the bookshelves in the library.

I climbed the stairs slowly, calling her name, holding onto the rail of the banister. I wiped my brow and was surprised to find it prickling with cold sweat. The hallway above was pitch dark and silent, without even the familiar whoosh of water in the pipes to break it. I poked my head into the study, which remained just as chaotic and frenzied as it had been on the first night, and then moved to the guest bedroom, my bedroom. It was exactly as I'd left it, as was the bathroom, the dirty towels folded neatly into a ball and placed by the washing basket. I reached down; one of them was still damp, just barely.

"Catherine?"

I stared through the banister at the gutted carcass of the top floor, where building lights had been strung up and the night sky peeked through plastic. And then, finally, I went downstairs to the kitchen, poured myself a glass of water and took out my phone. She wasn't here.

I remembered the storm, and the way she had moved drunkenly across the grass, the speed of her strides. Miss Carey was unwell. There was nobody to take care of her. She was prone to wandering, particularly at night. Perhaps it was this, the fear of her endangering herself, walking through the icy brook once more, that prompted me to decide.

My hands shook as I scrolled through the numbers, pressed the call button and waited.

"Hello?" Her voice, friendly but curious, answered on the second ring.

"Lucy, it's Ellen. We met a couple of weeks ago at the pub." There was a pause, then a cry of recognition.

"Ellen! Hello. How are things? How are you? I had my phone in my hand – playing Scrabble." She chuckled.

"I'm ok," I said, looking at the back door, at the small pair of boots festooned with cobwebs. "Sorry to call, Lucy. I'm just at Elver House."

"Ah, you're back!" she said. "Well that *is* good to hear. Steve told me you'd returned to London last week."

"I did," I said, still staring at the shoes. "I did. Unfortunately there was a problem . . . Boring stuff, technical issues. I've come back on a bit of a whim, really, but it was my fault so . . ."

"Well, it's lovely to have you in the village again," she said. "You must come over for supper one evening, you know. I don't expect it's very comfortable over there, not now the cold's set in. And my husband – you know, the one I mentioned to you – he'd be only too happy to run through the history of the house and the area, all that sort of thing—"

"That'd be great, Lucy," I said, cutting her off without meaning to. "Listen, I just wondered . . . I didn't tell Miss Carey I was coming back, and she doesn't appear to be here. I did try to ring ahead." I ran a hand over my eyes, feeling bone-tired all of a sudden. "She didn't answer. I just wondered if you'd any idea where she was?" I didn't sound hopeful.

There was silence. I pulled the phone away from my ear and stared at the screen, wondering if we'd lost connection. "Hello?"

"Ellen?" Lucy's voice had changed entirely. She sounded strange. There was a higher pitch to her tone, a disbelief. She was frightened. "What did you say?"

"Miss Carey's not here. I've looked all over for her." More silence. "I just wanted to check in, see if any of you might know . . . She might have moved out for a while, after all. The roof's half off. It's my fault, of course, I just—"

"Ellen," and now it was Lucy's turn to interrupt. She sounded more than concerned: there was a panic in her voice now, an intensity. "Ellen. What are you talking about?"

I tried to steady myself, but it was almost impossible. Perhaps, even as the moment hurtled toward me, I'd known all along.

"It's ok. I shouldn't have called. I didn't want to worry you." I took a sip of water, dreading the prospect of walking back along the deserted forecourt and through the quiet, overgrown path to the village. I'd go to the pub, to the light, the musky smell of spilt beer, the pumpkins drooping in on themselves, once jagged grins now reduced to lopsided half-smiles. Maybe they'd have rooms available; I'd have to call ahead and ask. It wasn't yet seven: if there was nowhere to sleep in the village I could find a car, I was sure, to take me to the nearest town and find a hotel. Lucy's voice came again, crackling briefly down the line before settling.

"Hello? Can you hear me?"

"Yes, I'm here."

"You said Catherine's not at the house. Is that right?"

"Yes. But I've worked myself up over nothing. It's been a long day. Sorry, Lucy," I stood up, crossed to the sink and refilled my glass, the phone balanced in the raised crook of my elbow. Pretending to feel much calmer than I was in reality seemed to be helping. Lucy said nothing; the line was still. "She must have had an appointment. Or she's out for a walk – she often did that at all sorts of times. I might come into the village, if you're around this evening."

I heard her sigh, then.

"Ellen, I'm going to come over, ok?"

"No, no," I said quickly, swiping my hand across my mouth. My lips were dry, my throat tight. "I'll walk over to the village, honestly."

"I'm coming. I'll be there in 10 minutes, maybe less. Alright?"

There was something in her voice, something low and urgent. She was holding back.

I could have ended the call then, rude though it would have been. I could have left at once. To this day, I wish I had.

"There's no need, seriously," I said. I wish I'd never phoned her. Her voice was quivering slightly. "I should have confirmed with Catherine first. I'll walk over to the pub, shall I? If she's back tomorrow maybe I could—"

"Ellen," she said. And then, more firmly, "Ellen. Listen to me."

She took a deep breath. Her voice was high, scared. "Catherine Carey . . . she's dead, Ellen. She died a month ago. She's dead."

CHAPTER TWENTY-FIVE

THREE THINGS HAPPENED at once. The door to the pantry swung wide, just once, and with enough force to bounce it back against the far wall. Outside, in the hallway and as though on cue, the grandfather clock chimed the hour. And I swayed on the spot, the glass insubstantial, slippery almost, between my fingers. I gripped it tightly.

"What did you say?" It felt like someone else was talking, like some foreign entity was forming the words, pushing them in a hiss of breath through my clenched teeth.

I heard voices in the background, low mutterings of conversation. *I'm coming with you*, said a man's voice.

"Ellen?" said Lucy. "We're on our way. My husband and me. It won't take us long. But I'd like you to do something for me. Ok?"

I said nothing, staring down at the taps, their tiny, engraved letters in the middle of the cross-head handles. Hot and Cold. Beside the sink a mug rested on the draining board; the mug I'd had in my bedroom the entire time I'd been at the house. I'd washed it up on the last morning, before I left for London.

"Ellen?"

"I'm here," I said. "I'm here." I held the phone away from my ear slightly, gazing around the room. I saw the shelves in the pantry, the multicoloured pickles suspended in their jars. The door had slammed open yet there was no draught in the room, no rush of air to account for it. I was aware of the cold and the sweat on my brow, but noticed with a sort of detached, vague interest that I felt nothing.

"Can you stay in the house for me?" Lucy's voice sounded far away, like the words were being transmitted through the kind of string telephones we'd made as children, travelling through upturned cups to reach us. "Just give us a few minutes. Where are you now?"

"At Elver House—" I said, mechanically.

Lucy interrupted. "Where exactly, Ellen?"

"I'm in the kitchen."

"Ok. That's good. And the front door was open?"

"It was . . ." I said. The words took a frightening amount of effort. "There was tape over it. The builders, I suppose. I just walked in."

"And you didn't lock the door behind you?"

Why would I? The only person who could do so – the only person with the key – was Miss Carey.

"No," I said quietly. "It's closed but unlocked."

"Good." I heard the sound of footsteps, of boots over ground. "I'm just walking to the car now. Jim'll put his foot down. Just stay in the kitchen for me, like I said, and we'll be there in a moment."

I ended the call, standing with my back to the sink. I leaned against it and tried to breathe, tried to swallow. I closed my eyes; they were suddenly sore, aching. Then, as though electrocuted, I opened them quickly and scanned the room. I stared into the pantry, moved forward and gripped the chair tucked under the table. The chair where Miss Carey had sat, where we'd spoken, where I'd cooked and eaten and listened. I breathed deeply again.

There were so many moments I could have walked away but this – *this* – was the most crucial. If I could have left the house at that point, walked through the rusting gates and turned down the track, I would have done it. I could have dismissed what Lucy said, told myself I'd heard incorrectly. I could have caught the train back to London and tried to forget about it, laughing it off with Laura when we spoke. I'd tell her about the return to Elver House, the bizarre ramblings of the local villagers with their jokes and jests, their eagerness to frighten the city intruder.

Without thinking about it, I called her name again. There was no response, no answering shout. But there was something here, something dark and brooding, like a twist of perfume lingering in the air long after the wearer has left the room. I rubbed my arms through the jacket, and fastened the buttons along its front. I pulled the chair out from under the table; its legs squealed in protest as I sat down heavily.

There was a soft tap at the back door and my head jerked up, snapped to attention, but it was only the first slow patters of rain beginning to fall. I made a tent of my fingers and rested my head on them, looking out of the window. I thought of the hours I'd spent in this house: the mundane work emails I'd sent, the cups of tea, the long stretches of silence. I thought of the bare cupboards in the kitchen, the mouldy items in the fridge. The way the only food in the house was stocked in the pantry, pickled and jarred and non-perishable.

She died.

I'd left Elver less than a week before.

A month ago.

Well, it wasn't possible. I stared at the raindrops coursing down the pane, now, and nodded slowly to myself. It wasn't possible. Miss Carey was elderly, of course. And she was not here. But I must have misheard. Or Lucy had the facts wrong. Or I was mad.

I picked at this last option, allowed my mind to snag on it. I chewed it over while closing my eyes once more, my fingernails digging into the underside of my chin. I turned the phone over and checked the date. It was November 9th, as I'd known it would be. It had been printed on the train ticket, collected from the station not six hours ago. I'd arrived on the twenty-ninth and left on Bonfire Night. Those were the facts. Catherine had circled the date in the calendar, the one on the fridge. *Writer arriving today,* she'd scribbled.

I stood, unable to be still, and pushed back the chair. I walked towards the fridge, lifting the calendar from its hook on the wall. Its page was still open to October and I flicked back to the month before. A neat, curling cursive gave evidence of a life: medications to be taken on certain days, reminders to phone people whose names, of course, I did not recognise.

The notes were made in different coloured pens, but the handwriting was the same in all the neat squares counting down the days until the end of the month. I turned back to October: there was a doctor's appointment scheduled for the 15th, a delivery earmarked for the 23rd.

And there, circled in red, was the note Miss Carey had shown me. The date of my arrival, with "today" underlined. The note she'd held out for me to see on my very first night at the house.

The night when I'd arrived to find it as it was now. Dark, empty, silent.

The entries for October continued much as they had during the month prior. There was a reminder on the 2nd to deadhead the roses, another on the 4th to call the Post Office. On the seventh day of October, there was a scribbled note about collecting a birthday card. And then, from the 11th day of the month, there was nothing. I flicked ahead to the next page, this month's, which was entirely empty.

What had she said, that first night? I peered closely at the dates, wondering. She'd been in touch with the agency some time before I arrived – had spoken to Laura, and some member of the sales team? At least two people had definitely spoken with her, I knew that. She'd have had to provide her details, her address. She must have emailed them afterwards too: in fact I remembered Laura copying me in, responding to Miss Carey's query about the start date.

I pulled out my phone and tapped a few key words into the search bar of my in-box – just two messages popped up, and I tapped on Laura's most recent. There it was, in black and white – the tentative, almost apologetic request from a member of the sales team. They'd spoken with Catherine Carey on the phone, and she wanted the writer to interview her in person. Laura's response was warm and reassuring, as always. She had telephoned to confirm, and they'd agreed on the start date. I looked up at the time-stamp: 10th September. Seven weeks before I'd arrived.

CHAPTER TWENTY-SIX

F OR THE NEXT quarter hour I sat, staring into the pantry, listening to the rain, barely moving. I did not want to see Lucy or Jim, but something fixed me to the spot, a paralysis I noticed only dimly.

Lucy was confused: it was the only explanation. Either that, or she'd muddled the dates. Or I'd misheard. Or, and this was the worst possibility – the one I cringed away from even as it came to mind – Miss Carey had indeed died, but over the weekend. I knew she was unwell. I knew the speed of her deterioration had increased.

My hands trembled against the phone, its screen blank. I wondered how I must look, how wired and strange. No one had asked me to come and yet here I was, unannounced in this old house when I could have left it, ignored it, turned my back on it all.

Maybe I was never meant to return. I wasn't supposed to be here. Perhaps there was something, at Elver House, or in the village as a whole, something dark and threatening, something I wasn't supposed to see. It felt ugly, sticky as flypaper and just as impossible to escape from.

I should leave. I could flee, without knowing anything more. I could have put it all out of mind and carried on with my life, my lovely life, the one that was all mine and which had been crafted like a house of cards, towering and higher every day, but fragile. And in that moment, moving so quickly I jarred the table across the floor, I decided to do just that.

The tape flapped in the wind as I pulled open the front door.

I grimaced as sheets of water infiltrated the neck of the jacket and began to run down my back. I'd return to the side track, where the driver had stopped and turned around. I'd avoid the forest. At this point, there was nothing for it but to put as much distance between myself and the house as possible. Maybe, when I was safely speeding back to London, I could phone Laura. She'd know what to do; she'd handle it.

I crossed the forecourt and set off through the overgrown grass, following the sound of the brook. Its tinkling was weak, but the sound was clear as the note of a bell through the rain, and soon enough I was approaching the perimeter wall, far off to the east, where the side gate was tucked away like a secret.

I knew that Lucy and Jim were coming. It had been at least 20 minutes since we'd ended the call. I didn't want to see them – didn't want any part of whatever was going on here, at Elver House or in the village. I needed to hurry.

The rain intensified and the wind howled like it had suffered a great and lasting injustice; I pressed ahead, flicking the torch on the phone from left to right and bowing my head, keeping an eye out for loose rocks, potholes in the meadow sprawling out before me. I squinted, trying to spot exactly where the small gate had been. I was definitely on the right side.

A flash of pink caught the beam: an unexpected and extraordinary colour in the bleak, murky landscape. I raised a hand to shield my eyes and squinted once more. I walked towards them. The gate had been here, just here.

The hydrangeas were waist-high, their stems a vivid, vibrant green. The deep, rich pink of the flowers emerged from within each basket of leaves, which were slowly turning red, fading and preparing for the winter's hibernation. A few petals had fallen under the weight of the rain like a scattering of confetti in the sodden soil. But they stood alone: the only flowers on the whole estate that I'd seen, and far from the main house. I edged closer, feeling the downward slope of the earth beneath my feet and realising, from the mud and pebbles sliding down around me as I walked, that it had recently been disturbed.

I reached out and touched one of the leaves, stroking its surface. I raised my torch and saw, just a few feet ahead, the unassuming wooden gate I'd entered through earlier. But the beam had caught something else, something shiny in the bed of flowers. I swung it back like a lighthouse.

There, nestled among the wet stalks and the fallen flowers, was a wooden board. Its solid oak was fresh and unblemished, the words upon it newly engraved. I crouched down, wiping water from my eyes.

Dedicated to the memory of Catherine Carey,
custodian of Elver House. 1936–2023.

CHAPTER TWENTY-SEVEN

I HEARD THE gentle rumble of a motor, then the engine cutting out. Car doors slammed and quick footsteps crunched across the gravel of the forecourt. Voices carried on the wind from the front of the house to where I sat by the flowerbed. They had gone inside. Minutes passed.

"Ellen?" It was Lucy. "Ellen, where are you?" The sound was faint, but growing louder.

I stood up, rubbed my eyes. I noticed with a sort of detached interest that I'd been sick. My coat was hanging from my arms and dripping steadily from each sleeve. While I'd been here, sitting hunched by the flowerbed, fog had crept up like a burglar and the rain had thinned to a spittle. In the distance, I heard Lucy continuing to shout. A man appeared at her side as I walked toward them. In his hands he held a large torch, and was scanning the grounds in a wide arc.

"I'm here," I called, in a voice that sounded nothing like my own – more a croak than a word. They turned to face me as I emerged from the shadows of the forecourt.

I saw them both framed on the threshold: Lucy's thick coat was unbuttoned, her scarf trailing along the ground behind her. The man with the torch stood just behind her, holding an umbrella in his other hand. His round glasses were streaked with rain.

"Ellen," said Lucy, and rushed forward, her arms outstretched. "Where have you been? We went inside but we couldn't . . ." She stared at me. "Come on, love, let's get inside."

We crossed into the flagstoned hallway once more: Jim was

gazing all around him, eyes scanning left to right and up to the stairs above. Like Lucy, he had a jovial, homely air about him – as they closed the door behind them I noticed the threadbare patches on the elbows of his jumper, the way he pulled a handkerchief from the pocket of his trousers to wipe the lenses of his spectacles.

"Christ, what a night," said Lucy, pulling off her muddy boots. "Are you alright? You're soaked." I said nothing, merely nodded.

"Do you want to come and sit down with us?"

I nodded, shivering.

"This is Jim," and she nodded to her husband standing behind her, who raised a hand shyly. They were both gaping at me but trying to hide it.

"We came as fast as we could," said Lucy. She eyed me nervously. "When did you get here?"

"I came in on the afternoon train," I said haltingly, struggling to appear composed. My hands shook and I shoved them deep into the pockets of the coat. "Lucy . . . what's going on?"

Lucy glanced over her shoulder at her husband, who nodded slightly and gestured toward the library. "Shall we go and sit down, Ellen?" His voice was soft, barely audible in the echoing hallway. We seemed to have brought some of the mist in with us – in the dim lamplight wisps of pale air danced like shadows.

"I think I ought to go," I said. Still my voice sounded alien to me, like I hadn't spoken in months or years. Each word was an effort. My throat felt swollen from the retching, and the coat was steadily dripping onto the floor.

Lucy looked down, then back at Jim. "I really think we ought to—"

"What happened?" I turned to face her, then looked to Jim. My voice rose, gathering strength. "I saw the wooden marker. Her dates . . . When did she . . . when—"

"Come on, love," said Jim, and he crossed the hall to the library, opened the door and switched on the lights. "Let's go in here."

Lucy gestured to my coat and I peeled it off and dropped it to the floor. And then I followed, reflexively, placing one foot in front of the other until I reached the sofa. Lucy sat beside me. Jim took the chair behind the desk, where I'd spent so many hours tapping away, recording, talking to Miss Carey.

Jim cleaned his glasses once more. He looked up at the shelves and then at his wife, who placed a hand on my knee.

"Ellen, we came as fast as we could," he said eventually. "Your call to Lucy was unexpected, to say the least. Could you tell me a bit about what happened?"

"When I arrived? This evening?" I stared at him. "I just got off the train and came straight here." I swallowed. "There was a problem with the interviews I'd done with Miss Carey. I wanted to explain to her what had happened. I tried to phone ahead but she didn't answer."

"What was the problem?" Lucy asked.

"I couldn't hear her on the tapes."

"Which tapes were these?" said Jim, leaning forward.

I explained about the project, about the agency, about the interviews.

There was silence.

"I knew you were staying here, of course," said Lucy slowly. "You said as much at the pub. But I didn't want to pry. You said you were working on a legacy project. About the house, about the village."

"Well, that would have come into it," I said roughly. "But we're not supposed to advertise the fact we're working with clients to write their memoirs." I saw a brief flash of comprehension on Lucy's face. "People want anyone reading their book to believe they've written it themselves. I'm a ghost-writer."

Jim fixed me with a long stare, then placed both hands on the table and lowered his head.

"And she contacted you? Catherine?"

"Not me personally. She contacted the company I work for."

The rain continued, as it always seemed to. In any other situation the sound might have been soothing.

"And that was some time ago?" said Lucy.

"I suppose a couple of months. I'm not sure exactly. But she'd provided all the background we needed, and my editor arranged for me to arrive on a certain date. Miss Carey had agreed to that date."

Jim glanced at Lucy, who dropped her eyes to the floor. "The thing is, Ellen," she began, "as I said on the phone . . . the dates don't match up."

I waited. Jim cleared his throat. "Lucy tells me you came to the house today as you'd wanted to see Miss Carey. To see her again, I mean."

"Yes, that's right."

"And by that," he frowned and placed his hands together on the desk, "I take it to mean that you have, in fact, met her."

"Yes. I lived here for a week."

"And you lived alongside Catherine Carey for all that time?"

"Yes. She wasn't here when I arrived, but she came back. And then I stayed here while we completed the interviews."

Lucy gave Jim a meaningful look and he nodded back at her, almost imperceptibly.

"Could you describe her, Ellen?"

"Why?"

He said nothing. "She was elderly," I said. "Late eighties. She was slim, skinny almost. Blue eyes, silver hair. Beautiful clothes, carefully chosen. Her nails were painted red on the first night I arrived." I'd no idea why I said this. "She was very apologetic when I turned up. She'd forgotten. But we got along well after that. She was kind. A bit absent-minded, but I put that down to age . . ."

Lucy sighed and leaned back against the sofa cushions. Her face was ashen now. She looked like she too might be sick.

Jim considered me a moment and then looked out of the library doors, to the garden. "I take it you went to the plot," he said.

"Which plot?"

"You mentioned the grave marker. She'd been very clear about it in her will, we heard. When the time came, she wanted to remain at Elver. Once the ground's settled we'll have it replaced for a proper stone. A plaque."

He turned back to us and gestured to the books on the shelves. "Most of her family were buried on the grounds, too," he said. "There's a family history somewhere here. Before the chapel was knocked down they'd have been interred in the crypt beneath it. But when it was demolished that was, of course, no longer possible." He sighed. "Her mother's there too, in the same plot. That was Catherine's wish. We honoured it. It was the least we could do."

CHAPTER TWENTY-EIGHT

I'D NO CONCEPT of time, no knowledge of how late it was. There was a sudden rush of water from the pipes above, but it sounded distant, as though the natural volume of the world around us had been tuned to just above a whisper. Lucy jumped slightly, then blushed.

Jim was still speaking. "When you were talking with Miss Carey," he said cautiously, "What did she tell you?"

I thought about this even while my teeth were starting to chatter. "She told me about her childhood. About her parents. About life here caring for her mother after her father's death." Lucy glanced quickly at Jim again, though his eyes were fixed on me.

"Those things are certainly all true," he said. "As far as I could tell, anyway."

"What do you mean?"

"Well, Ellen," he said, and he was clearly choosing his words carefully. He looked deeply troubled. "I'm trying to ascertain whether or not we need to call the police, to be quite honest with you. But what would we tell them?" He looked out of the window again. "That a woman pretending to be Catherine Carey lived here, for the entire time you were at the house? That whoever was speaking to you was an imposter? Why would anyone do that?"

Lucy shook her head. "There'd be no point," she said softly.

"Why not?" I asked. I was beginning to feel the cold now in a way I hadn't outside. It seemed to have seeped right down into my bones.

"Because there'd be nothing to gain from it," she said. "Catherine hadn't any family, or none that the solicitors could find. Elver House was classed as *bona vacantia* – an ownerless property, and as such it passed to the Crown."

"Who sold it," said Jim shortly. "It was wrapped up in under a week. Expedited. Must have cost a fortune to rush the sale through."

"Who bought it?" I asked.

"Some property tycoon. I've never met him. I doubt he's even been to the village itself. But he bought it." Jim gestured through the window to the front of the house. "Didn't take him long to start gutting it," he said through gritted teeth.

"But . . ." I looked down at the puddle forming around the bottoms of my soaked jeans. "But I spoke to the man managing the renovations." I pulled my phone out and scrolled through to my recent voicemails. I clicked, switched to speaker-phone. *This is Patrick Walsh returning your call.*

"That must be him, then," said Jim. "Bloke who bought it. Patrick Walsh."

"I spoke to him. Miss Carey had no idea why the builders had arrived." I frowned, trying to remember, and then – "He said . . . he said she understood."

"From what I've heard, Miss Carey had many offers for the house during her lifetime. Especially after she and her mother opened it up to the general public. He offered for it and, from what the police said, she accepted. Nothing official, of course, but a handshake of sorts took place. This would have been a few months before her death. He probably dressed it up as a renovation at the time, a facelift, rather than a total overhaul. She'd have hated what he's doing here."

Lucy nodded. "Absolutely hated it." She sighed again, stroking the arm of the sofa absently.

I remembered suddenly. "Hold on," I said, flicking to the recordings app on my phone. I found the shortest one, just a few minutes long, and clicked. The sound of a phone ringing filled the silent room.

Patrick speaking.
  Hi, Patrick. This is Ellen – thanks for phoning me back.
  Ah, Ellen. Not a problem. How can I help?

I heard my own voice trotting out the facts, enquiring about the builders, asking who'd hired them.

Well, I did.
  I manage the estate.

I paused the recording. "There, see? He just said it. He was the estate manager."

"He was managing Miss Carey's estate, Ellen," said Jim slowly. "Property. Possessions. Not the Elver estate."

Ignoring him I ploughed ahead, pressing play again.

I'm only here another day or so . . . Don't worry about it. Anyway, I'm glad we've spoken – I know Miss Carey will be relieved to hear it. I get the sense her memory's not quite what it was . . . Hello?
  You're breaking up. I didn't catch that.

I sat staring at the phone without moving. I could feel the blood coursing in its rhythmic circuits round my body. There was a slight ringing in my ears.

I was just saying Miss Carey will be relieved. And I'm sure it'll come back to her. She hadn't mentioned an estate manager so I thought it'd be wise to speak to you – on her behalf, I mean . . . Mr Walsh?
  . . . Could . . . repeat . . . not sure I understood.

His voice cut in and out. Moments afterwards, the three short beeps confirmed the connection had been lost. "The line broke up,"

I said slowly. Jim and Lucy said nothing. "He didn't hear that last bit, did he."

It wasn't a question. There was silence once more.

"Did the builders come into the house? While you were working?" Lucy turned toward me. She tucked a loose strand of damp hair behind her ear. It was like she was trying to coax information from a child who'd been caught stealing sweets, but wasn't prepared to admit it.

"Not while I was here," I said. I felt sick again. "But they'd been inside before. If Patrick Walsh was planning on gutting the place it makes sense. The study upstairs was trashed when I arrived. The drawing room across the hall looked like somebody had been inside, too." I thought of the boot-print, old and faded on the sofa. "But she saw them. We were chatting when they arrived."

"Did she speak to them?" Lucy asked.

I closed my eyes. All I wanted was to lie down, right here, and sleep. I thought back to the moment the men had arrived. We had stood in the doorway, Miss Carey and I, until she had turned and made her way back inside the house. And later, in the drawing room, we'd been startled by a tap on the window. I pictured the men's faces clearly. They had asked about the roof, if it was ok to start. Had Miss Carey spoken to them then? I didn't think so. And yet the image of the men outside the window niggled at me. I remembered smiling, mouthing good mornings and hellos and nodding. They'd both been looking at me.

"Ellen? Did she speak to them? Or your editor – did she have a conversation with Miss Carey at all?" said Lucy. I stared at her.

"She did. When Catherine first got in touch."

"After you'd arrived at the house, I mean. Didn't you tell Steve you'd stayed on longer than expected?"

I thought back to that first night. To Miss Carey in the guest bedroom, the way I'd phoned Laura, the speaker-phone. Miss Carey had spoken to me. Laura claimed she'd never heard her. *Ellen, what's going on?* And had I not asked Laura about exactly this, when the audio recordings picked up only my own voice, and no one else's? *She must have been quiet as anything,* she'd said. *I didn't hear a peep. Not once.*

Slowly, a fresh image replaced the memory of Laura's voice. A set of small boot-prints following my own through the wooded path of the estate, stopping abruptly at its boundary. I had continued on into the village, but whoever had been there too had remained behind.

"Ellen," said Jim, getting to his feet. He approached the sofa and crouched down before us. "I'm going to take a look around the house. Is that alright?"

When I said nothing, he nodded slowly. "Would you stay here? With Lucy?"

They thought I was mad. The knowledge arrived with a grim, final certainty. That's why they'd come – why they'd driven through the driving rain and the creeping fog to this remote, isolated place. They were worried about me. What I was saying frightened them. I looked from one to the other and saw it etched on their faces: the unease, the dread.

"It did happen," I said jerkily. "She was there. She was *here*."

CHAPTER TWENTY-NINE

JIM LEFT THE room. We heard him ascending the stairs slowly, a rhythmic thud which grew fainter until there was silence once more.

"I believe you," said Lucy, in a small voice.

I turned to her sharply.

"I believe you," she said again. "But I'm not sure Jim ever will. He didn't . . . well, he never saw what I saw."

I leaned toward her, holding my breath. Her eyes were wide and staring, fixed on a point over my shoulder. The seconds ticked by; I dared not move, convinced any distraction would shake her from the reverie.

"I was here in the house a lot as a child," said Lucy. "I came with my parents. My mother worked here for a time, once the majority of the staff had left. It happened in dribs and drabs."

I remembered Miss Carey saying the same thing.

"But there was always a summer fete, that sort of thing. The other village children loved it. For me, it was just another day: I was so used to the place, to the house and the grounds. I was always out exploring, while my mother worked. I must have been about eight when I first saw it."

She exhaled loudly, her eyes closing briefly. "I was down by the brook, watching the little eels. I had a net, and I was trying to catch them but they were too fast. At some point I must have got bored of it, because I sat back on the bank and started picking up pebbles, tossing them into the stream." She glanced at me and I nodded, once. "I must have thrown one further than I'd expected to, and I watched as it flew through the air, all the way to the other side of the bank, the opposite side. And there she was."

I waited, but she said nothing more. "Who?"

"I've no idea," said Lucy shakily. "I didn't recognise her. She was a bit older than me. A teenager, I imagine. She was watching me."

"A local girl? One of the staff?"

"No," said Lucy. "No. It wasn't like that. She was dressed in the strangest way. A long sort of dress, beautiful, embroidered across the front, with a lace collar. She was carrying a parasol, though it was the middle of winter. I'd never seen anything like it."

"What did she do?"

"Nothing at all. And neither did I. We just sat on opposite sides of the brook, looking at one another. I didn't know what to do. I felt like someone had pinned me exactly where I sat, like I couldn't move. Her hair was long, but it had been drawn into a coil at the base of her neck. There were curls either side, strands all twisted in on themselves. She had these great chestnut eyes, deep-set."

"Were you frightened?"

Lucy fixed me with a long stare. "I wasn't scared, exactly. It's hard to describe. I just . . . I just sort of *knew*. Years later, once I'd met Jim, we got talking about the house, about the Bassingtons and the Careys. He wasn't from the village originally, but he became very interested in its history when he moved here to live with me. Once we were married, I mean. He asked Mrs Carey – that's Catherine's mother – if he might borrow some of the family archives. When they opened up the house, he wrote all the pamphlets. And one morning I came downstairs and found a bundle of plates on the kitchen table. Copper plates, original photographs, before pictures were printed onto paper. Family portraits, that sort of thing." She inhaled slowly.

"I hadn't thought about the woman on the bank of the brook for years. Put it out of my mind, as children do. And then, as I was flicking through the pictures, there she was. It was a daguerreotype, a mirror-like thing, about the size of your hand. I recognised her immediately. The dress, the hairstyle, the face, the eyes . . ."

I heard a shuffle upstairs, a scrape of furniture on wood. "Jim came downstairs and saw me gaping at the thing. I asked him who the girl in the picture was, and he explained. She was the sister of Mrs Carey's grandmother. Lydia. She was 15 when she died of consumption." She paused and looked up at me once more. "I never told Jim."

Upstairs the shuffling continued, growing louder. I wondered, dimly, what Jim was searching for.

"Lucy," I said, "what happened to Miss Carey?"

Lucy said nothing for a moment, and then stood and walked to the window. She gazed out at the grounds, obscured by the fog. Then she turned back to me and spread her hands. "As far as we know, Patrick Walsh and his associates have done a very good job at hushing the whole thing up." Her face contorted suddenly into a grimace.

"Catherine had no idea about how to open the house up safely to the public. Neither she nor her mother ever saw the need for security. They lived in a sort of blissful ignorance." She exhaled. I could see the fury in her eyes, the grim set of her mouth.

"There were several break-ins over the years. Nothing terribly precious was taken, but it rattled the women, as you'd expect. Just opportunists. People who'd heard about the location, the size of the place, and thought they'd try their luck. Catherine only opened the house because her mother's care was becoming so expensive: the contraptions and devices she needed, the lack of any help."

The grandfather clock chimed once more. We both ignored it. "About six weeks ago there was another break-in. Miss Carey was here when it happened. There was no sign of a struggle. They didn't hurt her. That was something, I suppose."

I imagined the dark, silent house punctuated by soft footsteps. The creak of a board, the practised prowl of intruders, bent on taking what they could sell on and then fleeing through the forest.

I thought of the study, the upturned chair, the papers strewn across the floor. "The gardener arrived the following morning.

Catherine seemed quiet, he said, but otherwise well. I don't believe she heard the men, or disturbed them at all that night. But she was shocked. No doubt about it. When he arrived again, two days later, he found her at the bottom of the stairs. She'd fallen. I've no doubt the distress of the burglary caused her fall."

I tried to breathe and found I couldn't. I leaned forward, my head heavy. I opened my mouth, gasping like a fish plucked from the sea. Everything felt constricted, tight. Lucy seemed not to notice.

"For all we know they were just a pair of kids. I highly doubt they wanted to cause her any physical harm. She was taken to hospital, but there was very little they could do. She'd broken her leg and her collarbone, and there was some head trauma too. The shock was too much . . . She died in the intensive-care unit two days later. October 10th."

I thought of the calendar in the kitchen, its entries stopping so abruptly in the middle of the month.

"The fact that the thieves weren't disturbed, that we know of, made it harder to link the two incidents. They haven't caught whoever was responsible. They probably never will."

Lucy looked outside again. "Though the case remains open, it didn't receive much publicity. Ideal for someone like Patrick Walsh, someone who wouldn't want the circumstances of Miss Carey's death splashed across the media. Jim told me Walsh had a word with the village constable: asked him to make sure it didn't get out. There was a notice in the regional press that the house was already sold. I don't know what sort of contacts the man has, but the whole thing has been dealt with quietly. There wasn't even a death notice."

The seconds ticked by. Lucy seemed on the verge of something, like she was trying to hold her tongue.

"It just seems such a waste," she said finally, and looked directly at me. "A life spent trapped here because her selfish mother raised her to think there was nothing else. Uncaring, unfeeling. Somehow bringing up this child who silently agreed to stay with her when she could have gone anywhere, done anything. It wasn't Alice's fault she became so ill," she said haltingly. "But that only trapped Catherine further. She could never have left even if she'd wanted to."

Mrs Carey hadn't wanted her daughter: I remembered Catherine's sad, accepting descriptions, the way she herself had longed to start a family but felt unable to do so, unable to leave her mother behind. I thought of you, and the looks you'd quailed at in the café, the judgement despite the fact that, on paper, you were doing everything right. The questions put to me, the wheedling, insistent implication that if what you were doing was wrong, my refusal to do it was so much worse. No one was winning: not Mrs Carey nor Catherine, neither me nor you.

"There was a pair of gloves in my room. On the first morning," I whispered suddenly, remembering. "They were tossed into the fireplace. Plastic gloves."

Lucy recoiled. "In the fireplace?"

"Yes. I asked Miss Carey about them. She didn't seem . . ." I trailed off, remembering her reaction: the way she had turned away, refusing to hear any more, clutching at her throat. The seconds ticked by as the awful image hovered before us both.

"Lucy . . ." I began, then paused, struggling to find the words. "I don't – well, I don't understand. Why didn't you *tell* me? When we met in the pub. No one said anything."

She stared at me blankly. "We assumed you knew. You told us you were doing a legacy project – about the house, about Catherine."

I remembered the barman's discomfort as we spoke that day, the way everyone had shifted when I explained what I was doing there. They'd seemed wary of Elver, but there were any number of reasons for that. And I'd never said I was living alongside Miss Carey, had I?

I thought of Steve in the cab on that first night, the questions he'd asked. *You're a solicitor, I take it.* He'd assumed I was here to oversee the legal side of things. *Tie up loose ends.*

"People don't like to confront death," said Lucy. "We all just sweep it under the carpet. Pretend it didn't happen. I suppose if we'd been more open, acknowledged it, we wouldn't be sitting here now."

"You said you'd not been to Elver for years . . ." I said faintly.

Lucy nodded. "Not inside the house. I'd been on the grounds just weeks before. There was a small ceremony a week or so after she died: Jim and I were there, of course, plus a handful of other villagers. Walsh allowed that at least. She was buried here on the grounds. We planted the hydrangea bushes."

"She loved them," Jim's voice was hoarse. He stood framed in the doorway to the library. I hadn't heard him come down the stairs. He cleaned his glasses once more on the sleeve of his jumper. "There wasn't much more we could do, but we were glad to have done that for her."

"It was the strangest thing, though," said Lucy. "We'd bought blue ones. The same as she'd had just there." She gestured to the library doors. "But they seem to have changed colour."

Jim's face crumpled. He came and sat down beside me on the sofa, swiping at his eyes. Lucy came and stood behind him, her hands reaching out to find his.

"It's still just as it was," he said. "The study. They haven't even had the decency to tidy it up." He covered his face with his palm, then breathed deeply. "It's sorted now."

I leaned back, beside them both, and we sat in silence for what felt like a very long time.

CHAPTER THIRTY

W E SWEPT THE hallway of the mud brought in on our
boots. We wiped down the surfaces of tables, desks, the
kitchen counters. We hung the calendar back where I'd found it,
beside the fridge. We rearranged the sofa cushions, closed the doors
on the ground and first floor, and switched off the lights. Lucy
and Jim shot concerned looks at one another as we worked: none
of us speaking. I moved on autopilot, barely noticing what I was
doing.

The rain had stopped, for now, but the fog continued to hover
just above the ground. On the threshold we did our best to reattach
the builders' tape across the front door. The clouds had parted ever
so slightly, and a thin slice of moon peeked out from behind.

"Will you come back with us, to the village?" said Lucy, in a
small voice. "I don't think you'll find anywhere else tonight. You'd
be very welcome, Ellen."

I nodded once, tried to smile. "Thank you. I'll get the first train
back tomorrow."

"I can drop you off," said Jim gruffly. He seemed to have relied
upon Lucy to work some magic while he roamed about upstairs.
Whatever I thought I'd experienced, whatever I'd thought I'd seen
and heard at Elver House, he wanted nothing to do with it.

Lucy took my hand and we crossed the forecourt to where their
car was waiting, its tyre marks visibly haphazard across the gravel
from the speed with which they'd jerked to a stop.

"Just a moment," I said. Jim looked uneasily at his wife, but she
shook her head at him ever so slightly.

"We'll wait in the car," she said.

I set off across the grass, my head down, my hands deep in the pockets of the soaked jacket. It felt as though I hadn't slept for days. A headache was building with determined pressure at my temples. I crossed to the plot, the patch of hydrangeas, and crouched down once more. The flowers were bright and luscious, but in a few short weeks they would brown and wither.

For once, for now, Miss Carey had got her wish; the petals had changed colour as the soil she'd lain within became alkaline. I crouched down, touching the freshly hewn wood, and traced my fingers over the letters.

Hers was a story worth telling: a strange one, a sad one. A story nobody would have known about otherwise. I looked up, just once more, at the silhouette of Elver House, at the carcass of it, knowing it would soon be changed beyond all recognition, morphed into something she herself would never have recognised.

I squinted through the strands of fog to the space underneath the gutted roof and the missing porthole windows. I breathed in deeply, watching, as the burble of the brook continued on its course. I thought of the elvers, biding their time and waiting for the exact, predestined moment when the sea would call them home again.

On the second storey, where the rooms were still intact and where the study was now ordered, organised, set right, a pale disc reflected back in the moonlight. An orb, disembodied, shining. A slight movement, the quick rising of a thin arm, and then it was gone.

EPILOGUE

A CROSS THE SOUND from the Scottish Highlands, the isle of Raasay descends along the west coast of Skye like a pair of laddered tights, all coves and inlets. To the south Cuillins and munros stretch off into the distance.

Years later, long after I'd returned to London, we'd managed to find a weekend that worked. The baby was grown now, almost 10 years old.

You'd never asked about Elver House or the account I wrote of my time there: I doubt you'd read it; I hoped you hadn't.

In the immediate aftermath of the event, setting it all down was the only thing that helped. I was plagued by images of Catherine Carey on the stairs, her hand at her throat, her last strangled gasp. More than anything else, however, I found myself sleepless at the thought of her wandering the corridors alone: a spectre growing fainter by the year, confused and upset by what was happening around her. I wondered if she had known all along, or if she had required somebody to feel her death, to mourn it, in order for her to leave the house at last.

I thought of this with less regularity now, with less painful sadness. And Catherine's death had prompted something else, something I had never expected when I took on Laura's assignment all those years ago. It felt close to acceptance, a kind of gratitude for what I had and how closely I sought to protect it. I couldn't remain stuck in the past with you, either. We had to find a way to move forward, to take joy in a fresh reality. Change was healthy.

We'd been crossing a ridge, following the compass diligently, barely speaking with the effort of ascending. Our knees creaked more audibly now, our breathing was laboured. The flecks of grey in your hair had become more pronounced, and it gave you a wise, witchy air. I had new glasses on that day: a higher prescription, a thicker lens.

You'd stopped.

"This can't be right," you said, frowning. You spun in a circle, watching the needle swing from north to south. All around us a thin mizzling mist had begun to creep up, swirling past our ankles, obscuring our boots and the treacherous dips and plunging drops scattered across the ground.

I came to stand beside you. We took our bearings again.

"We're not meant to be descending yet," you said. "Can't you feel it?"

I tested the contours of the earth beneath my left boot, felt it sloping down. "We were supposed to continue along here for at least a mile before heading down."

We stared at the compass, at the wildly swinging needle, our heads together.

And then I remembered. There were sections on Skye where iron, once heavily mined across the area, confused the compass into false readings. There was magnetism in the air and we couldn't see or feel it, but it had thrown us off course.

"The fog won't last too long," you said briskly. "It never does. But I don't think we can keep going until it clears."

It wasn't cold, thankfully, and we sat down at the top of the ridge, sharing snacks and relacing boots, pulling our hats on as it started to rain. You shuffled closer beside me and spread the map open across our knees, running a gloved finger over the route. "D'you remember that time we got lost on a school trip?"

I shook my head; I'd no memory of it.

"We were only about twelve," you said. "We went on that long walk and missed the turning. It was a good hour before they found us, thinking we were about to catch up with the rest of the group any moment. Can you imagine . . . I'd be furious if that happened to my kid."

We sat in silence, listening to the rain.

"How's she getting on at school?" I asked.

"Ah, you know what she's like. What they're like, I should say, at that age. Cliquey little groups and secret passwords and all that. Friends one moment and mortal enemies the next." You smiled fondly. "I keep telling her she should enjoy it while it lasts. In a few years they'll all become obsessed with dates, boys or girls and drama and all the rest of it."

"Yeah, but they'll come back round to each other eventually," I said delicately. "They'll do all the partying and living together and sharing everything."

You gave me an appraising look, nodding. "Well, probably. But then they'll choose a person and live with them instead and pull up the drawbridge. For a while at least. I'm trying to explain to her it doesn't have to be like that."

You raised your eyebrow, just as you'd learnt to do years ago. "I mean, she doesn't have to stick around, feel beholden, make sacrifices . . . appease anyone. She doesn't have to put what she wants after what other people want for her." You looked down at the map again. "There doesn't seem much point in raising a girl to understand the value of friendship if we're really just training them to forget their friends, eventually. Opt into a life of duty."

I nodded, watching you from the corner of my eye.

"I don't want her to feel obliged to do anything . . . I don't want her hanging around like an afterthought, a ghost. You know?"

I nodded, recalling the flash of pink, the wooden board, the dripping of the taps. The curled, snaking tails of the eels, the translucent quickness of them. The dusty bottles and jars, the footprint on the sofa, the scaffold. The stacked old calendars, the years winding down to the point when they stopped, like the clocks of Elver House.

"I just don't want her to have regrets." You twisted the silver ring on your pointer finger; the wedding band was long gone. "Otherwise what's the point? Spending your days haunted by the things that could've been different, by a life cycle that's prescribed from birth. Like . . . I don't know. Like an eel."

I waited, not moving, barely breathing. I recalled Catherine's voice, unrecorded but remembered, lively and enthusiastic, playing out like a song. *Incredible creatures . . . Such a mystery.*

"They're carnivores," you said. I could hear the laugh in your voice. "Extremely adaptable. Omnivorous. That's what I want for her. An insatiable appetite for everything, for all of it."

I turned to look at you fully. Your lips were curved in a half-smile.

"You read the book," I said slowly. I looked down at my hands, exhaling slowly.

"Of course I did," you said. "It was yours."

You stood up in one fluid movement, folding the map in half.

"Come on, El," you said, holding out your hand. "The fog's clearing. Let's go."

THE END

ACKNOWLEDGEMENTS

HUGE THANKS TO Chris and Jen Hamilton-Emery for turning dream into reality, and for publishing this with such enthusiasm. To Lisa Moylett, for a decade of friendship and for taking the book on despite an enormous TBR pile, to Em, for reading the draft and giving such sensitive feedback. And to Lottie, for all the hours spent sitting across the same desk, and for being the best, most supportive friend since the 2000 solar eclipse.

This book has been typeset by
SALT PUBLISHING LIMITED
using Neacademia, a font designed by Sergei Egorov for the
Rosetta Type Foundry in Czechia. It has been manufactured
using Holmen Book Cream 65gsm paper, and printed and
bound by Clays Limited in Bungay, Suffolk, Great Britain.

If you enjoyed this book, do please leave a review on Amazon,
Goodreads and your favourite bookstore website.

CROMER
GREAT BRITAIN
MMXXV